girls who travel

girls who travel

NICOLE TRILIVAS

B
BERKLEY BOOKS, NEW YORK

BERKLEY

An imprint of Penguin Random House LLC
375 Hudson Street, New York, New York 10014

Library of Congress Cataloging-in-Publication Data

Trilivas, Nicole.
Girls who travel / Nicole Trilivas. — Berkley trade paperback edition.
p. cm.
ISBN 978-0-425-28144-4 (paperback)
1. Young women—Fiction.   2. Self-realization in women—Fiction.
3. Americans—England—Fiction.   4. Travel—Fiction.   I. Title.
PS3620.R55G57 2015
813'.6—dc23
2015030415

PUBLISHING HISTORY
Berkley trade paperback edition / December 2015

PRINTED IN THE UNITED STATES OF AMERICA

10   9   8   7   6   5   4   3   2   1

Cover photos: "Woman on Dock" © PlainPicture / Cultura.
Cover design by Sarah Oberrender.
Interior text design by Tiffany Estreicher.

Penguin
Random
House

One of my favorite childhood memories is of my dad taking me to the bookstore after dinner at the long-closed Sun Luck restaurant in Queens and letting me buy any book my heart desired. My father passed away before he could see this book published. This book is dedicated to his memory.

acknowledgments

First and foremost, I must acknowledge the two people who listened to me bitch about my writing struggles the most: Thank you, Jonathan Brierley. Words fall short of my gratitude for everything you do for me. You are my champion, my rock, and my hands-down favorite. You're also really, really funny and wonderful. Second, Georgia Stephens: Thank you for all those walks in Holland Park. Your support has never wavered—not for a second.

Next up, I must thank my lovely agent, Carrie Pestritto, for believing in me and taking a chance. It's been so great to do this together.

Thank you to the venerable Jackie Cantor; you answered my prayers! Thank you for *making* my dreams come true and for *being* an absolute dream to work with. My thanks also goes out to the whole Berkley team including Amanda Ng—thank you for being so wonderful to work with, and I hope to continue doing so for many more books.

Thank you to my mom, Maria, for taking me to the library and letting me take out as many books as I wanted (and then for taking me to Nino's for pizza after). And thanks to the rest of my family—Charlie, Sherry, and Jeremy—for the love. Oh, right, and a special shout-out to my sister Renee, who—in addition to being the original Mina—is just generally awesome and constantly helpful in terms of my writing and my life.

Thank you to the readers of my earlier work including: Ann Ehrhart; Amy-Lee Simon; Bayta Gideon; Carly Vasan; and Lauren Raggio;—you are all some of my favorite girls who travel, and we better keep running around the globe together, getting tipsy on local booze, and making to-die-for memories and questionable choices.

I would like to thank Wattpad, without which I may not even be here today, writing these acknowledgments in my pajamas (especially not without Marian Keyes and the Marian Keyes Short Story Contest). Thanks to Wattpad's Caitlin O'Hanlon for the backing, and tons of love to the Wattpad community—I've been absolutely floored by how loyal and caring Wattpad readers are, including Analise Anderson, an amazing stranger who generously helped me with early edits.

Thanks to Rick Del Mastro, who was always the best boss and who was the first one to give me space and time to write. Let's live our dreams, right, Rick?

Thanks go out to my Manhasset English teachers, Mary

Jane Peterson in particular, for the encouragement and sturdy foundation.

Thank you to my unofficial family, the Island, for all the love. Let's keep jumping international flights like buses. And I will always looove yooou.

And lastly, thanks, Daddy. I hope you're proud.

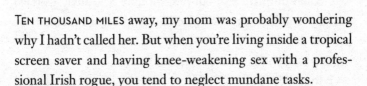

TEN THOUSAND MILES away, my mom was probably wondering why I hadn't called her. But when you're living inside a tropical screen saver and having knee-weakening sex with a professional Irish rogue, you tend to neglect mundane tasks.

Today. I will call her today.

I knew she was going to ask if I found out Lochlon's secret yet, and I had no update for her. Somehow, not knowing was bothering her more than it was bothering me.

"I don't get it, Kika," she protested during our last phone call. "You've been gallivanting around South India with some guy who admitted that he's hiding his past, and you still haven't gotten any details?"

But after a year of travel through countries that had obligatory coffee breaks and nap times, I had been slow-cooked into a state of tender, fall-off-the-bone relaxation.

2 · *nicole trilivas*

"He'll tell me when he's ready," I downplayed to my mom and to myself. Still, she wasn't buying it and was clamoring for more frequent updates from me.

I will definitely call her tomorrow, I decided as I got out of bed. I pushed the mosquito net aside, writhed into my clammy bikini, and left the beach hut. Feeling the sand against my soles brought up flashes of last night, when Lochlon convinced me that a midnight "swim" was in order.

"Get in the water, gorgeous." He didn't know that no one in real life spoke like the heroes of paperback romances, and I sure as hell wasn't going to be the one to correct him.

"And leave these"—he hooked his finger into the band of my bikini bottoms, snapping them against my skin—"safe on dry land."

I could do little else but nod dumbly. I vaguely worried that my inability to say no to him might present a problem for me one day.

Oh, but that day was not today.

I found Lochlon scribbling away in his leather-bound notebook in a patch of shade. He had dreams of becoming a writer, and I thought of him as my Irish Hemingway: all sun-shy skin and minimalist, declarative prose.

Before he noticed me, I found myself peeking over his shoulder at his notebook, proving that maybe I was slightly more curious than I let on. But he detected my presence and turned. Without speaking, he knitted his fingers into the fringe of my sarong and lowered me to my knees into the sand beside him.

"Mornin'," he hummed in his throaty Northern Irish brogue.

I put my face close to his, and he deftly slipped his hand

into the pocket of my sarong and onto my stomach. He slowly moved his hand up, up, up until his sandy palm cupped my—

"Ma'am!"

My face scrunched to a scowl. *Why is Lochlon calling me "ma'am"? What a horribly unsexy pet name.*

I rattled my head to dissolve the soft-focus soap opera scene from my memory and lifted my eyes to regard the strict eyebrows of a Long Island Rail Road conductor.

"Eek!" I squeaked like a chew toy. My face flared with heat, burning away my daze.

"Ma'am, I need to see your ticket," he repeated with a look that said, *Pull your shit together, lady.*

I rifled through my fatally boring winter coat and most-adult-looking handbag.

"I didn't realize you were talking to me," I chatted to buy time, "because I'm not used to being called 'ma'am.'"

I shot him a squinty-eyed smile in an effort to wring out some human emotion, but he gave me nothing.

"Aha! Here, good sir, is my ticket to ride."

He punched it without ceremony and moved on to the next train car.

"Next and final stop is Penn Station," announced the train's speaker in a grainy belch.

I sealed my eyelids and willed time backward to that sugary beach day. *What happened next?* I interrogated myself. *Was that the day Lochlon revealed his mysterious history?* But the pressure to remember all the details in the correct order made the specifics shifty. It was like the tighter I squeezed, the more slippery my memories became, like a beach ball in water.

No matter—there was no more time for reminiscing, anyway.

I buttoned my winter coat in preparation to join New York City's rush hour crush. Somehow, when I wasn't paying attention, I had become just another pleb carrying my chain-store coffee to a soul-destroying office.

My life was not supposed to be like this.

WHEN I FIRST came back from my grand backpacking tour around the world, I used the commute from my mom's house in suburban Long Island to the office to write out my memories from my year spent abroad.

The stories were for my website, Gypsies & Boxcars. Throughout my year overseas, I created the site for friends and family to follow me. I'd share stories and post pictures whenever I could, in the frantic but fruitless hope of remembering everything.

I didn't travel with much that year, so most of my wardrobe and possessions were acquired on the road, and something unexpected started to happen: People—strangers, even—began asking me questions. They wanted to know where I got the hand-painted glass bead bracelets or my bohemian leather belt. I got compliments on my jaunty hats and the patchwork, tasseled summer scarf, and the fabric journal I always carried with me. My mom always said I had an eye for that sort of thing, but I never truly believed it until the comments started rolling in.

In hopes of supporting local businesses, I began offering to buy the items and ship them to readers. For example, I blogged about my time in South India with Lochlon, and then sold a small inventory of sandalwood bead necklaces that I bought from the seaside shops near our beach hut.

My makeshift online shop was very Anthropologie—sans the inauthenticity and astronomical price point. Orders started coming in, and even with a minimal markup, I started making a small profit—which of course I promptly spent.

Regardless, it was then I realized that I could do this as, like, *a job*. I could travel around the world, tell my tales, and sell a small collection of local handicrafts that I personally scouted. There was a real market for authentic goods, for things not everyone had, for things not just "Made in China" or H&M.

Yet as soon as I got back home, business dwindled. I had no new goods to offer, no new tales to tell. And so until I made enough money to get back on the road, here I was, stuck playing the role of Cubicle Dweller in Corporate America. It was the part you had to play when you were in your early twenties and one teensy step away from financial destitution.

About to exit Penn Station, I crowded my hair into my wool beret and braced myself for the cold, but it still thwacked me with an unexpectedly cruel bitch slap. *And good freakin' morning to you, New York City.*

I hopscotched between honking yellow cabs and irritated businesspeople. New York was fuming with energy, the winter-white sun high and dazzling.

Despite being the obligatory plucky young girl in the big, sexy city and all that glossy sitcom setup, there was no promenading past the Chrysler Building in cute tutu dresses for me.

I reached my office building windswept and frazzled, my shoes click-clacking through the marble lobby as I juggled two venti coffees in one upturned palm.

According to my business card, VoyageCorp was a "corporate travel management company," which basically meant we planned business trips for CEOs more interested in high thread counts than high art. The only time I saw any desire for indigenous culture was when a client wanted a local high-class escort. Thankfully, those types of requests were usually reserved for my boss, Stephan Holland.

Placing Holland's venti in his office, I let the cold sunshine linger on my face and daydreamed of the beach again. My stomach panged at the thought of Lochlon—for the second time today, and it wasn't even 9 A.M. yet.

Plopping down at my generic desk outside Holland's office, I clicked through my email with Monday-morning indifference.

There was an all-hands-on-deck meeting in Dubai next week for our primary client, the Richmond Group, and every email contained yet another amendment to it. Holland was in a special sort of tizzy over the meeting, but it was hard to take him seriously when he considered missing the elevator a stage-one disaster.

"Aren't you looking fierce today," I catcalled Holland as he marched into the office, rattled and pink cheeked.

Holland sent his eyes toward the heavens. "Kika, not today."

"You're the one sashaying by me," I shot back.

Holland looped his coat onto the hook in his office and

looked as if he was about to say something biting, when he noticed his thick-foamed coffee sitting on his desk and thawed.

"Kika, you're a peach," he purred, switching gears. "Now, what is going on north of your forehead?"

I slinked off my knit hat and smoothed my hair. "There. It's gone."

"No, I actually like it. It's not at all office appropriate—what do you wear that is?—but it's très cute. Makes you look a little French." He ran his eyes over the mess on my desk. "And everyone knows that French women do everything better than us."

"Actually, it's Scottish. It was hand-knit by a brooding Highland granny—"

Holland outstretched his arm and wagged his finger *no, no, no* like he was in an R&B music video. The man had a flair for the theatrical and was an unfortunate over-actor. Holland wasn't interested in hearing the story about my trip to Scotland. He never was.

"Kika, you cannot get me off task today. I need everything confirmed for the Dubai conference—flights, airport pickups, dinner reservations, happy-ending massages—everything. If anything goes wrong with Ronald Richmond's trip, it will be my head on his plate."

"Richie Rich? Oh, he'll be fine," I said with a shrug. "I got it covered."

"Stop calling him Richie Rich. I almost called him that to his face the other day because of you. Ronald Richmond is very sensitive about his name—you know that."

I conjured the image of the perpetually red-faced man who owned the Richmond Group. Ronald Richmond was a fullname sort of fellow who could never be dwarfed to a friendly "Ron" or even the simple and bro-y "Richmond."

"Oh, please. He's offensively rich. Everyone knows his name," I reassured Holland.

"Yes, but the Richmond Group has more problems than Syria right now, so let's not contribute by screwing up the conference. I mean it, Kika."

I gave Holland a fake-serious salute and directed my vision back to my laptop with the intention of ensuring that the conference was scheduled down to the minute, but I got distracted by some uber-luxury travel porn on Barcelona—which was where Lochlon and I first met.

3

THE KABUL YOUTH Hostel in Barcelona was an acknowledged party spot located right in the palm tree–studded Plaça Reial, a plaza sporting a bubbling bronze fountain and drippy curlicue lampposts designed by Barcelona's own artsy kid, Gaudí.

My first morning there, I sat at a rustic table in the hostel's common area with a map and a cup of cold complimentary coffee. I had heard about a group of nuns who sold handpainted flamenco fans, and I was trying to find their convent among the spiderweb of streets in the hopes of buying some for my website.

Just then, a crowd of people came rushing down the stairs, dangling bottles of cheap cava and cans of beer in their swinging grips. Lochlon was leading the pack. When he noticed me, he froze in front of my table, causing a human traffic pileup.

The group jammed up behind him in a cartoonish way, each person slamming into the one in front.

"Oi, mind yourself, lad," said the kid behind him with a moody shove.

Wheeling away from the pileup, Lochlon sat down across from me at the table, staring at me the whole time.

I stared back as boldly and unflinchingly at him. *Who the hell is this guy? Do I know him?*

When he didn't speak, I leaned in and with a lilt of humor said, "Close your mouth, you big creeper."

His whole face lit up when he smiled.

"Can't help it, so. You're just . . . stunning, like," he said stupidly. "A natural knockout."

I couldn't help but blush at this straightforwardness, his informal charm. Before I could react further, his friends called out to hurry him along—they were already halfway out the door.

"Sure, I'm not bothered. I'll meet you there," he hollered back without looking in their direction. And so in the same swarmlike haste as their arrival, the group exited. It was abruptly peaceful again.

We sat face-to-face in a strange sort of staring contest. He looked away first and flipped up the corners of my map.

"Where you off to, then? I've been here two full weeks, so if you're in need of a bit of help, I'm your man," he said in a flirty flash of romantic foreshadowing or dumb hope or mere coincidence.

"Are you?" I laced my tone with playfulness.

We walked around the city for hours that day. He had no

clue where he was going, but that didn't matter anymore. I never did find those flamenco fans.

Instead, he taught me how to pronounce his name (*Lok-lun O-Ma-hoon*) in the animated Boqueria market. We talked of the cities we had come from while eating sugared churros on the steps of formidable churches with gargoyles for chaperones.

I had just come from Latin America and had a few months of travel left. But Lochlon, a serial backpacker, had just started a new journey and would be on the road for at least a year. He traveled until the money ran out, went home to Ireland to work, and then went back on the road. He was Peter Pan with dirty jeans and a brogue.

By the time night fell, we were talking of the places we would go to next while slipping through the side streets and back alleys of Barcelona's underbelly. I don't remember where we were going that night, but I can still remember the buzzing rush low in my stomach whenever I think of it.

The next week we would be on a train to the Pyrenees together, the pastoral countryside tumbling past us. Fallow yellow fields; stone ruins; farmers' cottages; dusty soccer games; sky, sky, sky. It was the beginning of a four-month-long "roadmance" where we traveled and, in effect, lived together. If he was Peter Pan, then I was Wendy.

After Spain, we went on to jump turnstiles on the Paris Métro; got kicked out of a glitzy, ritzy bar in Monte Carlo; and spent nights kissing over bottles of cheap Chianti in dreamy Florentine piazzas.

In Rome, he taught me it was okay to be a tourist and take pictures with the men dressed as gladiators. "If you act like you're above it, you're going to miss out," he told me. And he was right.

We splashed fully clothed in a public fountain in Zurich, *La Dolce Vita* style; climbed trees in a Berlin park, skinning our knees; and stayed up all night playing poker on an overnight diesel train to Greece with teenagers from Israel. We made love for the first time, hot and desperate and carnal, in Istanbul; and played "Never Have I Ever" on a budget airliner to Mumbai. He first admitted that he was hiding something from me on the Konkan Railway down south to Goa.

"There's stuff about me that you don't know, Kika," he told me as the train wheezed and jangled us along the thin railroad tracks that drew a line between the Arabian Sea and the Sahyadri Mountains. We had been on the train for five hours, and we still had more to go. *What is it about long journeys that breeds confessions?* I wondered then.

The sun shone through the window highlighting the freckles on my thighs. "Like what?"

"I've done some things in my past that I'm not proud of," he whispered, staring out the window greasy with fingerprints. Sweat oiled his temples.

I shrugged. "So has everyone." His words didn't worry me. By this point I had already made up my mind about him. This wasn't just vacation sex; he was really someone to me. And it would take a lot to change that.

But he creased his forehead seriously.

"No, you're not understanding me. You'd not be able to look at me in the same way if you knew." He looked deeply uncomfortable and tented his sweat-stained T-shirt off his chest.

"Why don't you tell me and let me decide that," I said without flinching.

But then, it was as if an emergency alarm had been pulled

in my brain. A warning image of my mom's face flashed in the speed of a strobe light: *Caution! Caution! Caution!*

"You're not married, are you?" I blurted, abandoning all casual coolness. My insides rippled at the thought.

That was mom's one rule: Don't fall in love with a married man. She had that rule because it happened to her. My father was a tremendously handsome (and tremendously married) Roman man she met while living in Italy. They no longer speak.

We didn't spring for the air-conditioned cabin, and my thighs suctioned to the seat as I shifted my legs.

"Jaysus, no, I haven't a missus."

I closed my mouth, but the alarm didn't subside. "Not even a mad wife locked in the attic? That still counts, you know," I prodded. This was one thing that my usually chilled yogic mother would panic over.

His head shook like a swinging door. But then a moment later he asked, "Wait, is that not the story of *Jane Eyre?*"

"Girlfriend? Boyfriend? Illegitimate children?" I fired, my brain whizzing faster.

"Would you stop? It's nothing like that at all." He fidgeted with a loose thread on the hem of his shirt, wrapping it around his finger until his skin went colorless.

"Was it something illegal?" I asked. "Were you in jail?"

"'Course not," he said, pinching his face like he'd just smelled something sour. "Is the question-and-answer period of the program over now? Look, I'm sorry I mentioned it. Forget it, yeah?"

He looked up at me with expectant, childlike eyes; this look was a departure from his usual self-assured swagger. His Adam's apple dipped in a hard swallow. My shoulder blades unclenched when he looked at me like that.

"Okay. One more question," I said. "Whatever you did, whatever happened—is it truly in the past?"

The train snaked through a mango grove, and the air grew sticky with the scent of rotting fruit and noxious diesel fumes.

Lochlon didn't even glance at the luscious, waxy mango trees and instead leaned forward, supporting his elbows with his knees.

"By God it is," he assured me emphatically.

A freight train going the opposite direction clattered parallel to us, momentarily blocking the view in filmlike flickers. In that moment, the worry burned away like a puddle in the blistering Indian sun.

"Then it doesn't matter to me. If this is the real you, then I don't care about what happened back then." The train plunged into the black shadow of a tunnel.

"You say that now. But once I tell you, you won't want anything to do with me."

A RUDELY SHRILLING phone yanked me from the Internet rabbit hole.

"Kika Shores, VoyageCorp," I chirped with counterfeit liveliness. "How may I assist you this fine day?"

I looked at Holland through his glass office, and he curled his top lip in warning. He had been observing my phone demeanor ever since he caught me answering the phone with "Kika Shores, Office Bitch." (I thought it was my mom calling. It was an innocent mistake that could happen to anyone.)

"Hi, Kika, it's Lynn, Madison's mother. I couldn't get you on your cell, and your mom passed on this number."

I winced and swiveled my chair to face away from Holland's office.

"Hey, Lynn. Yeah, this is my office number, but my mom really shouldn't be giving it out."

"Of course," she said with her heartland politeness, "but darling, I *must* say you do sound *very* professional!"

I loved mothers of young children; they were always easily impressed and quick to dole out praise. *Thanks, I have a big-girl job!*

"I was just calling to confirm tonight. I'll pick you up from the train station at six thirty with Madison and then drop you girls off at home. I should be home by midnight. I hope that's not too late for you, is it?"

I jerked my swivel chair one half turn farther, binding the curly phone cord around myself. I was babysitting her five-year-old daughter, Madison, that night. Why did she have to make it sound like we were having a playdate?

Madison's mom insisted that she pick me up from the train station, which was actually fine by me because it saved my own mother the trouble. Of course, the whole production made me feel like a teenager again instead of an early twenties college grad who worked in the city.

But I was desperate for the extra money babysitting generated. I had a giant credit card bill from last weekend when I took an impromptu trip to see a friend in Montreal.

"Thanks again for helping out. Madison adores you."

Babysitting came naturally to me—as an only child I always wanted younger siblings. I babysat all through high school and the summers between my years in college. In fact, I was our neighborhood's favorite babysitter. Shockingly, my college's career counselor wouldn't let me add this to my résumé, even though watching five-year-olds truly equipped me for dealing with fussy CEOs.

Holland emerged from his office bundled in his winter coat in preparation to go outside.

"Absolutely, so glad we were able to confirm that. Looking forward to working together in the future. Okay, bye now." I put the phone down before Lynn finished, and I rotated my chair in the opposite direction to face Holland.

"Something I can do for you, Mr. Holland?" I said, fumbling to unravel the phone cord.

"Kika—" he started forcefully and then cut himself short.

I offered him my most impressive Disney Princess smile, and he took a deep breath. The curiously bulging vein in his forehead throbbed up and down.

"Kika, I'm going to the last-call meeting at the Richmond Group to get any final requests. I'll send you Ronald Richmond's changes as they arise so that you can get started on them right away. Just please, I beg you, get everything confirmed. I'm getting a lot of pressure from the higher-ups on this one. I'm not kidding around."

"Right, Mr. Holland," I said far too cheerily to instill any genuine confidence. Holland put his hand to his temples, and his vein swelled again, but he walked out without another word.

As soon as he was out of sight, I shrugged off my itchy blazer to reveal a cottony soft retro T-shirt that said, in Russian: "Moscow Is for Lovers." (There was a highly probable chance that it actually said, "Stupid American Tourist"; I never checked.)

I tried to keep up a semblance of my true self whenever Holland was out of the office. Plus, work clothes were so binding and claustrophobic—wearing them was the fashion equivalent of being told to "quiet down." I was literally unsuited for corporate life.

The only thing about my work appearance that was wholly

mine was my summery, beach blond "Coachella hair," as Holland called it.

I heeled off my uptight office shoes and curled my legs in a lotus position in my chair, instantly feeling relief.

Contrary to popular belief at VoyageCorp, I wasn't an idiot. I was just understimulated and underemployed. But it wasn't like I was irresponsible or anything. I mean, how hard was it to set up and confirm meetings, right?

But then as if on cue, it hit me. *Oh no.*

I snatched my tasks list and flashed over it. There it was, inked in bright red pen and my own treacherous, loopy handwriting: *Set up last-call meeting with Richie Rich re: Dubai.*

I was so preoccupied with the actual Dubai conference that I forgot to schedule the meeting in New York *before* the Dubai conference—the one that Holland was en route to right now.

I frantically looked around like the solution was a physical thing that I could find if I searched hard enough. *Holland is officially going to shank me. Or worse, fire me.*

I started pacing, but then it struck me: Maybe Richie Rich was available to have a super-quick meeting with Holland. CEOs of multinational export companies weren't, like, constantly busy, right? He had to have five minutes to spare. I speed-dialed his personal assistant.

"Ronald Richmond's office," answered an impatient, too-cool-for-you voice.

I pictured his PA, Bae Yoon, adjusting her headset, which she always seemed to be wearing—even on social occasions—like it was some sort of high-tech fashion accessory.

"Bae Bae! It's Kika. You have got to help me," I started.

"Hold please," she said without emotion.

I tapped my foot. She didn't put me on hold properly, and I heard her whole conversation through the phone:

"Yes, I did just get it cut, Mr. Jørgensen. Do you really like it? You don't think it's too short, do you?"

Bae was a notorious flirt who considered bagging rich men pure sport. At any industry event she could be found shamelessly coiling up the arm of the wealthiest guy in the room like some poisonous snake.

I spanked my palms onto my desk: "BAE!"

"Forgive me, Mr. Jørgensen—oh, okay," (sickly sounding giggles) *"I'll call you Sven. What a privilege. Forgive me, Sven, but I have to attend to this call,"* Bae said in the background.

She came back on the line. Irritated, she asked, "Yes? *Who* is this?"

Bae and I spoke roughly three hundred times a day.

"It's Kika Shores, from VoyageCorp. Look, I have a serious problem."

Bae sighed, fluttering and wet like a horse. "Don't you *always*, though."

"No, seriously, this is not a drill. I repeat: This is not a drill. Holland is coming to your office *right now* to meet with Richie Rich, and I totally forgot to schedule it with you," I said in one breath. "Is there any way to get a meeting with Holland on the books, like, *now*, so they can meet?"

Bae let out another lengthy stream of air, which I *really* didn't have time for.

"So let me get this straight," she started in her snippy, nasally way. "You forgot to schedule a meeting with Mr. Richmond—excuse me, with *Richie Rich*—wasn't *that* what you called him?"

I dropped my head back and grimaced at the ceiling. She wasn't going to forget that anytime soon.

Bae continued: "—and now you want *me* to *find* Mr. Richmond, *interrupt* him, and tell him that he has a *meeting* with Holland, *like*, *now*, so that *I* look like the *screwup* who didn't put it in the *books*?"

(Sorry for all the italics, but that's how Bae Yoon really talks: *in* alternating *italics*.)

Bae always took this sort of superior tone with me because back in the day, we were up for the same personal assistant position for Richie Rich. A man named Prescott Darling, the father of one of the families I babysat for, was a financial advisor for the Richmond Group, so when he got word that Richie Rich needed a PA, he got me the interview, even though I was less than qualified with my tourism and travel management degree.

When Richie Rich chose Bae over me, he passed on my résumé to VoyageCorp as a courtesy to Prescott Darling.

Bae acted like she won this big competition when I really couldn't care less as long as I had a job. And at least for now, I had a job.

"Bae, please," I implored. "Just get someone—anyone—from the Richmond Group to meet with Holland. Look, he's been on my ass about Dubai, and if he finds out I forgot this, I'll be fired."

There was an unwelcome silence on the end of the phone.

"Will you now?" said Bae in a cool, clear voice.

Unexpectedly, I felt my bottom lip twitch. Sure, I didn't exactly *like* this job, but it was really hard to get one. I only got this position because of the personal favor.

Just then the situation became serious. If I lost this job, it would takes ages to get a new one, and I could kiss any hope of traveling in the immediate future good-freakin'-bye.

The line went quiet again. "Maybe I can help you," Bae finally said.

Now I was the one exhaling. "Bae, thank you so—"

"But you'll have to do something for me," she interrupted.

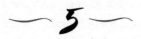

5

I PUT THE phone down and fell back into my chair with a relieved moan.

Bae consented to meet with Holland herself to go over the itinerary for the conference. She agreed to tell him that Richie Rich had something suddenly come up.

In exchange, I would need to run an errand for Bae since she was giving up her lunch break to meet with Holland and she'd be in Dubai next week because she was just sooo busy and important and cool.

But nothing to panic over. A few little errands bartered for job security? Done. Holland had another meeting this afternoon, so I could leave now and return during his second appointment, and he wouldn't know how long I'd been gone. My job was safe.

While waiting for instructions from Bae, I started prepping

myself for the outdoors. I left my blazer and work shoes behind and slipped on my (in)famous Dr. Martens boots, which I brought along to change into after work so I could be comfy at Madison's house. (Okay, fine, so it sort of was like a playdate.)

By the time I got downstairs and outside the office, Bae had texted me her order: "Pick up six Cronuts from Dominique Ansel Bakery. Anything else is unacceptable."

I thought to myself: *Enough with the damn Cronuts!* The croissant-doughnut dessert hybrid was still stupidly popular with tourists, and the bakery would be overrun this time of day with a line around the block. Not to mention that there was no way I'd snag *six* Cronuts without trading my immortal soul.

This task was obviously just designed to piss me off; since meeting Bae Yoon, I had never seen her put so much as a martini olive in her mouth.

Still, what Bae Bae wants, Bae Bae gets. I bundled up my coat and darted rabbitlike into the dank 34th Street Subway heading for Soho.

"YOU HAVE GOT to be shitting me," I said aloud as another text from Bae came through.

Some tourist in line for the bakery scowled at me and made her hands into earmuffs for her child's precious ears.

I had just waited in line for forty-five minutes to get the Cronuts and now *this*.

"One more thing," texted Bae directly after I let her know that I got her Cronuts—I was only able to snag three without resorting to sexual favors or the black market. Her next request was just plain cruel.

"Go to Orifice Depot and pick up . . ."—actually I stopped reading right there and *prayed* that she had made a very unfortunate typo.

She cannot be asking me to go to a sex shop for her, I silently contested. But when I read the rest of the text, my fears were confirmed. I texted her back: "You must be joking. Please, please be joking?"

Her response was instantaneous: "No."

In a follow-up text, she added: "And when you're done, make sure you leave the bags with the doorman of my apartment."

I said the word "fuck" aloud a few times, because it was *clearly* in order, and I begrudgingly made my way to the unbearably named store.

I THRUST (BAD choice of word) the phone up to the poor sales associate's face so I could be spared the embarrassment of reading Bae's list aloud.

"Please fetch me these things as quickly as possible, mm'k?" I piped, mashing the words together. But of course, it wasn't going to be that straightforward. Why did the sales associate have to be so damn thorough?

"Another question for you," he chirped (his third). "So this one comes in three sizes and colors. There's vanilla, then there's caramel, or the biggest one is called chocolate. Which one were you interested in?"

I threw up in my mouth when I saw what he was holding, and I inadvertently pictured Bae.

"Um, whichever. Really. I do not care," I squealed all too shrilly.

The sales associate, a peroxide blond who did not look old enough to be working in a sex shop, foppishly pinned his knuckles to his waist as if I was being difficult.

"Look, they're not for me. Can we please just get on with it?"

"Fiiiiine, suuuuuure," he said, bringing the item to the register. "Looks like someone needs the chocolate one," he muttered under his breath.

"Just ring it up." I checked my phone. I had been out of the office far too long, and Holland had already called me twice.

I dashed out of the X-rated store, out $65 and my self-respect. It wasn't like I was a prude, but call me old-fashioned for thinking that sex toy shopping shouldn't be outsourced. That's what the Internet and discreet brown boxes were for.

Now I was stuck toting around a neon-green shopping bag clearly labeled with the store's disastrous name and filled with things that would make Christian Grey blush. To make matters worse, Bae lived all the way downtown in the Financial District.

My phone buzzed again, but it was a text from Holland this time: "Where are you?!"

"In the fetal position," I almost texted back, but I left the text unanswered. I didn't have time to go downtown; I had no choice but to wait until after work to drop off Bae's bags.

SEVERAL HOURS LATER, I crammed a fluffy Cronut glaze-first into my mouth and chewed without taking any pleasure in it. To me, it tasted like tragedy.

(Okay, fine, it didn't *really* taste like tragedy—it still tasted awesome—but it didn't make me any less depressed.)

Beside me, a man in a suit discreetly shifted his eyes in my direction. I blatantly stared back without bothering to wipe off the glaze from the sides of my mouth.

"Vont von?" I asked him, my teeth caked with masticated dough. I held up the box and accidentally spat a few gooey crumbs onto his shoulder. He shook his head with disgust.

By the time the Long Island Rail Road train pulled into the Plandome station, there'd only be one Cronut left. I glumly licked a fleck of sugar off my fingernail and replayed the scene with Holland from earlier:

"Kika, where the he-ll" (he pronounced it with two syllables: ha-elle) "have you been?"

I would never be able to forget the appalled expression on his face when he caught me passing the packed conference room with my hands full of Cronuts, sex toys, and disgrace.

"Umm, delivery?" I croaked, as Holland stared murderously and I turned fifty shades of red.

"Let me say this to you so you can see it from my perspective: You messed up my meeting with Richie Rich, which means I won't have advance notice for any changes to the Dubai schedule. And then, instead of coming clean about it, you make me waste my morning going all the way across town so I have to hear it from that self-satisfied gold digger, Bae Yoon.

"'But Mr. Holland,'" he mimicked Bae's condescending voice, "'Kika *never* scheduled a *meeting* for you and Mr. Richmond. I haven't *heard* from her *all* day.'"

I nearly bit off my bottom lip at Bae's backstabbing, but Holland's rant wasn't done, so I let him continue.

"Then when I get back to the office you're not here and unreachable for the next hour. And when you do finally show up, I find out that you were out getting Cronuts and God knows what else, dressed like a college kid who just came home from 'finding herself' at a semester at sea!"

I didn't dare tell him that the dessert and dildo outing was Bae's doing, an obvious fool's errand in retrospect. It would just make it worse if I admitted to being so gullible.

His vibrating wrath was one thing, but then his shoulders drooped with disappointment.

"Your heart is not in this, Kika. I know you're not stupid,

but I also know that you're not taking this seriously, and that isn't fair to VoyageCorp. Or to me."

"You're right," I acknowledged to both him and myself. "I'm sorry. I'm not normally like this—" I began to protest, just to clear my reputation, but once I heard the puny words scrabbling from my mouth, I caught them and swallowed them back down. I had no good explanation. Holland knew that I knew. This wasn't the first time I had messed up.

"I'm going to have to let you go, Kika."

"Got it," I said softly. So I left my damn big-girl job, thinking: *If this job didn't mean anything to me, why does it sting so much to lose it?*

The one condolence was before I left I managed to schedule a messenger for a special delivery: The adult toy store bag would be arriving at Bae Yoon's front desk tomorrow at precisely 8:20 A.M.—the exact time that Richie Rich arrived in his office every day. At least I would get to embarrass Bae and eat Cronuts out of the whole debacle.

My train reached the station, jolting me back into the present. I looked out of the window as idyllic suburbia, wrapped in a hushed wintertime blanket, came into view. The grit and noise and drama of the city seemed far away now. A quiet snowfall swirled in the floor-length skirts of amber light dropping down from the lampposts.

I recognized Lynn's tan (or as she called it, "champagne") Mercedes. She flickered the headlights while hooting my name. I headed toward her with my face down, away from the blustering snowflakes.

ANY NORMAL GIRL who just lost her job would get to bond with
Bravo TV and butter. But not me; I still had to hang out with
a five-year-old. Not that I had any right to complain. I needed
the money more than ever now.

"I don't fink I'm awowed to watch dis," said Madison.

I set down the box of Lucky Charms cereal (I had extracted
most of the marshmallows, anyway) and quickly changed the
channel as some freakishly young, dead-eyed pop star humped
across the stage while her backup dancers shook what their
plastic surgeons gave them. Wasn't this the Disney Channel?

"Shit," I mumbled to myself. At this rate, I was gunning
to get fired from both jobs today.

"Can I bwaid your hair?" Madison asked me.

"Sure you can. I'm sorry I'm being such a crappy babysitter
today. I just had a horrible day; I got fired from my job."

Madison brought over a comb that smelled like synthetic cherry doll hair. "What job?" she asked.

"Exactly. You are one smart cookie."

Madison's eyes widened at the mention of a cookie—a girl after my own heart.

"Sure, I didn't like it there, but it was at least a way to make money for traveling. It's not that I want to be a backpacking bum; I *want* to work while I'm traveling. I need to acquire more merchandise for my website, you know? It was really starting to take off when I was last on the road, and I want to get back there so I can work on it full-time."

"Oh," said Madison looking thoughtful. "I can comb now?"

She reached up and promptly tangled the comb into my hair. (Side note: When did naming little girls after dead presidents become trendy? This weekend, I was scheduled to babysit a seven-year-old girl named "Kennedy" who, upon questioning, told me her favorite color was "glitter.")

"I knew you would get it, Madison. The worst part is that it's my fault that I got fired," I confessed. "Holland was right. I didn't apply myself. And, and, and . . . I just keep thinking about Lochlon, you know?" I sputtered.

"Yes, I know," said Madison, her sticky hands holding my head steady with toddler concentration. "Who's Lockin? Your boyfwiend?"

"Not really anymore, but he was for a while there," I said, knowing Madison wouldn't understand enough to judge me or pry for more info.

"Diego is *my* boyfwiend."

I turned and squared off with Madison. "Diego? Is that a boy from preschool?"

"Noooooo! He's from *Dowa de Explower*," she moaned impatiently. "Stop wiggling. Have you got ants in your pants, lady?"

"Christ. You sound just like Holland during the weekly status meetings, you know that?"

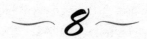

8

"MOM, WHAT ARE you still doing up?" I slung my bag slick with frost onto the kitchen floor and flicked on the overhead light. "And why are you sitting in the dark?" I glanced at the clock, which read 12:15 A.M.

"Kika, I called your work," my mom said over a steaming cup of calming honey lavender tea. She fingered the tea box, which featured one of those trendy pen drawings of a lady in Warrior II all Zen or stoned or whatever.

"Mom, I told you not to call that number."

"Well, I guess it doesn't matter anymore," she said carefully. "I made you a cup of tea."

I sighed. "Mom, it's fine. I'll get another job." I sat down next to her at the breakfast bar. She was in her pajamas, which actually looked no different from her yoga clothes, but I had a trained eye.

My mom nodded mutely, but I saw her recalling the three

months that it took me to get the job in the first place. Three more months of résumés, interviews, and desperation stretched ahead of me now as unpromising as a desert. No job. No money. No website. No Lochlon.

It was doomed to be one of those sad public defeats where I'd keep running into high school peers coming home from their Murray Hill apartments to visit their parents with their dry-clean-only blouses (who even says "blouses" anymore?) and jobs in finance. (Always, finance!)

"So what happened?" my mom finally asked.

"I'm a spectacular screwup."

"No, Kika. You weren't meant to be there." She tried to cup my hand, but I pulled away.

"Oh, cut the New Age bullshit for a minute. *I* messed up, Mom. Sure, I wasn't emotionally fulfilled there, but I should know how to suck it up in order to get to where I'm 'meant to be.'" I reeled in my tone. "Sorry. I'm not mad at you. I'm just really mad at myself right now. I'm actually shocked I lasted a year there." I laughed weakly.

My mom didn't laugh along. "It's really been that long?"

"Yup. And it's pretty sad that after a whole year of working in that office, I still have a pathetic bank balance hovering dangerously close to the negative. I mean, you'd think they would have paid me better."

My mom toyed with her bracelet and sighed. It was made of the mala beads I had bought her in Montreal last weekend. Suddenly, it was a lot harder to remember why I *had* to take all those weekend trips—using up every last vacation and sick day and spending all that money. Now, they didn't seem worth it. *I did this to myself, didn't I?* some voice of truth gulped.

I did a gusty yogi exhale for my mom's benefit. "Thanks for waiting up. I'm sorry I'm so cranky. I should go to bed."

"Okay. I'm teaching a power flow vinyasa class tomorrow at 9 A.M., if you want to join."

"At Heart 'n Ohm?" (Also known as our living room, which doubled as a yoga studio.)

She nodded. "You're going to be okay, Kika. Maybe this was a lesson you needed to learn the hard way, you know?"

"When I took this job I had this whole plan to save money and get back on the road to continue with the website. I don't know how I let myself drift so far from that goal . . ." I felt dangerously close to tearing up.

My mom's eyes twinkled with sympathy in the dim kitchen light. "Best-laid plans are always the ones that go to shit first. You'll figure it out."

I smiled at my mom's custom blend of earthy yoga jargon and sailor swearwords, and then I went upstairs trying to believe that she was right.

I FOUND MYSELF thinking of Lochlon as I bombed face-first onto my bed. I hadn't been with anyone else since him. I hadn't even *kissed* anyone else.

We spent our final few weeks together in South India, and I could recall the details of our life there as if it were a still life painting, a memory in thick oil paint. But despite the seeming perfection of our days, even South India wasn't far enough away to keep Lochlon's past at bay. And one day toward the end of my trip, everything was revealed.

I remember that day in vivid flashes: We had decided we would take a break from the beach and go into the city of Panaji.

India was my last stop, and soon my year of travel would be over. The money coming in from my website was still too meager to live on, and my tickets home had been booked and were nonrefundable—a fact I could not let myself forget despite Lochlon's persuasion to keep traveling with him.

He had another ten to twelve months on the road before his money ran out, and he was off to follow the "Banana Pancake Trail," a well-worn backpacker route from Goa to Hanoi.

After weeks on the seashore, the city felt oppressive and dirty and garish. Quickly wearied from the roaring traffic, exhaust, and yapping stray dogs, Lochlon and I found ourselves sitting at the very top of the epic, zigzagging staircase of the Church of Our Lady of the Immaculate Conception.

"The name just rolls off your tongue, doesn't it?" I remember him saying as we both gawked down at the city square below us, the high staircase making our vision blurry.

As we sat there, three tourists huffed up the infinite steps in our direction. Even from way up there, I could hear them making a big show of climbing the steps and moaning about their hangovers in distinct Irish accents.

"Look, it's your compatriots." I motioned at them even though Lochlon avidly avoided the Irish when we traveled. I assumed it was because he didn't want to feel like he was at home when he was abroad.

"Mental, isn't it?" Lochlon lowered his head. "Just look at the likes of them"—he gestured in their direction—"smokes in their hands as they're about to enter a church. They may as well have a pint of the black stuff in the other and complete the Paddy stereotype. Let's get out of here."

He stood and held his hand down to help me up, but I waved him away and stayed seated.

"Killing your cultural buzz, are they? Why don't you ever want to hang out with other Irish backpackers?"

Lochlon wouldn't answer my question and instead impatiently shook his arm at me again.

Still, I ignored him and instead cheered the women on. "Come on, you got this. You're nearly there!" I applauded their efforts.

One of the girls, dressed more like a Real Housewife than a sightseer, punched both fists in the air like a champion but looked as if she was about to pass out.

"C'mere, Kika," Lochlon murmured in his gravelly way. "Do you always have to talk with everyone?"

I craned my neck up toward him, shielding the sun from my eyes with my hand. "Oh, relax. I'm still exhausted. Let's sit for a minute more."

The first woman, a plump redhead, finally made it to where we sat. I fanned her with my hands, but Lochlon didn't even say hello.

"That climb was right bollocks," she sang out in a thick, melodious accent. "Holy Mary, Mother of God!" she added, finally focusing her eyes at me.

"Actually, no, I'm Kika. She may be inside, though," I said, gesticulating toward to the church. "And that's Lochlon."

She blotted the sweat from her hairline. "Lochlon, eh?" She eyed him up.

"Yup, he's Irish, too," I said, as if with that name I'd have to clarify.

"And don't I know you from somewhere?" she asked him with a slight lilt of apprehension in her speech. "You from Cork, are ya?"

The girl kept staring at him as her two other companions reached us and collapsed down at our sides.

"No, no. I'm not," he said, barely glancing at her.

"No," she confirmed slowly. "You're not from down south with that accent, are ya now?" She jostled her friend in the ribs. "I'm sure we know him, don't we?"

The three women examined him.

Lochlon brushed his dusty hands on his jeans and wouldn't make eye contact. "Right. We're off now." He snatched my elbow, and I let myself be tugged upward.

"Get moving, will you?" he whispered close to my ear.

I smiled apologetically at the girls, slightly embarrassed, as Lochlon led me down the stairs.

"What are you doing?" I could barely keep up as he took the stairs in twos, but I let myself be dragged in my bewilderment. "That was rude of you."

His grip on the crook of my elbow tightened.

"What the hell?" I said, twisting my arm away. As I trailed in his footsteps, I looked back and saw the redhead standing with her hands on her hips, scrutinizing us as we moved downward. We were now halfway down the steps, closer to the chaos of the street, but I still heard what she said next with perfect clarity:

"Lochlon O'Mahone." She waved both arms overhead.

I halted when I heard. "Did you hear that? She knows your name. Do you know her, Lochlon?"

Lochlon didn't try to take my arm again. Instead, he took off faster.

"It's Ireland's own Lochlon O'Mahone, feckin' him, it is!" I heard the redhead exclaiming to her friends. It wasn't a question; she *knew* his name.

"Look at your man leggin' it!" She laughed, motioning to Lochlon, who was hiding his face with his hand. She did some strange dance move, thrashing her hips front and back in an overtly sexual way.

"Lochlon?" I called down in confusion. "Who is she?"

But Lochlon wouldn't stop or answer me, and instead broke out into a panicky jog when he reached the street. "I'm so sorry, Kika," he hollered from over his shoulder.

I looked down at my feet. I was frozen in the middle of the staircase like I had suddenly sprouted roots—I wanted to go up and ask the girl how she knew Lochlon, but I wanted to go down and follow him at the same time.

At the top of the stairs, the girls' laughter reached me in clouds of sound. They jumped up and down and rushed into their bags, their camera phones appearing a moment later. A barrage of flashes glinted in our direction. They were taking Lochlon's picture. I swore I could hear the rapid-fire, automated *click*, *click*, *click* from here. My legs made the decision for me and transported me down the stairs.

Lochlon had darted into beeping traffic like a skittish buck crossing a highway. He disappeared behind a brightly decorated bus for a moment. I craned my head back and forth, searching for him, and finally caught sight of his shirt as he ducked into a narrow side street.

I hitched up my peasant skirt and sprinted after him.

"Lochlon, will you wait up?" I called, but I knew he couldn't hear me over the traffic. We didn't have cell phones, so I couldn't lose him now. I was actually worried that if I didn't catch up with him I might never see him again.

My sandals bounced off the hot asphalt as I turned onto the backstreet, finding him again. When I got close enough, I extended my arm, and I knocked him hard on the shoulder.

"Gotcha!" I couldn't help but hoot, as if we were playing a game of tag.

He whipped around, his face stained with worry as he looked behind me to see if we were being followed.

"Sorry," he mouthed, fully out of breath.

"Lochlon," I wheezed, bent with my hands on my knees. A million questions swarmed my head. *Why are you running? How did those girls know your name? And why were they taking your picture?*

But only one question made it out of my mouth.

"Holy shit. Lochlon, are you, like, *famous* in Ireland or something?"

10

I ZEROED IN on Lochlon and fired my questions like a slingshot right between the eyes. "Does this have to do with your confidential past?" I demanded now that I had caught my breath.

"Just calm down a minute, will you?" he said, pressing his palms toward the ground as if signaling to a rabid dog to stay, staaaaay.

Like winding up a pitch, I sucked in the air to start my objection. But Lochlon forfeited before I could hurl my words his way. "Look, I'll tell you everything, yeah? Let's just get out of here."

I looked around and just then realized that we were standing in an alleyway spackled with graffiti and warm piss.

"Come on now," he said, offering me his upturned palm.

I looked down at his hand and hesitated.

"Look, I didn't mean to grab you like that before." He looked down. "I didn't hurt you, did I?" he asked, changing his tone.

I sighed, shook my head, and gave him my hand. We walked silently to a nearby outdoor café garlanded with blinking Christmas lights and whirring with Bollywood music, and we ordered our favorite drinks as if this was just any other day.

My legs jiggled under the table in the shade of a blue plastic umbrella. Curiosity zinged through my nervous system, and our mango lassis vibrated on the tabletop from the tremors. Even the stray dog that had been sleeping at our feet whined in anticipation. I was too intrigued about his bizarre behavior to be angry about the way he had run from me before.

"I can't believe you're going to tell me!" My stomach somersaulted.

"You wouldn't be a little less eager there, would you now, Kika?" Lochlon looked disturbed by my near giddiness and kept looking around as if those Irish girls were going to show up at any moment.

"I think you'll feel better once you get it off your chest," I crooned.

"Okay. I'll tell you. Just know that I'm sorry—I'm so sorry that I had anything to do with it. Yeah?"

"Stop being dramatic. Out with it." I straightened in my chair. *Maybe my mom is right and it was foolish to let our relationship get this far without knowing. What if what happened in his past really is a deal-breaker?*

"Well, I should tell you first," he stalled, "that this is what people were into in the early 2000s in Belfast, okay? It wasn't just me. I swear it. Lots of lads were there."

"Just tell me," I coaxed, doing my best to keep a tranquil air. "Start at the beginning."

Lochlon scraped the plastic chair away from the table, ignoring his mango lassi.

"Well, I suppose it all started with an advertisement—they were looking for boys." He spoke slowly, the verbal equivalent of dragging his feet.

"Boys?" I repeated. "In an ad?"

"Yeah, they weren't spelling out what it was for, but you could put it together because it was so popular at the time. They were after young boys and, you know, decent-looking ones. Fit and in good shape and all that. You need to look good in that industry. They don't care what you sound like." He shrugged.

"I had just turned sixteen at the time . . . so young and stupid. It was nearly ten years ago now," he said. He didn't look at me but continued talking like he was reciting a monologue.

"It was supposed to be easy money—I'd no interest in it otherwise. So I went on me own, didn't ask anyone to come along. Didn't even have the nerve to tell anyone I was going." He paused then for a long time as if he were reliving that day in his head.

"Where were you going?" I blurted when he didn't continue. My stomach moved on from somersaulting to performing a whole Olympic floor routine.

He narrowed his eyes at a group of Indian teenagers at the table next to us, even though they weren't paying us any attention. Then, he leaned in. "You know, to the audition!" he whispered dramatically as if he had just lifted the cloak off the whole thing. "They recorded us. It was just about how you looked on camera, in the *videos*. Oh, Kika, I don't know why I did it. And now I'm to live with this for the rest of me life!" His voice splintered.

I sorted the information he had just provided me with: the easy money, the audition, the videos, and all that stuff about having to live with it for the rest of your life.

"Oh my God!" I gasped, suddenly getting it. *Porn! He's talking about doing porn!* I tasted the mango lassi ascending in my throat. The look on my face must have showed him that I had figured it out.

"I'm so sorry." His skin was splotched pink in mortification. "That's why I didn't want to tell you. You'll never look at me the same way, will you now? No. How could you?"

I felt something akin to jealousy thinking about the girls who had recognized him. I pictured the Irish girl humping the air. *Those girls saw him naked. The whole world saw him naked*, I realized dumbly. I knew it was illogical, but it felt like an infidelity. I wanted to be the only one who knew him so personally.

Lochlon continued talking very fast. "You can't imagine my shame, Kika," he babbled on.

I shook my head. "How could you do it? It just seems . . . so unlike something you would do. Were you that desperate for money?"

"But that's the worst bit. We weren't at all successful. I mean, if we were, even *you* would have known about us. There's big money in it, of course."

"Us?" I whispered.

"Of course," he nodded matter-of-factly. "It was a group thing, you know. You can't really do something like that on your own, could you now?"

I thought about it. *No, I guess it took at least two to tango—and to make porn.*

"But Kika, the videos"—he gulped—"the horrible, shiny matching outfits, the harmonizing, the dancing, the works— I mean, if I at least made some money out of it—" He spoke in a disjointed jumble.

Wait. What?

"It was a right disgrace. And the thing is, those videos, they're still out there. On the Internet, like. Not that anyone would want to watch them. We were truly rubbish. Thank the Lord we never really got out of Ireland."

"Dancing?" I repeated in confusion. "Matching outfits?" *What kind of weird pornos did he make, exactly?*

He nodded with downcast eyes.

"Yeah, the rest of the lads and I had a whole dance routine in the video for our first single, and since we were marketed as the Irish answer to 'N Sync, we even did . . . some Irish step dancing . . ." His voice trailed off as if he couldn't bear to continue.

"Sometimes Irish people still recognize me and take the mickey out of me—like what happened back there." He angled his head toward the direction that we had just come from. "That's why I try to avoid them. It's a right embarrassment."

My hand shot to my mouth. "Are you saying that you . . . were in a boy band?"

Lochlon looked up at me.

"Um . . ." He sounded confused. "Have you only just realized that now? Yes, that's what I'm saying. What had you thought I was going on about this whole time?"

"Oh my God, Lochlon, I thought you were talking about doing *porn!*"

"What?!" His jaw dropped open. "How'd you figure that?"

"You said they were auditioning boys for videos!"

"I meant *music* videos," he protested. "God almighty! I *wish* it were porn! That'd be fine. Rather cool, do you not think? Being in a shite failed boy band is far worse. I'm *still* paying for it! You wear *one* shiny suit and do *one* Irish step dancing sequence—"

I busted out in laughter and quickly concealed it with a fit of coughing when I saw the heartbroken look in Lochlon's eyes. *Keep your face looking normal*, I demanded to myself. But I had to bite my lip because I couldn't stop picturing Lochlon reenacting Riverdance in lamé pants. It hit me: *Those girls on the steps were mimicking his dance moves.*

"I cannot believe it. You? In a boy band? But you're so—" I looked him up and down, scanning over his scruffy face and basic, untrendy man-clothes.

Lochlon crossed his arms, looking vaguely insulted.

"Wh-what is it?"

He frowned. "Do you not think I'm a good-looking enough lad?"

I couldn't help but laugh out loud right in his face this time. "No! I'm sorry—I didn't mean that—you're *very* good-looking. It's just that you're so . . . dark and moody." The wrong words were stumbling out, but I could do nothing to stop them.

He stabbed the bottom of his drink with his straw. "Well, every group needs a bad boy, don't they now?" He pouted in all seriousness.

I dug my nails into the heels of my hands to smother my giggles. I felt my face growing purple. "Yes," I said, mirroring his sincere mood. "You are right about that."

Appeased, Lochlon refocused. "But Kika, you must know I'm a different person now; I'm a serious writer and traveler. I'm to be published one day. You know that, don't you?"

I was silent for another moment, strangling another fit of chuckles.

"Still, I understand if you want nothing more to do with me. I was a right loser for doing something like that."

Lochlon showed me his eyes. His irises were wine-bottle green, a beautiful, jarring shade that had no business being someone's eye color.

"Lochlon," I announced, ensuring I had his full attention. I studied him over. *He isn't any less attractive to me*, I thought with an *ahh* of relief. I still wanted to sleep next to him. He was still mine.

"Yes?"

"I. Don't. Care." (Of course I had a million questions, but I knew that Wikipedia could answer them.)

"You . . . you don't?"

"Of course I don't! Who cares if you were in some silly group ages ago?" I asked, fanning out my arms. "I assumed your dark past was going to be *way* darker than this because of the way you were going on and on. I can't wait to tell my mom that it's nothing serious—"

"But it *is* serious. I'm still getting slagged on by the lads at home," he said, interrupting me with adolescent touchiness.

"Forget them. I mean, whatever, it *is* sort of funny. But who cares?"

He chewed his bottom lip.

"Thank you for telling me," I said. "That must have been really hard for you."

"'S okay," he mumbled.

"This doesn't change how I feel about you," I reassured him then.

He looked at me suspiciously. "So you still want to be with me?"

I showed him my answer.

TAKING ADVANTAGE OF my newfound open schedule, I spent the
rest of the week with Madison, which did little to lift my
mood. I peeled off the lid of my third pudding cup, feeling
vaguely ashamed. At least I had the decency to save one for
Madison's lunch box tomorrow—I wasn't an animal.

I licked the buttery chocolate lid as Madison played with
her high-end American Girl doll, every upper-middle-class
kid's prized possession. Madison was less interested in the
pudding and more interested in Kirsten Larson (the doll) and
her inadvertently chic Peter Pan–collar dress.

Raiding the snack cupboards was one of the unspoken
perks of babysitting. I unabashedly stuck my tongue into the
pudding cup to lick out the last bit, and Madison gaped up at
me with her long-lashed doe eyes.

"Don't judge me. You don't know my journey!" I told her.

She just stood there. "Kika, can I cowor?"

"Of course you can color, Madison." I couldn't help but grin at her adorable lisp.

I pulled down her craft box crammed with construction paper, markers, and that white glue that looked like marshmallow fluff—no wonder kids were always trying to eat it. My cell phone rang just as I plunked her at the kitchen table with a sheet of fresh white paper.

A strange number with far too many digits flashed on my phone. My heart pounced: *It's an international number; it must be Lochlon.*

After Lochlon told me about his candy pop past, we became closer than ever. Still, I wasn't prepared for what would happen once we parted ways: We actually kept in touch.

Lochlon emailed and called me from all corners of the globe.

"I don't get it," I asked him recently when he was calling me from Cambodia. I clarified over the dodgy phone line, "I mean, you're off living the dream. Why are you wasting your time calling me? I love hearing from you, I just don't . . . get it."

I was scared of what his answer would be, but I was more scared of not knowing.

"You don't get it?" he mimicked back, entertained. In the background, I heard horns of tuk-tuks beeping and children shrieking with delight—his world was still uproarious; his life still crackled with wonder.

"Gorgeous," he said almost shyly. "I want you in my life. I want you in my life in any way I can get it. And right now, if that means just over the phone, then I'll take it."

Even though he couldn't see me, I smiled then.

"But with any luck at all it won't always be like this. And if I'm to have anything to do with it, I'll make sure of it," he told me. I knew then that we were both invested.

Madison snapped me back into the present moment: "Your phone's winging, Kika."

"Thanks, doll face," I told her as I pressed my phone to my cheek. "Hello?" I asked, my voice hopeful and urgent. According to his last email, Lochlon should be in Indonesia by now. "Lochlon?" I asked into the phone, already dreaming up the interior of the Southeast Asian Internet café he'd be calling me from—sticky keyboards, plastic palm trees, bad electronic dance music.

But it wasn't Lochlon.

Instead, a high-pitched female voice pummeled through the phone and into my ear: "Lamb!"

There was only one woman it could be: Elsbeth Darling. And to her, everyone—from her husband to her spinning instructor—was dubbed "lamb." Before I could respond, she plowed on: "Why, oh, why didn't your mother tell me you were babysitting again?"

"Um, hi? Elsbeth?"

"Of course it's me, Kika. Can you hear me okay? I'm calling from London."

I heaved myself onto the kitchen countertop. "My mom told me you guys moved there. How is it?" I kicked my dangling legs. "That's why she didn't tell you I was babysitting, I guess. Besides, I'm not *really* babysitting." I instantly regretted saying that.

As if Elsbeth picked up on this, she said, "I know you're

not *really* babysitting. You have that job at VoyageCorp that Mr. Darling got you. As if I could forget."

Elsbeth's husband, Prescott Darling, was the financial advisor to Richie Rich who passed on my résumé to VoyageCorp. So, in effect, the Darlings got me the job from which I had just been fired.

"Right," I said. I didn't have the heart to tell her I got sacked, knowing it would get back to Mr. Darling and he would think I was an incompetent free spirit (but wasn't I, though?).

"How are things going over there? Mr. Darling and I were wondering about that . . ."

"Um, good. Fine," I fibbed.

"Oh." She sounded dissatisfied.

"I mean, it's *great*. I'm getting a big promotion soon." I squirmed at the lie and willed my mouth to stop moving, but it was no use. "You know, just clocking in my face time, doing due diligence, going big or going home. Total win-win scenario!"

I blathered out clichéd business jargon in the hopes of confusing her into silence. "I'm just babysitting during my downtime to make some extra money, you know," I said in conclusion.

But Elsbeth Darling didn't know, because her whole world consisted of downtime and she certainly never had a need for money. I visualized her life as a looped Parisian perfume commercial. I imagined she spent lots of time kittening about on chaise longues and whispering.

"Of course, of course." Her voice surged emotionally. "Oh, Kika, the girls and I miss you *terribly*."

Elsbeth used to take yoga classes with my mom, and, oddly enough, the two of them became friendly. Because of their friendship, Elsbeth took me on as a babysitter and I got to spend whole summers bonding with the Darling girls, Willamina (Mina) and Gwendolyn (Gwen), and their aquamarine inground swimming pool. But my sunscreen-scented memory suddenly vanished when my eye caught Madison.

She had uncapped every single one of her Mr. Sketch Scented Markers and was exuberantly huffing them like a practiced druggie.

I put the phone on speaker so I could wipe the rainbow colors off Madison's nose. Give them all the bourgeois names you want; all children will act like feral drunks when your back is turned.

"It's great to hear from you, Elsbeth. I really miss you guys, too," I said truthfully. "How is London?"

"Well, that's actually why I'm calling, lamb," she said. "Mr. Darling and I are *very* happy, and Mina's wonderful, too—you know Miss Popularity. She's the reigning queen of Harrington Gardens School for Girls.

"But Gwen isn't doing as marvelously. I think she's homesick. She doesn't speak to any of the British children in school, and she isn't clicking with any of the French au pairs we've hired."

"Oh no," I said. Gwen was a willful girl who was dazzled by her older sister; scarily skilled at karate; and harbored dreams of being a spy when she grew up. "Well, a spy or a ballerina," was how she officially put it.

It was hard to remember a time when she wasn't so precocious. When I first started working for the Darlings, Gwendy was going on her tenth month of what her world-renowned child psychologists called "selective mutism." She refused to talk to anyone outside of her immediate family and even stayed completely silent during kindergarten. The doctors blamed it on social anxiety, but now that I knew Gwen, I like to think she was just bored of everyone babying her.

When Elsbeth hired me, she explained that I wasn't to take Gwen's silence personally. I didn't, but I still found myself chatting to her, even though her mother told me she wasn't paying any attention.

One day, while I was ranting about the creepy, babyish *Teletubbies* show that Elsbeth was always plopping her in front of, Gwen started giggling aloud. Shocked at the sudden sound coming out of her mouth, I asked her what she was laughing at.

"The bat-shit bonkers Teletubbies!" she said, repeating my words back verbatim. Ten months of not speaking and her first word was "bat-shit"—can you imagine?

But Elsbeth ignored the distasteful specifics and gave me all the credit for getting her to talk again. And from that day on, Elsbeth never reprimanded me for my foul mouth again.

Over the phone line, Elsbeth continued: "Mina was studying the French Revolution in school and had made a model guillotine for her European history presentation, and my little Gwendy took it upon herself to torture the au pair with it. The whole thing was getting very *Les Misérables*, so I've just had to let go of another au pair," said Elsbeth in a blasé way.

She then added: "Of course, it wasn't just that they weren't getting along; I also found out that she was *fired* from her last job. Fired and she didn't even tell me! Can you imagine just omitting such an important detail like that from your future employer?"

The squirm-inducing scene from my own firing swirled in my mind's eye.

Then Elsbeth's voice rose in amusement: "But you should

have seen the '*Vive la Revolution!*' banner Mina and Gwen made when she left. Very creative."

I laughed aloud at the image and felt a sudden twinge of sentimentality.

"Anyway, my point is we really need a nanny Gwen is comfortable with—someone who can make her transition smoother. In the end, she wasn't even speaking to the nanny; she was just chasing her around. We can't have Gwen regressing and refusing to speak again. Do you see?"

"Gotcha," I said tentatively. *Why is she telling me all of this?*

"We want you back, Kika. We want you here in London."

Sure that I had just started to hallucinate, I didn't dare speak. But Elsbeth Darling continued, undeterred by my lack of reaction.

"Mr. Darling has already secured a visa. And we have plenty of room here at the town house. The house has a whole servants' quarters. Not that you'd be a servant or anything. Lord no, how very feudal, am I right? But what I'm saying is you'll have your own space and even your own entrance from the street so that you can come and go as you please."

I shook my head. *Is this really happening?*

"Kika, did the phone cut out?" Elsbeth heightened her octave and slowed her words. Sounding as if she was talking to an ancient great-aunt, she tried again: "What. I. Said. Was—"

I interrupted: "No, Elsbeth, I heard. I just . . . can't believe it." I swallowed deeply and audibly. "Are you my fairy godmother or something?"

Elsbeth chuckled. "Oh, lamb, you'd be doing *us* the favor. You worked miracles on Gwen, and you're the only one we can trust her with."

"Are you sure I don't have to, like, give you my firstborn? Because if so, you can definitely have it."

Elsbeth laughed as if unsure I was joking. (I wasn't.)

"You're the first one we thought of for the job. Plus, I know moving here is a nonissue for you. You've always been the type of girl who loves a fly-by-the-seat-of-your-pants adventure, am I right? And, lamb, I know you have a job and a whole life over there. You can take your time deciding. I know you'd have to give up the VoyageCorp job, and that's a *major* career decision."

Right then, I knew my chance had come to tell Elsbeth I'd been fired. *But will she still offer me the job if she knows?*

I started rationalizing an omission: *If I moved to London, no one would know me, and no one would know I got fired from VoyageCorp. The thought relieved me. Elsbeth would never find out, so what was the point in risking it by telling her now?*

Unaware of my inner struggle, Elsbeth went about convincing me. "Your job can't be paying you enough if you still have to babysit. And not to make it about money, but we'd offer you a very competitive salary in GBP . . ." Elsbeth Darling trailed off meaningfully. "Oh, Kika, say you'll come?"

"Christ on a bicycle. Are you kidding me? Of course I'll come!" I shot-putted my body off the kitchen counter.

"Brilliant. Just brilliant," Elsbeth drilled into the phone.

Elsbeth had certainly altered her way of speaking since she moved. She sounded like a one-dimensional caricature from an American-produced period drama.

"Damn, Elsbeth, you're really getting into this British thing. You sound just like Madonna with that accent."

"How dare you! I *at least* sound like Gwyneth Paltrow."

It was good to know that Elsbeth wasn't above making fun of herself—even with her new overdone inflections.

"I have to give notice at my job first," I (white) lied.

"That's expected. So you can be here in two weeks? By the middle of February?"

I agreed and hung up the phone after promising to follow up with Mr. Darling's assistant to solidify all the details.

"Madison!" I barked.

Madison froze and stared up at me with a lemon-scented yellow marker buried halfway up her left nostril.

"Do you realize what this means?"

"No . . ." Madison said, slowly removing the marker and looking abashed.

"It means"—I swiped her up—"that I'm moving to London!"

"Wike 'Wondon Bwidge Is Fawwing Down'?" Madison asked eagerly, picking up on my excitement.

"*Exactly* like 'London Bridge Is Falling Down.'" I was moving to London where people said, "Cheers, love," where the alphabet ended in "zed," and where there were Cadbury Creme Eggs all year round—not just for Easter. I swirled Madison around the kitchen.

"Faster, faster!" she yelled, and I obliged until we collapsed on the honeycomb-tiled kitchen floor.

"Chwist on a bicycle." Madison sighed, holding her spinning head.

"Oh shit. Madison, please don't say that in front of your mother." I winced. "And you may want to avoid saying 'shit' in front of her as well," I added for good measure.

EARLY THE NEXT morning, I wrote Lochlon an email about the latest developments in my life:

"I got a new job in London," I wrote like it was no big deal. "Hopefully I'll get to travel all over Europe while I'm there. I feel like my life is moving in the right direction again—I can't believe I'm getting this opportunity."

In my mind, I could see my mother rolling her eyes about the "travel all over Europe" remark, and I deleted it before clicking "send" with determination.

A band of early-February sunshine slowly made its way across my face, and I leaped from my desk with unnatural morning energy. Now *this* was how my life was supposed to be.

My backpack, as well-worn with love as the Velveteen Rabbit, slumped in the corner of my room.

"Cheer up, buttercup," I told it. "We're busting out of this joint in two weeks."

Long ago, I learned to pack light, using only my backpack and collecting goods along the way. Rolling luggage is all well and good for packaged group tours on shiny buses pumped with recycled air, but nothing beats a well-packed backpack for the stair-filled metro stations and the cobbled lanes of Europe. I prided myself on my portability.

Growing up, I used to have a lot more stuff around. I was one of those girls who was the contents of her closet. My friends and I spoke about shopping in a language that was insisting and self-defending—we *had* to have new, pricey things because we thought we *needed* them.

But I couldn't keep up with these girls, and once I started traveling, I stopped wanting to. Instead, I found my own course to be passionate about. I strove to form a collection of once-in-a-lifetime experiences instead of designer attire.

Even now, my life didn't run in alignment with theirs. I wanted none of the things they wanted: not the clothes, the McMansions, the 401(k)s, the husbands, or the silver gadgets named after fruit. I had no interest in the swag of adulthood, of normalcy.

I looked around my childhood bedroom with my outdated furniture and ratty bedspread. After college and my year abroad, I didn't bother buying new stuff. Acquiring more things just meant more stuff to leave behind.

"Hi, Kika. Want some coffee?" my mother asked through my closed door, interrupting my manifesto.

"Yes, please," I called.

She entered my room and set a swilling cup of coffee (free-trade Guatemalan) onto my desk. "I wasn't sure if you fancied a spot of tea instead," she said in a laughable English accent.

"Coffee is brilliant, Mumsy," I responded with an equally offensive twitter.

"Kika, I'm so excited for your next soul journey."

"Mom, I'm so excited, too." I didn't give her a hard time for her yoga-teacher speech and even spewed out some of my own. "I feel like the world is opening up for me in a positive way, like I'm getting a second chance. I couldn't handle job searching for another three months."

"Good. Remember that when you're with the Darlings."

"I'm going to be Mary freakin' Poppins. I'm going to give it my all. If I fail at a job again, I want it to be because of real reasons, not because I was too lazy."

"That's exactly what I was getting at." My mom seemed relieved that I got there myself.

"Besides, it's the Darlings. Mina and Gwen love me. How hard could it be?"

"Famous last words, Kika," she warned before escorting herself to the door. "And maybe you'll actually make some money this time," she added. I knew she wasn't being malicious, only honest. Somehow that made the comment land harder.

"I'm off to teach downstairs," she said.

"I'll be down in a minute," I called behind her.

I did yoga on occasion, too, but mainly because it made my mom happy. As far as I was concerned, the greatest benefit of yoga was being bendy enough to tie your shoelaces without crouching all the way down, but I never told her this.

Even though I didn't do yoga daily, my mom and I were

more alike than not. She passed on her free-spirited penchant for swearwords, Scandinavian features, and impossibly long femurs to me. I secretly hoped that I wouldn't become the heir of her bad luck with men as well.

As far as I knew, the only thing I inherited from my dad was my Mediterranean first name, Francisca (which strangely got shortened to Kika), and my dark eyes and eyebrows, which somehow still worked on my otherwise Nordic coloring and frame.

I've never been a "Francisca" with her Italian sensibilities, sky-high stilettos, killing-it red lipsticks, and knowledge of fine wine.

I was always a "Kika"—foulmouthed and sweet toothed. (No matter how much quinoa my mom fed me, I always wanted what was never around—pure sucrose.) I was raised to rock a bohemian wardrobe and a pair of secondhand Dr. Martens while listening to folk music.

A normal mother would be a bit nervous about my move to London, but my mom was used to it. She no longer said to me, "I am confused about your life," like my well-meaning high school friends, or, "But what do you want to do when you grow up?" as my grandparents asked.

And thankfully she didn't ask me (like a presumptuous stranger once did): "What are you running away from?" (Short answer: Nothing. Long answer: Nothing, asshole.) Instead, my mother let me be myself. And even before I had a self to be, she let me figure it out on my own.

At sixteen, I spent the summer in Panama building houses with Habitat for Humanity. In high school, I suffered through a year of finicky Latin just so I could *veni, vidi, vici* and *vino* my way through Florence during the senior trip. In college, I studied abroad every other semester. But I only started to get a sense of who I wanted to be when I traveled alone.

There are many reasons why girls should not travel alone, and I won't list them, because none of them are original reasons. Besides, there are more reasons why girls *should*.

I have the utmost respect for girls who travel alone, because it's hard work sometimes. But girls, we just want adventures. We want international best friends and hold-your-breath vistas out of crappy hostel windows. We want to discover moving works of art, sometimes in museums and sometimes in side-street graffiti. We want to hear soul-restoring jam sessions at beach bonfires and to watch celestial dawns spill over villages that haven't changed since the Middle Ages.

We want to fall in love with boys with say-that-again accents. We want sore feet from stay-up-all-night dance parties at just-one-more-drink bars.

We want to be on our own even as we sketch and photograph the Piazza San Marco covered in pigeons and beautiful Italian lovers intertwined so that we'll never forget what it feels like to be twenty-three and absolutely purposeless and single, but in love with every city we visit next.

We want to be struck dumb by the baritone echoes of church bells in Vatican City and the rich, heaven-bound calls to prayer in Istanbul and to know that no matter what, there just has to be some greater power or holy magic responsible for all this bursting, delirious, overwhelming beauty in the great, wide, sprawling world.

I tucked my passport into my bag. Girls, we don't just want to have fun; we want a whole lot more out of life than that.

IF THIS WERE a movie, I'd jet off to England in one of those highly stylized, jump-cut montages set to the rhythm of an upbeat sound track.

At the airport, I'd hug my mom good-bye—good-bye for now. Because it's always "good-bye for now" with me.

And we're clear for takeoff. The camera would do a long-tracking shot framing the plane, all silver and glossy, bisecting woozy heights at impossible velocities. (Or maybe there'd be one of those cartoon planes puttering across a map.) Then the lens would zoom in for a close-up inside the egg-shaped plane window, where I'd rest my head back on the airline seat. And the audience would think: "There she goes, Wendy en route to Neverland."

• • •

Of course it wasn't as refined and cool as all that. In real life the trip was fraught with first-world problems including the standard-issue flight delays; a KGB-grade interrogation by UK border control; and the realization that I may or may not have forgotten to pack clean underwear. But still, I had arrived!

The Darlings arranged for their personal driver, Clive, to pick me up from Heathrow in a "British racing green Audi" (as described by Mr. Darling in the email). I watched England whiz by through the open window, the wind gusting my hair in a cinematic way. Once we were on the motorway, I felt my eyelids getting heavy, as if hypnotized by the BBC radio host's charming accent.

"We're nearly there, love." Clive startled me awake. The purring car braked in Stanhope Gardens, a leafy, manicured block of residential town houses that were impossibly big and white. The houses, crafted for another, more regal era, were set in a square shape with a large fenced-in garden in the middle.

Clive opened the car door for me.

"Thanks, but I've got it," I said as I wrestled my backpack out of his grip only to plop it on the footpath. "I just want a second to compose myself before going in," I explained.

He gave me a chauffeur-ly head nod, said, "Very good," and left to park the car.

I stood in front of the still-sleepy square of houses forming and memorizing my first impressions. The Darlings' house was alight in that curious, sallow morning light, and a ghostly fog tiptoed over what was officially known as the Royal Borough of Kensington and Chelsea. My Southwest London post-code apparently was, like, *posh*. (I only knew what "posh" meant because of the Spice Girls.)

What I wanted (what I really, really wanted) was to observe everything before it got too familiar, too normal, and under-appreciated. First impressions were only fun to think about after you knew better. I relished that little wave of pulse-quickening fear and excitement that travel splashes on our faces, as if to wake us up and remind us we're alive.

I exhaled a swell of hot breath into the winter air, ready for whatever was ahead for me, and I walked toward my mysteri-ous destiny.

BUT MY MYSTERIOUS destiny would have to wait.

Ruining the picturesque morning scene was a homeless guy slumping on the sunlit doorsteps of the house. His body blocked my access to the front door. *Of course.*

I coughed conspicuously, but he didn't react. I tried again: "Good morning, sunshine."

He stirred at my chipper voice but moved leisurely, taking his time untangling his long limbs. Up close, I could see he was actually very nicely dressed in a heavy blazer with an upturned collar and expensive-looking shoes—this guy wasn't homeless, just disheveled. It was like he was on his way home from a bar and just sort of fell asleep here.

"Rough night?" I asked.

He studied me. His expression was that of someone unim-pressed.

"Do you need help getting a taxi home?" I asked, undeterred by his unresponsiveness.

He seemed about my age, and hey, we've all been there. Well, not *there*, per se—*I've* never passed out on someone else's stoop—but we've all had *those* nights.

I nodded eagerly. "Taxi? Home?"

"Another bolshie American." He spoke under his breath. He then gave me a scolding sneer like I interrupted his nap, which I supposed I had.

"Yes," I said in a loud voice, demonstrating that I heard him perfectly. "I am American. I'll try asking in British: You, good sir, are sleeping on my front stoop. If I could trouble you to move?" I spoke in the politest Queen's English that I could manage this early in the morning.

He made a face but didn't move from my path. Patting his pockets, he looked around himself, first to one side and then the other.

"Um, dude, you're in my way—" I began again, but he interrupted.

"That is not possible, I'm afraid," he said haughtily. I smelled alcohol on his breath. His light eyes were rimmed pink from the lack of sleep and the night of drinking. He reminded me of one of those albino-white bunnies with the demon-red eyes.

"I'm Aston Hyde Bettencourt," he said and then paused for dramatic effect, like it meant something to me.

"Ashton? Like Ashton Kutcher? I didn't know real people had names like that," I said.

"How dare you?" He looked genuinely offended. "It's *As*ton, as in Aston Martin; as in, as in, Aston Hyde Bettencourt," he stammered, now rising. He buttoned his blazer and smoothed the lapel.

I stared at him. "Got it. *Ass*ton. Emphasis on the *ass*."

"Yanks," he eked out through closed teeth. "I live here. So you, madam, are actually on *my* steps, and I'd kindly request that you sod off and leave me be."

"Well, *I'm* Kika Shores, and according to my new employers, I live here." I took out the crumpled printout of the email with my new address on it and flapped it in front of his unshaven face.

He reluctantly took the paper like it was a used tissue. "*Kika?* Your name is Kika, and you're taking the piss out of *my* name? Sounds like the name of a French poodle."

Before I could retort, he said, exasperated, "You're thirty-four."

"How dare *you!*" I patted my hair down. Sure, I just got off a transatlantic flight, but I didn't look thirty-four. "I'm twenty-three. How old are you?"

Aston stared at me unblinkingly. I glowered back.

"No," he mustered with the barest civility. For a moment I thought he was going to add, "stupid." *No, stupid.*

"The house you're looking for is number thirty-four—it's next door." He tilted his head to the left where the next house sat at an obtuse corner angle. "This is thirty-two. In case you have trouble with the numbers in the future, you'll remember this door is red and yours is blue." He spoke like a wicked kindergarten teacher, deliberate and patronizing. "Now off you go."

I snatched the paper back. "Oh, I'm dismissed, am I?"

"I think I bloody well know where I live," he said more to himself than to me. He began lifting the potted plants to peer underneath. "I did manage to get through Oxford, after all."

He dragged a key from beneath a planter; the metal scraped against the slate.

I scoffed, hitched my backpack on my shoulder, and hauled it over to the house next door. Out of the corner of my eye, I saw him scrutinizing me.

"What a snob!" I said loud enough for him to hear as I rung the bell of number thirty-four, the blue door.

From inside, I heard the dead bolts twist. As my door creaked open, he disappeared into his house. I uselessly hoped it would be the last I saw of him, though that seemed highly unlikely.

14

"ELSBETH!" I SQUEALED too loudly. Behind me, a tree full of garden birds darted off in a dewy puff of clucks and feathers.

"Kika!"

I shucked off my bag, dropped it down in the foyer with a dead-body thump, and entered Elsbeth's perfumed embrace.

"Oh my God, Elsbeth, you look emaciated." I wrapped my arms around her with concern. It was like hugging a bird with an eating disorder.

"Oh, Kika," she pooh-poohed, "you're so flattering!"

I blinked my eyes rapidly and managed to keep a straight face.

"Don't tell your mother, but I've been supplementing the yoga with barre classes. You must come. Not that you need to, with your mother's genes. You, lamb, look like a Danish supermodel. You're just naturally magnificent."

"Mmm, Danish . . ." I licked my lips in Pavlovian response.

Elsbeth was a German drill sergeant when it came to exercise, and as far as she was concerned, fatty food was the enemy. I, on the other hand, just couldn't get on board with fake ice cream products with skinny cows on the box (cows were *supposed* to be plump!).

"You poor thing, you must be starving. There's breakfast in the conservatory. And you'll be able to see the girls before they leave for school. Go on."

"In the conservatory?" I suddenly felt like I walked into a game of Clue. "It was Miss Scarlet in the conservatory with the candlestick!" I announced in a pompous accent, erecting my pointer finger in the air.

"I know, I know. Having a conservatory is so over the top."

"Oh, stop. You love it."

"Clearly," Elsbeth said with a demure smile. "This way."

She led me through the light-filled house, her clapping heels echoing off the high ceilings. The house was tastefully decorated in what Elsbeth would describe as "clean lines and neutrals": slates, milk whites, and Elsbeth's favorite color, beige.

She was supremely groomed as well—fragranced, hair upswept, and polished with understated makeup despite the early hour.

Her naturally curly hair had been pressed into submission by a flatiron. I'd actually never seen her hair curly, but allegedly she had corkscrew ringlets. When I last babysat for the Darlings, Elsbeth would have a girl come once a day to straighten her hair and do her makeup—an indulgence she still appeared to partake in.

"Straighter," she'd command. "Make me look *Asian*," she'd

insist to the girl, who actually was Asian, but hearing it still made me cringe.

When we reached the back of the house, I saw the girls before they saw me. They sat at a breakfast table in a sunny glass room filled with palms and tropical greenery. The table was laid with ballerina-pink rosebuds in stout vases; orange juice in beading carafes; and well-steamed and creamed coffee in cups with matching saucers—this was how the Darlings rolled.

"Holy shit. Look at my little hobgoblins," I squealed, unable to hold it in a moment longer. My silly nickname for the Darling girls had stuck a long time ago, and using it again was my way of hoping that Elsbeth would keep making concessions for my big mouth.

"Kika!" they chimed in unison. The girls were outfitted in prissy school uniforms with blazers, ties, and kneesocks.

Gwendy, now seven, leapt up first. "Kika Shores!" she shrieked. "Kika! Kika! It's me: Gwendolyn Prudence Darling III."

I seized Gwen under her armpits and whirled her in the air, completely confident that I would have no problem keeping her talking.

"Gwendy," I exclaimed, "I know it's you. How could I possibly forget anyone so freakin' adorable?" I gave her a suffocating hug and set her back down. "You are the prettiest hobgoblin ever."

"Actually, Kika"—Elsbeth tapped me on the shoulder and motioned for me to lean in as she whispered—"we're trying this new thing where we don't compliment the girls on their looks. We're attempting to instill the notion that one gets praised for merit, for things like academics, over superficial things like appearances. You understand, don't you?" she murmured apologetically.

I nodded my head, impressed. "Nice. I can still call them hobgoblins, right?"

Elsbeth smiled. "Oh, Kika. You always make such a lively splash."

I went over to Mina, now thirteen. She had matured since I last saw her. "Mina, how absolutely *intelligent* you look."

Mina stuck her tongue out the side of her mouth. Elsbeth tried to butt in, but Mina snapped, "She's kidding, Mother."

I stroked her dark curls, which mercifully hadn't been flat-ironed. "What's up with these getups?" I motioned at their uniforms. "You guys didn't tell me you were going to Hogwarts."

"I know, right? I just want to die," moaned Mina.

"I want to die, too!" mimicked Gwen excitedly, bouncing up and down in her storybook pinafore. She still obviously hadn't grown out of the older-sister-worship phase.

"I missed you guys so much. How is everything?"

But Elsbeth cut me off. "Later. You will be able to catch up later. You girls have to get to school. And I need to get to the gym. Go on now, Clive is waiting out front with the car." The girls protested but still filed out with military-perfect posture.

Gwen waved good-bye energetically. "Bye, Kika, bye!"

"See you later, alligator." I winked.

"Bye, Mom, bye!" Gwen called next, just as enthusiastically. "Have fun at your twirling class."

"*Spinning* class, lamb. Yes, thank you, I will," said Elsbeth Darling as she shooed the girls out.

"WELL, I WAS going to paint it—cream colored, perhaps, or eggshell—" Elsbeth signaled to the soaring walls of my room. "But then I said to myself, 'This color *is* Kika. I should keep it.'"

The rest of the Darlings' South Kensington house was a bit cold and clattery and taupe (Elsbeth's fancy way of saying "beige"), but my room had been spared. It was delightfully twee with celestial blue-green walls, a small balcony, and even a doll-sized fireplace.

"I love it." I rapped my knuckles against a rosewood writing desk. "I feel like I'm living in Downton Abbey."

"Oh, and here are your keys. The skeleton key is for the private garden out front, in the middle of the square of houses. Only residents of Stanhope Gardens get access to that park, which is why it's locked."

Elsbeth then promptly excused herself—she was going to

the gym. "But call my mobile if you need anything, anything at all."

Since it was Friday, she gave me the day off. She told me most weekends I'd have to myself, and if I needed to watch the girls, we'd make up those days during the week. She left me with an advance on this month's salary. When I converted it into dollars, it roughly equated to what I would call "a damn near shit-ton of cash"—more than twice what I made at VoyageCorp.

I mentally started planning my first weekend trip: *I wonder if Malta is warm this time of year?*

I wrote a quick email to my mom and followed up with a slightly longer one to Lochlon: "You wouldn't believe the Darlings' town house," I started, but as I typed, I was surprised to see a message pop up from the very man I was emailing. I rushed to open it.

"Glad for you about the new job. That's class, isn't it? How'd you get on with the trip?"

I couldn't read fast enough:

> I have news myself: Looks like the craic is over for me for now. Da's ill so I'm to go back home to the farm for a short while. My mother's insisting, so I know it mustn't be good. Suppose the upside is that we're to be on the same continent again—for a wee bit, anyway. Maybe everything happens for a reason.

My pulse deepened and thumped like a bass beat in my ears. My eyes and my heart moved at different speeds. I read the email again and again. *Is Lochlon's father dying?*

Lochlon wasn't close to his father (we'd bonded over having absent dads), but my heart throbbed for him at this news: His dad had liver problems, and it had to be serious if his mom asked him to come home from Asia.

Poor Lochlon and his poor family. He was the eldest of five; his youngest sister was only eleven. They were still so young.

But then, an uncensored blip of pleasure bubbled up inside me: *Lochlon is going to be nearby in Ireland.* Immediately, I was ashamed of the insensitive thought.

I tried to regain focus: *This isn't about you. His father is dying*, I reminded myself.

Still, I knew he was quoting me when he said, "Everything happens for a reason." It was far too American a phrase for him to use, so I knew that the same thought had occurred to him: We were going to be very close to each other. Lochlon's family lived outside of Belfast. That was just a hop, skip, or a jump (my geography needed some polishing) from London.

"So sorry to hear that," I wrote back immediately, hoping he'd get my message while still at the Internet café and that my words would provide the slightest bit of comfort. "Please remember I am here for you. If there's anything I can do, let me know."

I signed off with my new number, since Elsbeth already had gotten me a phone.

The knot of conflicting emotions tightened in my stomach. To busy myself, I emptied my backpack into the freestanding wardrobe. There was not one "blouse" or "sensible-sized heel" in sight.

I surveyed my ripped jeans (ripped from overwear, not factory fashion holes); my shabby boots; and my dirty blond hair.

I looked like myself again, not a corporate imposter leeched of all color. Technically, I was far from home, but I already felt closer to who I really was.

I tried to keep my persistent happiness from bleeding over into thoughts of Lochlon back in Ireland, caring for his dying father, but it wasn't easy.

Even though this was the first time that I had legit reason to think that we might actually meet up again, I had already imagined our reunion with embarrassing frequency and in bodice-ripping fashion. It helped that he had actually ripped my clothes off me on more than one occasion in his sudden and passionate way. I could still recall the tingling, lusty head rush of being naked in front of him. A year's worth of fantasizing left me desperate to feel that way again.

— *16* —

A FEW DAYS later, I accidently ruined the girls' dinner by taking them to the Kensington Crêperie, where we ordered dessert crêpes roughly the size of Hula-Hoops. The café was cozy and bathed in warm, earthy light, which spilled out of the fogged-up windows like honey. Through the cobblestone plaza outside, people rushed home under winter-bare trees and a misting of frosty rain.

I made the girls bring their homework, but so far Gwendy and I had just been chatting while Mina filtered in and out of the conversation, mainly staying focused on her cell phone.

"Mina and I both go to the same school. But Mina's school is in a different building from mine, because she's older. Mina's the most popular girl in her school—I know it. And she's also the prettiest—even though Mom says we can't say that. And she also is the funniest." Gwen swirled the Nutella around her deconstructed crêpe.

Mina's thumbs scurried over her phone. She hadn't eaten much of her banana crêpe. I eyed it longingly, though I'd just polished off my own (fresh strawberries, white Belgian chocolate, Chantilly cream, and magic).

"Jeez, how much are you paying the hobgoblin for these endorsements?" I nudged Mina.

She skimmed a look away from her phone screen for one solitary second. "What can I say? Gwendolyn has an excellent and observant eye."

"I have *two* excellent eyes," corrected Gwen, all abuzz in a souped-up sugar high.

"Do you want the rest of my crêpe, Kika?" Mina asked, noticing that it was the object of my lovestruck gaze. "I don't want any more."

"Seriously?" I asked. "Oh, come on, eat it. Carpe diem!"

"Huh?" Mina frowned.

Gwendy studied her face and then replicated it. "Huh?"

I sighed and dragged the dish in front of me. "It means 'YOLO' in Latin," I told them before sawing off a bite.

Mina went back to her phone.

"So Mina," I said, trying hard to keep her attention. "Who are you texting?"

Mina shielded her phone from me. "Um, no one."

"Is it a boy?"

Gwen made the obligatory *oooooh* noise.

Mina glared at us. "I'm texting Peaches Benson-Westwood, my best friend at school. She's, like, really, really rich. And the most popular girl at school—well, we're both equally popular."

"Peaches Benson-Westwood? Do all English people have three-name monikers?" I thought of that guy from the other day: Aston Hyde Bettencourt. I only remembered his name because it was so snooty and ridiculous.

The phone absorbed her full attention again. "Pretty much."

But then, Mina turned toward the sound of giggles coming from the table next to us. I leaned over her shoulder and stole a glance at her phone screen. She wasn't texting at all—she was playing Candy Crush Saga.

She turned back around, and I ruffled Gwen's hair as a diversion. "And what about you, Gwen? No friends at school yet?"

"Nope!" said Gwen cheerfully. "Mom says I don't play well with others!" She beamed with pride.

"And why is that?" I asked.

"Because the other kids are crack babies."

I spat out my cappuccino, and Mina and I keeled over laughing. Gwen looked very pleased with herself for making us both laugh.

"Where'd you learn that?" I asked incredulously.

"From Mina." She pointed her finger at her sister.

Mina retorted just as quickly. "Hey! Don't blame me, you little crack baby."

"And TV," Gwen added. "From *Law and Order: SUV*. Dad watches it."

I didn't bother correcting her.

I pictured Mr. Darling. I had only seen him for approximately eight minutes total since I arrived. "You all right, Kika?" he had asked me, or rather demanded of me.

I just nodded and stared at his tremendously bald head, listening to him smack his nicotine gum in his mouth. That was the extent of our interactions, which was fine with me, because

I was secretly kind of scared of him, even though he had always been generous with me.

Once, he asked me what I wanted to do with my life, but when I told him about Gypsies & Boxcars, he asked me all sorts of intimidating questions about returns on investments and import taxes. I rambled on until he stopped listening, and he just mumbled, "How amusing . . ."

"Kika, what's a crack baby?" Gwendy asked me, breaking my thoughts.

"It's something little hobgoblins like you should not be calling the other kids. And I think if you stop calling people names, you'll make some friends," I added.

Gwen considered it for a moment. "But they all think I talk funny. And they laugh at me when I say the wrong words."

"Is that why you won't talk to them?" I asked, pulling the crêpe away before she drizzled Nutella all over her math homework. (There would be no criminal waste of Nutella on my watch.)

I scooped Gwen onto my lap. "We can learn all the new British words together so you'll know what they're talking about, okay?"

Gwen nodded bravely.

I tried again: "You see, it's like a secret code," I cooed in a hushed voice with a mysterious glint in my eye.

This got her excited; Gwen loved mystery. "A secret code?" she repeated, enthralled.

"Yup. And we need to crack it. The question is"—I eyed the people around us and flipped up the collar of my shirt in mock suspicion—"will you help?"

Gwen nodded vigorously. "Does a bear shit in the woods?!"

I looked at Mina. "We are going to have to watch our mouths around this one."

"Word," said Mina.

"Word," I said back.

"Word," mimicked Gwen, soberly nodding her head in the same stern way Mina nodded hers.

As the girls packed away their schoolwork into their backpacks, I stole another look at Mina's phone to confirm that she definitely wasn't texting anyone. But why would she lie about something like that?

A DARK, THROATY voice tumbled over the line: "Hiya, gorgeous."

It was Lochlon. (Of course it was Lochlon; who else called me "gorgeous" besides Italian maître d's?)

Lochlon had flown into Belfast a few nights ago, and here we were, already chatting on the phone at a decent hour for the both of us. Life was so much easier now that we were in the same time zone.

"I can't believe you have a cell phone," I gushed.

"And why not? This is modern Ireland now. We even have color telly," he told me with cheerful sarcasm.

"It's not that; it's just the fact that I can reach you whenever I want that gets me excited."

His voice went raspy. "Do you want to know what it is that excites me?"

I was sitting outside on the stoop in front of the Darlings' house, and I looked around. "Oh, I'm sure you're going to tell me."

Out of the corner of my eye, I spied movement from the house next door. The red door opened, and the nasty neighbor, Aston Hyde Bettencourt, came out whistling. *He's probably drunk again*, I judged.

Meanwhile, on the phone Lochlon proceeded to tell me in meticulous detail what it was exactly that excited him: ". . . thinking of you lying down on the bed under me, your wrists above your head—"

"Lochlon, I'm in public," I muttered into the phone, making accidental eye contact with Aston. He caught my eye for a moment and looked as if he was trying to place me. Maybe he was too drunk to remember me from the last time.

"You in public, eh? That makes the fantasy a wee bit hotter, doesn't it now?" Lochlon breathed. "And then tugging off your—"

"Shh!" I hissed loudly into the phone.

Thinking I had shushed him, Aston stopped whistling and whipped around to shoot me a disbelieving look. He sneered and rapidly stalked off down the street before I could let him know I hadn't meant him.

"Lochlon," I begged, "I just can't take it," I mock-cried into the phone. "Stop right now."

But he was unrelenting. "Oh, you can take it, I think."

I swallowed hard to compose myself and then changed the subject, because I could feel myself coloring in hell-hot lust. It had been far too long.

He snickered on the other end of the line. This was just how he liked me: squirming and impatient for him.

"So how is everything else?" I asked, clearing my throat. He already told me he didn't want to talk about his dad, so I ducked around that subject. "Have you seen your old friends?"

"I have, and you know what's really at me?" he asked rhetorically. "Everyone and everything"—he stopped to give his words weight—"*is exactly the bleedin' same*. Nothing changes, so. Everything is just as it was. Bit depressing, that is. At least they've stopped taking the mickey out of me, so I've nothing to complain about."

"I felt like nothing changed when I first came home, too," I said. "It was almost disappointing. But also comforting, don't you think?"

"I suppose. Places don't really change, but I suppose if you're gone long enough, you're the one who's doing the changing," he said.

I reflected on the unique alienation I felt when I first returned home from my year of backpacking. I was a stranger in my birthplace, feeling as if I had lost all sense of belonging there. And that was weirdly okay. I used the sensation to underscore the belief that I *didn't* actually belong there. It was then that I understood the mixed thrill and isolation of belonging nowhere and everywhere.

"I couldn't ever live here again. It's arse-backward," he complained. But then he upped his mood. "So, gorgeous, when am I to come and see you?"

I pulled the speaker away from my mouth so that he didn't hear my girly reaction. I had been waiting the whole phone call for this to come up.

"You mean visiting me? But what about your dad? You just got there," I said, keeping my pitch level.

"Yeah, sure, not straightaway. It would be best to wait until it evens out. But maybe in a few weeks' time I may come to London and see you, yeah?"

"How long are you going to be home for?" I asked in a breathy voice.

He brushed off this question again. "I'm sure I'll be back on the road in no time. So, what's the story? Am I to book tickets?"

"That sounds great." I tried not to come off as too enthusiastic. "I have weekends off," I said with nonchalance, like I wasn't planning the most important weekend of my life or anything.

"Brilliant."

I could sense his smile on the other end of the line. I loved his unshakable smile. It was so authentic and contagious.

"It's done, gorgeous. I'll give you a ring back when I get some dates sorted. And don't make like you haven't been thinking about me since I told you I was to be in Ireland. I know you well, I do. You want this. You want this as bad as I do, Kika."

Suddenly, I just knew that I'd hear it: He was going to tell me he loved me.

Not right now or anything, but at that moment, I just knew that one day this man would say those words to me.

I had already confessed my feelings to him at the end of the last trip. I left him and my life of travel in a train station in South India, on a foggy morning. I remember being so jealous that he got to keep traveling. I was envious but happy for him and angry and depressed and seething and blissful. I felt a thousand things when I left that morning, but mainly I felt heartbroken.

We spent our last night together in the $4-per-night beach hut that we had called home for the month.

He lay on top of me, his hips pushing into mine, his skin hot from the perpetual sunburn he'd worn since arriving in sun-scorched India. He brushed my hair from my face like he wanted to say something. But he wouldn't.

And so I wiggled out from underneath him and wrestled myself on top of his waist, his hands firm on my hips. The flimsy glass lightbulb swayed in the mosquito net and tossed junglelike shadows on the bamboo walls. The hut smelled of salt and sunscreen and incense and sweat and anticipation.

"I want to say it," I told him then, hunching my back so that my sea-sprayed hair dusted his bare chest.

He shook his head with a thin smile. "Don't do it, gorgeous," he cautioned playfully.

I pressed on. "You don't have to say it back," I said, fully meaning it. I knew I couldn't leave the next day without telling him, without him knowing—without *me* knowing. And so I said it: "I love you."

For a moment, everything was effortlessly still and noiseless in a way you can't describe. This sort of quiet is a rare thing in India.

"I'm not saying it to guilt you into saying it back," I rushed on. We already had the timeworn conversation that hundreds of travelers had before us: We spoke of "letting this be whatever it was supposed to be." We would see what "happened on its own." We "wouldn't force it."

The whole dialogue was such a backpacker cliché, and there was a small part of me that was worried that we'd never speak again after this—like so many other travelers before us. And so I said those words to him because I never wanted to regret *not* saying them.

— 18 —

WHEN I GOT off the phone with Lochlon, I went back upstairs to my room to find a pile of glossy shopping bags amassed on my bed. The bags were the color of my mom's wheatgrass shakes and said "Harrods" in gold script.

Resting in front of the bags was a piece of heavy-stock paper regally embossed with Elsbeth Darling's initials in a haughty serif font.

Lamb, the note began in elegant cursive.

> *I noticed you only came with a backpack, so I took the*
> *liberty of grabbing you a few things while I was*
> *shopping today. (You know I couldn't resist.)*
> *I forgot to mention that there is a party next*
> *weekend with Mr. Darling's colleagues, and we'd like*
> *you and the girls to attend. Since I neglected to tell you*

about the evening events, I thought it only fair that I undertake the shopping.

Enjoy!
E.

I knew better than to get excited. Elsbeth's generosity was the stuff of legends, but it didn't come for free. I dumped out the bags one by one, letting the expensive factory-fresh fabrics wrapped in delicate tissue paper pile on the bed like the spoils of war. There was even a small tub of wrinkle cream—*Elsbeth!*

My eyes spotted some hot pink satin, and I snatched at it with the sort of speed that even alarmed me. Had Elsbeth actually gotten me something I'd like?

But the electric magenta was actually the exquisite lining of a conformist black sheath dress designed for a put-together woman ten years my senior. On the high, tasteful neckline, Elsbeth had clipped another note. I could just picture her doing it, thinking she was being so sneaky.

For the soirée next Friday, she wrote in her private-school penmanship, all graceful loops and privilege.

Elsbeth was up to her old tricks again.

When I first started babysitting for her, I was still in high school, and she'd tried her hardest to "improve" me.

"Why don't you let me straighten your hair?" she'd prod, running her hand over my voluminous waves to smooth the constant halo of frizz that accompanied each strand. But I never let her.

"You make everything look stylish," she would tell me when I showed up in thrift store getups or one-of-a-kind vintage finds, but then she'd leave me piles of her "old" clothes, cardigans from Ralph Lauren and expensive shoes from Brooks Brothers. She always got me tremendously chic Chanel perfume for Christmas, but I never wore any of it. The Chanel perfume made me smell like an old lady (albeit a *French* old lady).

I always had the feeling that if I let her change even one little thing about me, it would be an "If you give a mouse a cookie" predicament. You know: "If you give a mouse a cookie, he'll eventually expect your ATM number."

First, she'd want to straighten my hair, then my clothing would go, and before you know it, I'd be a mini-Elsbeth with a rich banker husband living on Park Place and collecting $200 for passing Go. That was all well and good, but just not me. She didn't get that.

I frowned at the note. I knew that now that I lived with her, telling me to wear the dress was not merely a suggestion.

"So, WHAT IF I told you I was a South Kensington bird walking around in Harrods frocks all day long?"

"Who's Harrod?" asked my mom on the other end of the phone when I finally called her a week later. "Did you already meet a new boy? Are you sure he's single?"

It had taken me a while to call my mom with an update on my life, and my stomach sank with guilt when I heard her animated reaction.

"I just mean I'm quite posh, Mummy," I explained.

"Yeah right. I'll believe it when you part with those Dr. Martens boots."

I chortled, picturing the face that Elsbeth always made when I wore them—like she just found a horsefly in her arugula.

"How's life in London?" asked my mom.

"So you know *Bridget Jones*?" I asked eagerly.

"Of course," my mom said. "Single girl figuring out life and love in London!"

I copied her enthusiasm: "Walking through Piccadilly Circus! Shagging hot Brits!" I stopped short and deadpanned: "Yeah, it's nothing like that at all."

She laughed.

"I'm kidding. I love it. Gwen and I are already besties again. Yesterday we went to see the statue of Peter Pan in Kensington Gardens. We invited a girl from her class to come along, too. I've been on a mission to get her to open up to her peers, and she seems really receptive to it."

"That's so sweet," my mom said.

"Yes, but Mina has been very closed off lately. Something's up with her." I thought of her lying about text messaging.

"Thirteen is a hard age, and she's in a new country. But you'll crack her."

I went out onto my tiny balcony, wearing only a navy sweater that drooped off one shoulder from years of wear. My mom once told me that the cable-knit sweater belonged to my dad. I wasn't sure if it was true, but I liked the idea. This was all I had left of him and all I ever really wanted from him.

"So, have you made any friends yet?" my mom asked hopefully, because to her I was still ten years old.

"Well, Elsbeth has a cleaning lady around my age. She's from Poland and is obsessed with American pop music, so I hang out with her when she cleans, and we dance around the house singing Lady Gaga." It was a delightfully uncomplicated friendship.

"Oh no," my mother said in discomfort.

"Don't worry. Elsbeth is never here when she comes. Elsbeth says she feels guilty watching her clean, so she always makes sure she's out of the house. Plus, we don't always goof off—I help her clean whenever she lets me."

"How often does she come?"

"Every day."

My mom groaned. Though my mom and I grew up in an affluent area of Long Island, we were both still a little prickly among the super wealthy. For me, it was because I converted everything into traveler's currency. I'd calculate money into potential days spent abroad, and that gave me a strange financial perspective. What some women spend on handbags, I could live on for a month in Central America.

My mother always had money until she flew the coop to go to Italy instead of Dartmouth, where both her parents went.

"I just wanted to see Botticelli's *La Primavera* in the Uffizi," she liked to say all casually with a relaxed shrug whenever I asked her why she chose Italy over Dartmouth.

She told me that when she found out she was pregnant, she'd stare at that painting for hours, always looking at Spring, the fair-haired pregnant nymph scattering petals beside the muses. She said people used to tell her that she looked like that figure from the painting, all windy haired and serene eyed.

"I guess there can't be too many people your age in such an expensive area," my mother said.

I looked down from the balcony. Because of the way our house was turned on a wide angle, like a joint, I could see the entrance to the house next door. On the doorstep sat Aston with an acoustic guitar. *He probably doesn't even know how to play that thing*, I thought to myself.

"Well, my neighbor is my age."

"Oh?" asked my mother, sounding more faraway now. I heard the sink running on the other end of the line, and I could picture her washing out her morning coffee cup, which said, "Namaste, bitches," on it.

"Yeah, but he's a total snob. One of those upper-crust British brats. Aston Hyde Bettencourt. He, like, told me straight-out he went to Oxford. And he was drunk at seven A.M."

"Well, who knows what things are really like for him? Mo' money, mo' problems," my mom said sagely (and absurdly).

"Speaking of having too much money, the Darlings are making me attend social events with the girls to make sure they don't get into any 'tomfoolery.' Elsbeth's word, not mine. So I shall be rubbing elbows with young royals any moment now. Not like I have a choice. Elsbeth even bought me all these boring conservative clothes to wear so I don't embarrass her."

"Ah, champagne problems."

"Exactly, but still, I wish she'd stop trying to change me. Or at least let me pick out the clothing."

"That would be fun. Speaking of fun, have you planned any trips yet?"

I pulled my sweater down over my fingertips, and when neither of us spoke, I could hear faint guitar chords mounting from Aston's steps. My ears perked, caninelike. *I guess he actually can play that thing.*

"I'm sure by now you have every weekend from now until summer booked!"

"You know what, Mom?" I didn't wait for her to answer because she'd never guess. "I actually don't."

Despite the assertion in my words, I couldn't help but think about how great a weekend in Malta would be right now. But I pushed this thought aside. Something in me made me deposit the money from that first paycheck instead of booking that trip.

It was a spur-of-the-moment decision: I was walking past the bank and just decided to do it. Funnily enough, ever since I made that first deposit, all I wanted to do was make another. It felt *that* good.

"I decided to wait awhile before traveling—so I can save some money," I told my mom now.

"No!"

"Yes. I mean, maybe I'll go away in a few months or something. It's just that, immediately, when I got this job, I started thinking about all the trips I could go on. And that's not the point of being here, is it? It's to work and save money. I literally cannot afford to let what happened at VoyageCorp happen here."

"Ah, so the young grasshopper is learning."

"Let's see how long my resolve lasts . . ." I was purposely avoiding spending too much time on the Internet for fear that a flight sale would pop up or that a friend would invite me somewhere.

"What brought this on?" my mom asked.

"Well, the other day I met this artist who has a stall on Portobello Road and sells this kiln-fused glass jewelry that she makes in a studio in her garden, the most beautiful pendants, earrings, and bracelets. I was thinking the old readers of Gypsies & Boxcars would love her stuff, so I want to relaunch the site. But I want to do it right this time. You know, invest money into it and make it self-sufficient."

"No trips booked? Investing money into a business? Making it self-sufficient? Is this really Kika that I'm talking to?"

My pride made me blush. "I've been doing some reading online. But there's still a lot to do. I have to line up more artisans besides this British artist, which means I'll eventually have to travel again. So I guess I have to work out finances, you know, make a budget and business plan. But I'm crappy with numbers. I'll need someone to help me."

"Don't put yourself down. Just listen to yourself! If you keep at it you could really do this. And it sounds like your mind is in the right place for it now."

Just then, a melody of guitar strings wafted over to me like the smell of home cooking. The sound made me lose my train of thought and forget all about my website.

"Thanks, Mom," I said distracted. *Is that really Aston playing?* "I should get going . . ."

As if Aston felt me staring at him, he looked up and noticed me on the balcony. He gave me the slightest of head nods in civil salutation. I hung up the phone.

The chords were haunting. The twanging notes were just one minor key away from full-fledged, unabashed sadness.

The acoustics were better when I reached the street; the music grew louder with thick pastoral soul. The rustic melodies of my childhood resounded: the scratched records my mother would play in the drowsy summertime with every window in the house wide open. The memory of the smell of sticky ice pops and freshly cut July grass flooded over me.

I followed the harmony in a trance until I found myself standing in front of Aston, arms crossed over my chest to protect myself from the cold.

Aston noticed me but didn't stop his vigorous strumming. He closed his eyes for a moment and hummed along.

Lost in playing, he only briefly made eye contact with me in a sharp flick of those pink-rimmed, insistent blue eyes.

He struck the final chord, and the sound fell from the air in perfect gradation. And then it was deafeningly quiet. In that moment he looked so artful: a timeless indie-folk troubadour against the red door with its antique brass knocker shaped like a lion.

I felt the vibration rattle in my rib cage from the ghost of the long-gone note. I realized I hadn't blinked in quite some time.

"I . . . I . . ." I started, but I was not exactly sure why I was hovering over him like this. I was not exactly sure how I even got down to the street.

20

I STOOD THERE feeling clumsy and uncool, with a cow-eyed stare on Aston. Though it was freezing, I felt a hot bead of sweat slide down the arch of my spine like a tear.

"Right," he said, fracturing the trance. "I suppose I'm disturbing your sensitive ears and you want me to piss off inside with my offending racket."

I bristled at his brittle delivery, scowling reflexively. *Why does he have to be such an abrasive asshat?*

"That's quite fair," he said. He hoisted himself up with his palms on his knees and then tousled his already messy hair.

I opened my mouth to correct him. But then he shrugged off the guitar strap from his threadbare merino wool sweater. His shirt followed his arm upward, and the motion revealed a band of taut lower stomach just above his loose, low-slung jeans.

My belly did a little flip at the sight of the pristine skin of his lower abdomen, striped with a line of fine blond hairs that led my eyes lower and lower and lower.

"Yes, what is it?" he asked, tugging down his shirt over his belt buckle.

When I realized I was blatantly ogling his waist, just above the button of his jeans (dear God I hope he didn't think I was staring any lower than the button of his jeans!), I shook my head violently so that my bangs tumbled into my eyes. "Nothing. Nothing," I said overbrightly.

He turned from me and walked up his short stoop and into his house, closing the door behind him with a clank that banged me back into consciousness.

— 21 —

"No! I DO." Celestynka butted me out of the way with a radioactive-yellow Lycra-clad hip.

Unable to think of a better comparison, Elsbeth prepped me for meeting Celestynka by telling me: "Celeste likes to dress like . . ."—she rolled her eyes thoughtfully before settling on an adjective—"like . . . Vegas!"

"It's just a cereal bowl. I can wash it, Celestynka." I jockeyed for a spot in front of the sink.

"*Cele-STEEN-kah*," she corrected. "No *Cele-STINK-kah*."

"Maybe I should just stick with calling you 'Celeste,' like Elsbeth."

"No, you call Polish name. Is better," she insisted with both hands, waving them with silent-movie gestures.

I vaulted onto the countertop as Celestynka diligently

washed my single cereal bowl with disturbing robustness. (You'd think it wasn't about to go into the dishwasher.)

"I see you talk yesterday with Mr. Bettencourt from the next house. Is nice boy, ah?"

Celestynka was my age but already married with twins, and she was obsessed with the fact that I wasn't. Of course, you'd never know she was a mother with her rail-thin hips, which were always attired in a smattering of tooth-achingly bright, candy colors.

"You know Aston?" I asked her.

"Yes. I clean for him, too. This is why Elsbeth employees me. She knows of me from him. You see?"

I felt terribly lazy as she began to mop the kitchen floor. "Do you need any help?" I asked her.

"No. I clean. You mind babies," she ordered, sloshing the sudsy water around.

"The babies, as you call them, are in school right now." Celestynka was under the impression that Mina and Gwendy were the same age as her own newborn twins.

"So tell me what you know about this Aston character," I said.

"I don't know nothing. I only clean. Always clean. For him and *Babcia*."

"Who the hell is Babcia, his girlfriend? Babcia?" Just saying the name left me with an icky taste in my mouth. "Is she some graphic artist from Reykjavík with that name?" I stopped myself then, realizing I was babbling.

"No, she *Babcia*," she stated louder as if saying it at a higher volume would help me understand. Celestynka looked at me impatiently, as if my Polish language studies were not moving fast enough for her taste. She tapped her temples and closed her eyes to think. "The mother of his mother."

"Oh, he lives with his *grandmother*." My tongue unfurled from the roof of my mouth.

"Yes." Celestynka looked pleased. "His *Babcia*. This is what I tell you!"

"Where are his parents?"

"I do not know. I only clean. You like him, eh?" she asked hopefully with a little spark in her eye. "*Babcia* good lady. She open many schools for girls. And she know everything about everyone. Aston very kind boy."

"Actually, I think he's a bit of an asshat." I unsealed a bag of organic trail mix and started fishing out the chocolate chips. It was like World War II with the sugar rationing in this house. I had to get Elsbeth to stop being such a tiger mother when it came to chocolate.

Celestynka looked confused, and I knew it was because of the word "asshat," but I kept talking.

"He's kind of an elitist. But I saw him the other day playing guitar, and it was, I don't know, nice. I guess. Surprising."

Celestynka stopped mopping a moment but then quickly resumed. "Ah, you think he is nice looking? See, I tell you."

I snorted at Celestynka's encouragement. "I just liked his *guitar playing*. And stop trying to marry me off. I do have someone, you know."

"You do not."

"Oh, but I do," I said with an exaggerated coquettish pout. Celestynka wrinkled her nose up and down like a rabbit.

The mop clattered onto the marble floor. "Why you no tell me you have boyfriend?"

She looked genuinely affronted, and I couldn't help but laugh. Celestynka raised her eyebrows and haughtily picked up the mop.

I quickly explained: "Well, he's not exactly my boyfriend. But it's this Irish guy, Lochlon. I met him when we were traveling. He's coming to visit me soon."

I couldn't help but let the corkscrews of excitement spiral and swirl into my voice. My mouth eased into a woozy smile. I hopped off the counter to distract myself from the rush of feeling going straight to my cheeks. *He is just coming to visit; it doesn't necessarily mean anything significant, does it?* Still, I couldn't help hoping that this would be the first of many visits that would result in our relationship officially resuming.

As if Celestynka read my thoughts, she asked: "You will marry this man?"

The question plunged me into a preteen hypersensitivity. "Oh, I think it's too early to tell," I tittered.

"Is not. You know sometimes. Yes? This is a very American way of believing, I think."

Celestynka thought of herself as a very modern girl because she married for love. I got the impression that where she came from, a small fishing village on the Baltic Coast, this didn't happen too often. She was braver than a lot of people gave her credit for. She first traveled to London alone and then met her Polish husband here.

"I'm just ready for Lochlon to come. I'm worried that I may jump the next guy who plays folk guitar," I joked, momentarily remembering seeing the straits of Aston's lower stomach, mere inches from his—I ousted the unnerving thought from my head and refocused on the conversation.

"Lochlon is my first real love, though. He was my *real* boyfriend, anyway."

Though Celestynka's English wasn't perfect, her comprehension was usually spot-on. "Is good thing. Aleksander is my first love. And Lochlon, you are his first love as well?"

"Well, I'm not his first girlfriend, that's for sure. Once, he mentioned a girl from his hometown who he broke up with before he left to travel. But they just grew up together, you know? They, like, got together by default."

He only ever brought up his childhood sweetheart, Bernadine, once, in blasé sort of way, which made me think it wasn't a sloppy or weighty breakup.

Still, I had secretly wondered if he had run into her since returning home. I knew his town had more sheep than people. But I didn't dare ask him about her. I knew I wasn't supposed to remember her name.

"Yes, I know how this is. At home, many people never leave. They stay in the same town all of their lives; they wed the boy in the house next door. Then you live next to your mother. Done. Over. A whole life in one town." She hacked down her forearm, the gesture reminding me of an axe splitting wood.

"Yeah, that's the same impression I get with Lochlon's town. All he said about the breakup was that they were two very different people."

"Some people want the world. And some people want home," said Celestynka.

"Lochlon and I want the world. He's home in Ireland at

the moment, but just temporarily. He's going back to Asia, and maybe I'll meet him there when I save enough money."

Of course, I hadn't mentioned a word of this to Lochlon, but he obviously planned on living his whole life traveling, doing odd jobs and writing along the way. And I could fit into that life just fine while working on Gypsies & Boxcars.

"Aleksander does not like travel," said Celestynka unexpectedly.

"He doesn't? But he's in London," I said.

"Yes, is here like many Poles, for better life, more money, nah, nah, nah." She swished a bucket of clean water over the already sparkling floor, and I leaped onto the counter again to avoid the incoming tide.

"But not you. You came for exploration and love." I didn't know how she could be with someone who didn't like to travel. I could never be with someone who didn't appreciate adventure.

"Is true. My mother says, 'Celestynka, you are not right in the head!'" She knocked her skull forcefully. "She no like that I do not marry the butcher's son."

We both laughed.

"Is only funny because I left." She shrugged.

$$\sim 22 \sim$$

"So you're going to be on your best behavior tonight, right?" I asked Gwen as I knotted the oversized bow on her frothy party dress. She looked like a tulle cupcake.

We were getting dressed in my room since Mr. Darling, Elsbeth, and Mina were out to dinner already. Gwen and I would meet them at the party later. Elsbeth and I had decided that a fancy dinner followed by an even fancier party would be pushing Gwendolyn's attention span and our luck.

I wasn't sure I had the attention span for it, either. Not to mention the last time I went to some prissy, white-tableclothed restaurant with Elsbeth, I made a blatant fool of myself:

"Where did that sommelier go?" Elsbeth had inquired aloud.

And then, I had stupidly asked: "How do you know that guy's from Somalia?"

I still recoiled thinking about it. Even Mr. Darling let out a yap of a laugh, and he *never* laughed.

I smoothed my hair in the Venetian smoked-glass mirror and inspected the boring black dress one final time, seriously tempted to defy Elsbeth and change into a different one.

"Hey, Gwendy? Did you hear me?"

When she still didn't respond, a flurry of motion behind my back caught my attention, and I turned around to find her half buried in my wooden wardrobe between the hanging clothing.

"Whatcha doing in there?" I asked, burying my head into the closet beside her.

She knocked against the back of the wardrobe: *clack, clack, clack*, then put her ear to the wood to listen intently.

After an inpatient pause, she said, "Oh, you know, I'm just making sure you didn't get the wardrobe with Narnia in it. If you did, I'd be super jealous."

I nibbled into my bottom lip to keep from smiling.

"Should we get this show on the road?" I asked, passing over her velvet coat.

We both shrugged into our coats and made our way outside to wait for Clive with the car. He was supposed to pick us up after he dropped off the rest of the Darling clan at the party.

I gingerly steered Gwen down the icy front steps.

Just then, a voice from the street yanked my attention up: "You look, erm . . . clean."

It was Aston, lurking right in front of our stoop. I sighed. *Fuck off, Aston Hyde Bettencourt.*

I was about to say something in response when I noticed the

same thing about him: He was cleaned up, too. His mop of dirty blond hair had been slicked back, and he appeared to be wearing a tuxedo under his overcoat. Maybe this is what South Kensington boys wore to the bar on a Saturday night, for all I knew.

"Excuse me?" Aston said.

Oh shit, did I really tell him to "fuck off" out loud?

"Hello!" Gwen said cheerfully. "Fuck off, Aston Hyde Bettencourt!"

My face went crimson, but Aston laughed. It was the first time I had ever heard him laugh, and it sounded genuine, not at all hollow or pretentious. But then he ruined the unassuming laughter by speaking.

"Fine job you're doing there. Really making her into a model citizen," he said to me snarkily.

I ignored him and crouched down next to Gwen. "Listen, Gwendy. I'm a total potty mouth." I heard Aston snigger again, and I exhaled loudly through my nose. "But you cannot repeat what I say. Even *I'm* not supposed to talk like that. Got it? You have to swear to be on your best behavior tonight."

Gwen offered her little finger for a pinky swear. After we had linked pinkies, we pounded fists.

I stood back upright and met Aston's gaze again. His glacial blue eyes were so forceful that I had trouble meeting his stare head-on. I looked out into the night for any signs of Clive with the car.

"Right then. I just meant you look different. You don't often dress like this," he said a bit softer.

I looked down at the plain black dress and tugged my coat around me, ashamed. For the first time, I felt like hired help meant to be unnoticed—unlike in daily life when the Darlings treated me like part of the family. At least I managed to keep my hair wavy and wild, even though Elsbeth practically chased me around the house with a flatiron earlier today.

"Yeah, well, this is what working people have to do," I lamented into the night.

"So because I live in South Kensington, I've not worked?"

I stopped for a moment. Before I could come up with a snapping retort, I remembered him playing folk guitar the other day, and it dawned on me that all I'd been doing since I'd met him was making assumptions.

"Um, Aston, the guitar the other day—" I began, realizing that I never told him that it didn't bother me, and I actually *liked* his playing.

"Yes. Point made. No more guitar." He about-faced.

"No!" I said more fiercely than I meant to just to get his attention back. "It's that—"

"Kika, I need to pee like an effin' racehorse"—Gwen yanked at my coat—"but I'm trapped in my party dress!"

I took her hand in mine. I knew she was copying my language again, and Aston deliberately laughed in my face once more. *Why do I have to have the mouth of a pirate hooker?*

"Don't worry, Gwendy, I'll help." I turned back to Aston to finish my thought, but he had walked into the street to hail a passing black cab.

Gwen started doing what she called "The Wee Dance," so I shuffled her back up the steps and unlocked the front door, so that there would be no accidents in overpriced party dresses.

By the time we finished and got back downstairs, Clive was waiting with the car, and Aston was long gone.

23

THE PARTY WAS at this glamorous place called the Wolseley in Green Park. Gwendy and I craned our heads to check out the soaring ceiling veiled in fairy lights and tinsel, making it look wintry and festive. Men with unflinching faces, like those of the Buckingham Palace guards, wielded gleaming silver trays of bubbling champagne.

When the string quartet picked up their bows, Gwen swirled her hips. "Come on, Kika, shake your moneymaker like the rent is due!"

But Elsbeth had warned me "to keep the Kika to a minimum tonight."

"I don't think we can dance here," I told Gwendy as I admired the clusters of ladies in serenely graceful floor-length gowns and the men in freshly pressed suits.

"But why not?" she whined, already bored.

"Because our dance moves are so much cooler than everyone else's, we're going to make them jealous for having all the fun. These people are far too sensitive," I said with some truth to it.

Gwen nodded soberly. "I understand, Kika. I *am* a fabulous dancer, after all."

"Let's get you a Shirley Temple."

Mina stayed close to Elsbeth's side, and Mr. Darling worked the crowd of strangers while cradling a Cuban in his mouth like a cartoon villain.

On the way to the bar, out of the corner of my eye I spied someone I knew. I did a double take. But, no, it couldn't be *him*.

Actually, *it could be him*. Mr. Darling was working for the Richmond Group in London, so it very well could be him. It was Richie Rich! More commonly known as Ronald Richmond, as in the Ronald Richmond who passed on my résumé to VoyageCorp, the company I had been fired from.

I ducked behind a granite pillar, and Gwen followed me without having to be told to, clever, intrigue-loving girl that she was.

"Who are we hiding from?" she stage-whispered while flipping her eyes from side to side like a spy.

"The enemy." For right next to Richie Rich stood none other than Miss Bae Yoon, aka the Bitch Who Cost Me My Last Job.

— 24 —

I CURSED MYSELF for not telling Elsbeth that I had been fired from VoyageCorp. Then I remembered I had made it worse and smacked my head with my palm; I'd had the sex toys delivered to Bae's office after I was fired. After that little stunt, Bae would never miss the opportunity to retaliate by blabbing the details of my firing to the Darlings. If she said anything about me losing my job because I showed up at the office with sex toys, I was *done*. Elsbeth would fire me on the spot at the mere waft of scandal. You can't talk yourself out of something like that.

Gwen started getting restless, and gluing myself flat against the pillar was making the people around me uncomfortable.

"Can I have my Shirley Temple now?" she moaned.

"Yes. Yes, you can." I clasped her hand in mine, and we stalked across the room in a half crouch.

Why didn't I let Elsbeth straighten my hair and cake me

with makeup? The dull black dress, although a good start, was not enough of a disguise.

"Look!" Gwen indicated across the room directly where Richie Rich and the vile Bae Yoon were looming. (I decided that she needed an epithet and "the vile Bae Yoon" just had the perfect menacing ring to it.)

"What is it, Gwen?" I questioned.

"It's Aston."

I craned my head through the crowd. *It is Aston.*

Rich people really did live in a small world after all. Questions floated into my head like comic strip thought bubbles: *Why is he at this party? And why in God's name is he talking to none other than the vile Bae Yoon, whose hand—no, it couldn't be—is resting on his shoulder. Why is Bae touching him?*

The vile Bae Yoon lobbed her head back in laughter, as if Aston had just said the funniest thing in the whole world, which, to be honest, was highly unlikely. The boy did not have a sense of humor.

"What the hell is she doing?" I swung behind the next granite pillar, and Gwen followed suit.

"Whooooo?"

"The vile Bae Yoon," I said distractedly. *Could Bae's dress be any shorter? I could almost see her—*

"Is she your archnemesis?" Gwen asked, saucer eyed.

I blurted out a laugh. "Yes, actually. She tried to sabotage me."

"Which one is she?"

The one who's dressed with her bits hanging out, I wanted to say.

"The girl Aston's talking to."

"Is she his girlfriend?"

"Ew, don't be disgusting." I felt my fingers compress into fists. "I mean, no, she's not. But they do look like they know each other, don't they?"

I was a bit shocked by my outburst, but I chalked it up to nerves. I was obviously stressed. *But why* is *Bae all over him like that?*

I thought it out: She usually only came on to moguls, but perhaps Oxford brats were her type, too. Surely Aston was some trust fund baby. He looked at home among the glitterati. Of course he'd be talking to ego-stroking and eyelash-fluttering Bae Yoon.

"Come on, let's go to the bar. You can be my spy." I plopped Gwen atop a too-tall barstool and took a seat next to her, finger-brushing my hair onto my face so I looked less recognizable—and more like a bush child.

"Good evening, madam. May I—"

I cut him off. "Two Shirley Temples!" I positioned myself away from Aston and Bae. *What could they possibly be talking about?*

"Make mine a double," insisted Gwen, and the bartender nodded gamely.

The bar was backlit and glowed like a cathedral window. I swiveled Gwen's barstool toward Aston and Bae. "Ok, my little secret agent. Tell me what they're doing. I can't stare at them. They may recognize me."

Gwen waggled her head, taking the task very seriously.

"Aston just put his hand in his pocket," she said excitedly. "And now—what's her name again?"

"The vile Bae Yoon."

"What does that mean?"

"It's just her name. It's a mean name, actually. Just call her Bae." I felt slightly remorseful about being a bad influence on Gwendy. "What's Bae doing now?"

"Um, she's just talking. A lot. And laughing."

"How about Aston?" My head was down, and I dug through my clutch (Elsbeth's) as if it were an unexplored archaeological site.

When Gwen didn't answer me, I looked up just in time to see her lift a martini glass in both hands and bring the pink liquid (a cosmo?) to her lips.

"No!" I moved to snatch it away. "Don't drink that!" My hand clipped the martini stem, and the pink drink splashed right into my face.

"Oh, balls!" yelped Gwen, which I have to admit was a little better than, "Oh, shit!" which was what I barked.

I ducked under the bar and pulled Gwen off the stool. The whole party seemed to be looking at us. My dress was drenched in—I licked my lips—yup, definitely a cosmo. *People still drink those?*

I crouched with my finger on my lips. Gwen and I swapped severe, horror-filled glances.

"Sorry, Kika," she said.

I swatted the apology away and pretended to be tying my shoe . . . except I was wearing high heels. So I pretended to be tying my high heels. *Good one, Kika. Very believable.*

Luckily, Gwen was unscathed, and I was wearing black, so the stains weren't immediately visible on me—but I was soaking wet.

"That wasn't my Shirley Temple, was it?" Gwen asked sheepishly.

"No, baby. It wasn't," I confirmed. "It's okay, though. We're going to make a run for it—to the bathroom."

Gwen's eyes sparkled.

"Not really a run, just a very fast walk. But look normal, okay?" I was talking to both her and myself.

We emerged from under the lip of the bar and began power walking across the room. I saw Mina and mouthed for her to take Gwen. Without missing a beat, she was by my side ushering Gwen away. An undercurrent of being hunted loomed. I walked toward the bathroom corridor as fast as I could. Then, like a shot ringing out from across the room, I heard it: that unmistakable, tetchy voice calling me out like the damn tattletale she always was. "Kika? Kika Shores?"

The vile Bae Yoon had found me.

~ 25 ~

MOMENTS AFTER I reached the safety of the bathroom, the door pitched open with a gust. Posted in the doorway was Bae Yoon with her hands on her hips looking like Kim Jong-un in Louboutins.

I willed myself not to speak first. Instead, I blotted the drink from my dress. I felt glaringly unglamorous and not at all impossibly aloof, which was the look I was going for.

"So it is you," said Bae.

"What are you doing here?" I asked her in monotone, studying the Australia-shaped stain on my bodice.

"I could ask *you* the same question. I'm here on *business*," she said with an intonation of pride, the subtext being: "because I'm sooo important."

"It is, after all, a party hosted by the Richmond Group. Remember them?"

"I guess it was too much to ask to never see you again," I remarked dryly. I pushed by Bae and moved out of the bathroom. But then, thinking better of it, I stopped short just outside the ladies' room door. Leaving the secluded bathroom corridor was a bad idea; I didn't want to expose Bae to more ears.

I made a move to go back into the ladies' room, but Bae was one step ahead of me and blocked my way.

"Oh, I see," crooned Bae. "You're working, aren't you? You're the girl who hands out the towels in the bathroom."

I frowned at her. "Bae, you cost me my job." I finally looked in her eyes, black and bitter as espresso.

Bae intersected her twiggy arms. "You cost *yourself* that job. And you know it."

I stayed quiet and hateful. I silently begged her just to *go away*. But because of my lack of protest, Bae knew she had me.

She continued, a shark who had scented blood: "I'm on to you, Kika Shores. I saw the way you treated that job; the way you treated everyone else's time like it was less important than yours; the way you ran around major corporate headquarters in your cheap granola outfits, flaking out on meetings, taking *nothing* seriously. I just made sure you got what you deserved. And you did *not* deserve that job."

She held up her hand to block my way. "Basic bitches like you don't *get* to be in my world."

I was both seething and charred by her words, but deep down I knew *she was right*. I *had* been an awful employee. She was right about it all: I'd called out sick just so I could go to Florida with my mom for a yoga conference; I'd leave early even though I knew others would have to pick up the slack for me; I'd spend weekends away only to show up Monday morning straight off a red-eye and completely useless with exhaustion. I had nothing to say.

"I went to Wharton, you know. I *sweat* high-level excellence," she spat. "To think you even *applied* for my job!"

The horrible visual of Bae sweating excellence interrupted my personal shame spiral and made me crumple up my mouth. *Does she not hear what comes out of her mouth?* I bit my lip white. She may have been right about who I was in my past job, but I was changing—wasn't I? *I deposited my first check instead of spending it!* This private act, though meager and long overdue, made me stand a little straighter.

Even though she was right about me in the past, she still had no right to treat me so poorly. Not here and not now—when I was trying. Suddenly, I snapped.

"Oh, enough criticism, Bae. You may have your MBA, but everyone knows that all you want is an MRS. Looks like I'm not the only one who's unprofessional." I savagely baited her.

She sputtered for a moment like a car trying to start. "I mean, where did you even go to school?" she spat. "What did you even major in? Recreational Studies? You may as well have majored in 'fun.'"

She regained her stride, all viperlike and furious: "Listen to me. I don't know how you got into this party"—she leaned into me, her finger daggering my face—"but mark my words, Kika Shores, I *will* find out why you're here and I *will* destroy—"

"There you are!" A booming bass voice reverberated through the bathroom corridor, cutting Bae off mid-threat. We both swerved our heads toward the full-throated call.

Oh shit, it's Aston. My face blushed hotly when I thought about how much he had overheard before announcing himself. *Please don't let him have heard Bae telling me off,* I begged to whichever deity would listen.

"I've been scouring the whole room for you." Aston hushed us with his authoritative voice and paraded down the corridor toward Bae.

"And may I say, aren't you a vision?" he said when he got close enough.

Bae visibly melted and let out an inhuman giggle that sounded more like she was gargling on the blood of virgins. I made the slightest of gag faces, which Aston may have seen.

"Oh, Aston," Bae said in an infantile voice, "I was just—"

But to both our surprise, Aston walked right past Bae and slid against me. He put his hand familiarly on the small of my back, and I couldn't help but react.

I immediately changed my posture and bolted upright, rod stiff at his touch. My mind felt like it was free-falling. *Aston's hand is on the small of my back.* I had the urge to make a squeaking sound.

"There you are, my . . . poodle," he cooed, looking sweetly into my eyes.

I opened my mouth in protest, but with a shiny smile, he bopped me on the ball of my nose in a gesture that I couldn't believe was done in earnest.

Poodle? Did he just call me poodle?

I didn't know who was more surprised—Bae or me. His hand rested confidently on the bend of my waist, right on that feminine part where it tapered in like a vase. He was acting like we had known each other forever, like we were, I don't know, *intimately acquainted* or something.

I took a quick survey of Bae's reaction: She was purple with anger and perplexity. Seeing her like that made me smile—first at her and then up at Aston. He was quite tall, I realized, now that he was this close to me.

I mentally unruffled myself and tried to play along. "So, um, you've, um, found me . . ." I said to Aston.

Bae looked scandalized. Aston looked encouraging. "You've found me, my . . . English muffin." I almost ruptured in laughter, but Aston radiated like he was a damn Kennedy. I wanted to hug him. I actually wanted to hug him.

For a second, I let myself just enjoy being *beamed* at by him, and, I don't know, I actually fell for it myself for a moment and felt—special.

"Aston!" Bae yapped, snapping me out of the trippy trance. She coughed to compose herself. She knew she was coming off too strong and visibly tried to reel herself in. "*Asssss*ton," she stressed with babyish aggravation in her voice. "What? How?" She playfully rolled her lips into a pout. "So, how do you, um, know Kika Shores?"

I pushed my breath through my nostrils and hoped he wouldn't mention anything about me working for the Darlings. Bae would make it her mission to get me fired. But then I felt the slightest of nips on my waist. *Play along*, it told me.

Bae waited anxiously, not speaking, but blinking her eyes very fast as Aston torturously took his time answering.

He brushed his hand along the small of my back warmly and looked at me a moment too long, smiling that daze-inducing smile. I grinned back, trying to keep the confusion contained to my pupils only. *What are you doing?* I silently asked him.

Trust me, his gaze insisted back.

Strangely, I did.

"Kika is my date tonight, of course. Lovely, isn't she? We're quite old friends," he said with gentlemanly ease. "Isn't that right, poodle?"

This kid was a pro. I shined at Bae and said nothing.

"Oh," she said smiling back—albeit excruciatingly awkwardly. "I thought she was working here—"

Aston cut her off with a pompous laugh. She automatically stopped talking, sensing she was on the outside of some sort of inside joke.

"Right. Not like anyone dating you would be working here. I was just—" Bae cringed at herself as if she just realized how dumb that sounded.

"You're the only one working tonight, Miss Yoon," said Aston. "In fact, even Ronald Richmond was about to do a shot. Even he's taking the night off."

I chuckled at the image of Richie Rich doing shots, and Aston laughed along with me. Weren't we just the perfect magazine couple? All white teeth and dumbass nicknames.

Bae shriveled from us sheepishly. "All right, I better get to it, then. Great to see you again, Kika."

I seized her arm, her skin waxy and reptilian. I stopped myself from recoiling and put on an innocent guise. "But wait, Bae, wasn't there something else—"

"Nooo," she said lightning fast, drawing out the last letter. "I didn't know you were here with—" She stopped herself from saying anything else stupid.

"That was all," she chirped, her voice clipped. "I do need to attend to Mr. Richmond. If you'll both excuse me."

She wobbled down the carpeted corridor as fast as she could. Teetering on her skyscraper heels, she didn't look back. And it was a good thing she didn't, because she would have been stunned to see what we did next.

— 26 —

ASTON AND I collapsed into what can only be described as schoolyard giggles. Our outpouring of laughter—balled and extra juicy from being jailed up—was louder and lengthier than it should have been.

"Aston," I laughed, folded over, hands on my thighs. "Aston." I tried again to contain myself. "Wh-what are you doing here? Wh-what *was* that?"

I stood upright and wiped the mascara from under my eyes.

"What was that?" Aston sniffed back a laugh and got serious again. He plopped down on a leather ottoman lining the corridor that led to the bathrooms. "I should rather ask you, *poodle*."

His voice had an underlying good-natured quality to it that I'd never noticed before.

"Oh my God," I gushed like a teenager. "I almost *lost* it

when you called me that. Did you see her face?" I flopped again into peals of laughter, but Aston was now much more reserved.

His voice got low and careful. "What was she going on about? Was she threatening you, Kika?"

"She's clinically insane." I sniffed and flattened my dress. "Well, actually not that insane." I dropped down next to him on the bench, closer than I'd meant to, but I couldn't just slide over now, could I?

"If I tell you, do you promise not to tell anyone?"

Aston rolled his eyes but held out a disgruntled pinky finger.

I smirked and coupled my pinky to his in a binding swear. For the second time tonight, I was overaware of our touching. I pulled my pinky away and combed my fingers through my hair.

"Bae Yoon and I worked in the same industry together in New York. The Darlings sort of got me the job through their friend Ronald Richmond, you know, the guy who owns the Richmond Group." I gestured in the direction of the party.

Aston shook his head, but he let me keep talking.

"I lost my job because . . . because of my own fault, really." I swallowed hard. Saying those words was still unpleasant— especially saying them to someone like Aston. "But the Darlings don't know I got fired, and I'm trying to keep it that way—just because I don't want them to think that I'm not taking this job seriously."

"Is that all?"

"Well, I was really unprofessional in New York. But I'm trying to change: I've kept Elsbeth's schedule for the girls; I've never been late picking them up or dropping them off.

I've done everything asked of me. I'm even wearing the dress Elsbeth picked out for me tonight."

He looked me up and down. "I can see that, but I mean was that all about Bae Yoon? She appears to have it out for you."

"Yeah, she does, because I didn't realize the value of the New York job, and she did. She took it as a personal insult that I was so blasé, which I understand. But she doesn't have to act so condescending all the time, you know?" I didn't wait for him to answer me. "She humiliated me by making me run this bullshit personal errand—I had to buy sex toys for her. And I don't want that to have any effect on this job. I can swear all I want, but Elsbeth would definitely fire me at the first mention of 'sex toy.'"

My cheeks flushed at my oversharing. The word "sex" hung in the air between us, and I had the urge to flap my hands to make it go away as you would a foul odor.

Aston moved his mouth to the side. "I believe I understand," he said in his usual curt and growly way. (Finally, back to the Aston I recognized.)

"Well, I should go." I stood and felt the warmth between us dissipate. I regretted it instantly.

I looked down at him. "But what about you?" I asked. "Why are you here? Who does Bae think you are?"

Aston tossed his head in quick dismissal.

"She knew my father, who was someone. And by her level of fawning over me, you'd think I was his second coming and whatnot. His company is why I'm here tonight. But I've no real part in it, I'm afraid."

I nodded. Typical Bae sniffing out the wealthy. My cell phone buzzed with a text from Mina asking where I was. Gwen must be getting restless.

"I have to go." I frowned. "I am being summoned by a thirteen-year-old."

Aston gave me a half smile. In the shadowy mood lighting of the bathroom corridor, it nearly could pass as warm. "Good night, Kika."

I smiled back and started to walk down the corridor toward the show and pageantry of the party, but then something in me made me turn around.

"Aston?" I called.

He stood at the sound of his name, hands in his pockets. His hair was a little messed up, which made him look boyish and . . . cute.

I spoke on impulse: "Thank you. You know, for saving me. And keeping my secret."

He didn't move for a moment, but then he gave me a courteous head tilt before turning in the opposite direction toward the bathrooms. But I couldn't bear him looking all stony again.

"I misjudged you," I called out louder than I meant to. But it made him turn back and face me again. *Just don't stop looking at me like that*, I found myself wishing.

"It's quite all right, Kika," he said. "I shall let you get on. Those mad girls need you."

I stared at him for a moment longer and then turned to walk back to the party, a smile itching the edges of my lips.

I was just in time to see Bae at the doors, about to leave. She whooshed her coat over her shoulders. I caught a glimpse of the label. It appeared that the devil actually *did* wear Prada.

She saw me watching her and gave me a brave wave good-bye. She actually looked a bit frightened of me. Because I was an absolute child, I narrowed my eyes at her, just to give her an extra bolt of panic. But then I granted her a courteous wave back. I was the clear winner; there was no need to rub it in her face—no matter how much I wanted to. Plus, I couldn't forget that when you boiled it down, she had been right about me.

Bae Yoon noticeably exhaled as she exited. It was the first time I had ever seen her leave a party alone.

ON THE WAY back home, Mina sat in the front of the car, strumming her fingers to the car radio. Gwen slept on my lap, as peaceful and innocent as a cherub in a Renaissance oil painting. As we passed under the streetlamps of the silent Kensington streets, her baby face was momentarily splashed in peach light. Elsbeth and Mr. Darling, those party animals, would stay out later, but it was time for me to get the girls to bed.

My mind reran the conversation I had with Aston. Something bothered me. He said "was." He said his dad "was" someone. Past tense.

I underscored the conclusion from earlier in the night: I didn't know Aston at all.

27

"You have no work today, yes?"

Whack. Whack. Whack.

Before Celestynka gave me a chance to answer, she swatted the rug three more times in quick succession. I grimaced at each impact, trying my best to hold steady.

Instead of spending the sluggish Sunday in bed, I was helping Celestynka beat rugs outside. Earlier in the day, I had helped Mina and Gwen organize their closets, and then we went down to the charity shops to make donations. The confrontation with Bae yesterday was a good motivator for me: I was so grateful for this job. I wouldn't make the same mistake of taking it for granted.

Celestynka raised the broom for another assault.

"Damn, how can someone so skinny hit that hard?"

She bared her teeth but didn't stop the dusty battering.

"Polish. Girls. Very. Strong," she said, separating the words to coordinate with the vehement wallops.

"I promised Gwen I'd be her backup dancer later, but after that I'm free for the rest of the day." I coughed into the grime.

"Good. You come to my flat tonight. You will see my babies."

I wasn't sure if it was her English or something she did intentionally, but Celestynka rarely made requests—she made demands.

THAT EVENING, I went over to see her.

When she opened the door to her Ladbroke Grove flat, the roasting air flooded into the stairwell.

"Quick, quick! Come in before all the heat runs away."

I rushed inside and we closed the door behind us quickly, as if we were being chased.

Celestynka's work clothes were conservative compared to what she wore on her free time. Tonight she rocked what could only be described as Barbie-pink booty shorts and a baby tee that said "Bad Girl" on it.

"What are you wearing?" I asked her outright. "I mean, don't get me wrong, if I just popped out two babies and looked like that, I'd be showing it off, too."

"This is no thing," she said, separating the words. "In Poland, all the girls show off their skin. *If* they have nice body. Sometimes even if body is not so nice, they show. In London, everyone wears plain clothes. Nothing so fun. Nothing with—" She motioned to the "Bad Girl" stenciled on her shirt.

"Sparkles?"

"Yes! Diamonds! Showstopper! Fancy, fancy! Get the Polish look! Baby, I was born this way," she said, copying beauty commercials and candy pop songs. She shimmied her shoulders and ran through foxy, catalog-style poses.

"I bet Aleksander likes it."

"Oh yes," she agreed. "And how is your Lochlon?"

I had called Lochlon that morning after helping Celestynka. As I recalled our conversation, uneasy emotions fizzed up inside me and made me feel like a shaken-up can of soda.

"He comes to see you soon. You call him today, yes?"

"Yeah, I did. He's good, I think." I bent my fingernail backward agitatedly. "He had a long night at the pub. He said he was out with his friends all night, so he was very quiet on the phone because he was tired."

I clung to these caveats, but the truth was he had barely said two words to me. I told him the whole story of the Wolseley party, but he didn't seem to be listening. In fact, I was pretty sure he was still drunk.

"Yes? This is all?" Celestynka asked.

I didn't know why I wasn't confiding in Celestynka. I guess it hurt my feelings that he didn't seem to care that I had finally gotten rid of Bae Yoon. I was disappointed, I supposed. But that would just make it true, saying it all aloud to Celestynka like that.

"Yup, it's all good," I chirped. I shoved the discontent down and began mentally paving over it with logic: *I'm overreacting. I know it's nothing, and my experience proves it.*

Once, after we both drank too much in Prague, we spent the next day walking along the John Lennon Wall—a wall bedecked in hopeful, inspiring graffiti. We didn't speak the whole day, not because we were mad or tired of each other, but just because we both were comfortable enough to be quiet in each other's company.

We held hands and walked beside the wall for hours, then we sat on a bench in front of it and closed our eyes for some time.

The wall was a sacred site. During communism, there was no creative freedom, so it meant something now to be able to express yourself with art.

Before we left the wall behind, Lochlon took out a green marker and wrote our initials. Afterward, he spoke for the first time all day: "Let's come back and visit this one day, yeah?" he said in a haunted and drowsy voice.

Our blocky, childlike initials would forever stand there, leaning against each other for eternity. And other lovestruck kids would come from around the world and see them there, forever scarred and sacred as a first tattoo.

That day at the wall became one of my favorite memories of our time together. I purposely replayed this scene to myself as if to prove that he was *always* reserved after what he would call a "long night on the sauce." *There is no point in reading into it*, I instructed myself again.

But Celestynka offered no relief from my batty thoughts. "You are worried?" She sat down at the kitchen table.

"A little," I confessed. "I mean, he's definitely a little depressed. But wouldn't you be if your dad was ill and you were forced to come home?"

"Yes, of course. But I am meaning with you. Things are okay for you, Kika?"

I tapped my fingers on the kitchen table to some inaudible song. "Sure, I just have to see him again, you know? He's coming for two days mid-March—just before I leave to go on vacation with the Darlings."

Celestynka frowned but changed the subject. "Come see my babies."

She ushered me up and into the living room where her two roly-poly babies were squirming on the floor like two happy glowworms. Celestynka's eyes twinkled.

"Oh my God, they're so cute. All cheeks and giggles," I said.

"The name of this one is Kasia, and this is Janek." She swooped them up, each one astride a hip.

Celestynka heaved them at me one after the other as if they were sandbags in an assembly line. I didn't know which one was which. (I learned that with babies—especially babies with Polish names—it was best not to make assumptions about gender.)

"Look how adorable you guys are," I cooed and bounced them up and down as Celestynka grinned like a maniac.

"Where is Aleksander this evening?"

"He is at work today. On Sunday as well he works. Come. I make tea."

We paraded the babies into the kitchen, and Celestynka gathered the sheets of paper off the kitchen counter and then came to sit beside me.

"Finances for the house," she mumbled, stacking the papers into a neat pile on the kitchen table.

The sheets looked professional and intimidating, especially to someone like me who was afraid of basic arithmetic.

"Aleksander does them on Excel or QuickBooks or something? Impressive."

Celestynka laughed. "Aleksander does not know how to work computer. Not even for porn!"

We both laughed at this.

"I do these," she said, smoothing the paper as if it were creased.

I must have looked surprised, because Celestynka defended herself.

"Yes. Is me. I take courses in accounting and business in Warsaw before I leave. I am always very fast with numbers. But here, because my English is no good, I cannot get job accounting."

"What? That's amazing that you know all of this." I pried the papers from under her arm to look over them, but they may as well have been written in Sanskrit.

"Numbers are the same in any language, this is why I like. But I cannot do good interviews, so I clean houses." She shrugged like it was not a big deal.

"But that's ridiculous—I'll help you with your English, Celestynka. We can practice while you clean. You speak English well. You just need interview practice. We'll have you ready in no time."

She looked rapturous for a moment. "You will teach? Because there is no time for me to take school, and with no one to practice. Alek only speak Polish, because many builders are Polish. He no needs," she explained adamantly.

"I'll practice with you. Don't worry," I told her, grabbing her hands to stop her from taking out one of the babies' eyes with her long fingernails.

Celestynka twisted her hands away, the happiness draining from her face. "But I cannot give money."

"Celestynka, you don't have to pay me."

She shook her head. "But I must do for you something."

"You must *do something for me*," I said, correcting her syntax, her first lesson. But she just bowed her head in agreement, thinking I was asking for some sort of payment.

I sucked my mouth in for a moment. I looked at the sheets. "I've got it! I'm trying to start a company, but I'm crap at math and money—maybe you can help me organize a budget and business plan for it."

I knew in the upcoming months, as I started making more money, the enticement to just spend it on a trip would also grow. I thought of the marshmallow experiment; the one where a child is offered an option to eat one marshmallow right away, or get two marshmallows fifteen minutes later.

Throughout my life I had always been the "marshmallow now" sort of girl. I had always chosen to stuff that fluffy, sweet, gooey marshmallow into my mouth whole. Why wait? There were no guarantees that there would even be a later! And so I gobbled up life before it could grow stale: I took that time off, I spent every cent, kissed the boy, took that trip. I didn't like my gratification delayed. I liked it now. At a moment's notice.

But ever since I put away the money from my first paycheck, I felt a slight and almost imperceptible shift in my mood: I had resisted my natural impulse and the temptation, which may have been the very first mature, certified adult conduct I'd ever participated in. And I wanted to continue this behavior; to keep depositing everything I could into that savings account, which I had started calling my "more marshmallow money."

"You need money help?" Celestynka shook her head. I spoke too fast, and she didn't quite understand.

"This!" I snatched the papers back from her again and laid them out on the table. "I need you to make one of these for me, for my website."

I figured that if I had a plan in place for Gypsies & Boxcars, it would be easier to save; I could see where the money would eventually be going, instead of just watching it pile up in some black hole bank account. Celestynka could help me figure out how much money I'd need to get Gypsies & Boxcars started again. She could help me with a budget, a business plan, and deadlines and dates. She was the missing piece.

"Do finances? For you? I can do this."

"I know you can!" We were both roused now by the simple accomplishment of comprehending each other, and even the babies seemed excited by proxy. Kasia (or Janek) belly guffawed in that gurgling, bouncy baby way.

"Okay, teacher, I have first question about English," Celestynka started shyly. "Is silly, but I no understand. Tell me, Professor Kika, what is difference between 'Fuck you,' 'Fuck me,' and 'Fuck off'?"

I tried not to laugh. "Okay, pay attention," I told her. "This is of *crucial* importance."

~ 28 ~

A WEEK LATER, I went in search of Elsbeth in the hopes of getting some information about Aston. I was missing some vital chunks of his story, and I knew Elsbeth was just the well-connected, loose-lipped woman to ask.

I found her in the sitting room, washed in midday sun, and reading a serious novel with a cobwebbed man on the cover. She looked up brightly when I came in, as if she were just dying to be interrupted.

"Hey, Elsbeth. Sorry to disturb you. I just wanted to ask if we could have a little chat sometime today, obviously not right now because you're reading, but whenever you're free."

Elsbeth placed her finger along the seam of the fat book. "Now is fine, lamb. What's up?"

"Are you sure? I can come back . . ." I motioned to the door.

Elsbeth shook her head vigorously. "Please, Kika. Take a seat," she said, sounding a little desperate.

I jangled my shoulders. "Okay. I just wanted to make sure that you're happy with how everything's been going with the girls."

The overstuffed upholstered armchair moaned with old age as I sat. The fabric was opulent in an overdone Marie Antoinette way, but uncomfortable as hell, demanding perfect posture out of me.

"Yes, Kika. Mr. Darling and I are very pleased. How sweet of you to ask. I love the initiative you're taking by escorting them all around London. Mina was telling me about all the museums they've been to with you. But remember, you *do* have weekends free. I hope you don't feel obligated to spend time with the girls—though they love every minute with you."

"It's okay, I like taking them to museums on the weekends." I dawdled. "So that party last weekend was fun. The girls were very well behaved."

"Weren't they?" She beamed. "I introduced Mina to so many people, and she dealt with it all smashingly. Of course, I barely saw Gwen, but I saw you two running around playing a fabulously creative game of some sort."

I bared my teeth self-consciously. I guessed she didn't see me spill that drink and hide under the bar.

"So, um, at the party I ran into our neighbor, you know that guy Aston Hyde Bettencourt? I didn't know he was going to be there . . ." I let my sentence trail off like a fishing line.

Elsbeth made a throaty noise. "Lamb, of course Aston was going to be there. The Richmond Group is Mr. Darling's main client at the moment. Why, you know that."

"What does Aston have to do with the Richmond Group?"

She paused for a moment and rested her hand on her chin. "Oh no, but of course, you wouldn't know, would you?"

"Know what?"

"Oh, how silly of me. I should have explained earlier." She removed her reading glasses and placed them in her lap. "It was just that I didn't realize you two were friends, but of course you would be: two bright, young things in an old-moneyed neighborhood like this. There are not too many people your age around here, are there?"

I scrunched my eyebrows, fully intrigued now. "So, what is it?"

"Hmm? Oh right. You want to know about Aston. Aston's grandfather is Sir Richmond Bettencourt," she said.

I waited for her to continue.

Elsbeth held off a moment longer to give me time to figure it out, but when I didn't make any motion of comprehension, she continued. "Sir Richmond Bettencourt, the founder of the Richmond Group," she clarified.

I squinted at the information. "What? But Ronald Richmond owns the Richmond Group."

"Oh no, lamb. He runs the North American division, but his last name is a mere coincidence. The Richmond Group is named after Aston's grandfather's first name. His grandfather is now deceased, though."

I dismantled the information then reassembled it in the context of my own life: *So Aston really is a rich kid, like, a super-rich kid.* No wonder Bae was all over him like white on rice.

"This whole square of houses actually belongs to the Richmond Group. That's why we live right next door to

Aston; it's corporate housing of sorts since Mr. Darling is consulting for them exclusively at the moment. At least we'd call it corporate housing in America; I'm not sure they use that term here."

"Elsbeth, what about Aston's father? He's not around anymore?"

Elsbeth shook her head.

I slowly put it together. That was why Bae backed off so quickly when he said I was his date that night: He owned an empire. The bigger picture took shape: Bae worked for *him*. He could *fire* Bae! But before I could flesh out my retaliation fantasy any further, Elsbeth snipped through my thoughts with what she said next.

"Both of his parents have passed. A tragic car crash, only five years ago, I think. Aston was still at school at Oxford I think, or Cambridge—one of those schools. So catastrophic and untimely."

My hand cupped my mouth to stifle a gut-socking gasp. "No," I whispered, but Elsbeth didn't hear.

"They both died instantly. That's why he lives with his grandmother—there's no one left. Poor soul! Not that his grandmother isn't a good influence. She's a big patron of women's education. She basically started Harrington Gardens School for Girls, where Mina and Gwendolyn go. I haven't met her yet, but supposedly she's always there . . ."

I stopped listening to Elsbeth.

When Elsbeth saw that I wasn't paying attention, she stopped talking. We both sat in a motionless silence, the blow of shock and sadness blunting me into wordlessness.

"Oh my God." The handful of interactions I'd had with

Aston came flooding back to me in a sickly montage, crippling me with heart-stopping regret. "I had no idea. Elsbeth, I've been *so* rude to him!"

"Oh, Kika, you're never one to be rude. Just a little, um, free with your words sometimes, but never in a malicious way. Besides, I'm sure he's tired of people walking on eggshells around him, anyway. He probably just wants to be treated like a normal boy."

When I didn't respond, she asked, "So what happened between you two? You're friends?" Elsbeth rounded her eyebrow.

"Well, not really. But we talked a bit at the party—I just feel so terrible. I can't imagine losing my mom." I got up and walked to the window, which coincidently faced Aston's house.

"We just got off on the wrong foot." I flicked my gaze back at Elsbeth in camaraderie. "We're just from very, very different worlds," I clarified, as if this would explain it all.

"Now Kika, don't be a snob," said Elsbeth, snapping shut her book.

The clap made me plop back down. "Me? The snob?"

"Yes! Reverse snobbery. Prejudice. Don't hold it against him that he's well-off. Elizabeth Bennet was quite prejudiced against poor Mr. Darcy, remember? And just think how wrong she was about that."

I tucked my hair behind my ear. "I don't think there was anything 'poor' about Mr. Darcy. And if I remember correctly, he snubs her first."

Elsbeth wiggled uncomfortably. "Well, lamb. There's nothing wrong with you two being friends now, is there?" she asked. "He's a very respectable young man. Even the tabloids can't dig up much dirt on him, save the occasional snatch of dating gossip. They all want to make him out to be an international playboy, pinning him with this girl and that one, but they never have any real scandal."

Elsbeth continued: "And you could use a friend, a new girl in a new city like this."

I smiled at Elsbeth, knowing she thought Aston was just the perfect catch as an orphaned, wounded billionaire. With maybe a nice set of abs and a penchant for acoustic folk guitar . . .

I felt my ears get hot, and I chided myself for thinking about that little bit of his stomach that I had seen that day. I wish I never saw it.

Still, I knew what I had to do.

~ 29 ~

I SNUGGLED INTO my bed, concentrating on the whiskey-colored lamplight worming its way through the half-drawn curtains. I never fully closed my curtains. I liked to be woken up by sunshine.

Sleep refused to come to me. It was obvious why: *I want to make things right with Aston. I want to—I don't know—tell him that I liked his guitar playing!*

It weighed heavily on me that he thought I disliked it. In a plea bargain deal with my insomnia, I resolved to stop by Aston's house first thing tomorrow morning after dropping the girls off at their early morning choir practice.

Clive usually dropped the girls off at school, but as the weather grew steadily milder, I started walking them there. Mina would make me turn around at Gwen's school, so I wouldn't embarrass her at the older kids' entrance.

"I can go the rest of the way myself, Kika," she whined. I always gave in.

MORNING CAME QUICKLY. Too quickly.

As I made my way toward Aston's house, I felt the tightness from last night return to my stomach as if I had just taken my belt in a notch.

Face-to-face with the shiny red door, I lifted my hand to create a sharp rapping sound. The moment my hand dropped, I got the urge to bolt.

A few painful moments later, the door opened.

"Kika." Aston sounded surprised. "Everything all right with the house?"

"Yeah, fine. It's nothing like that." Now that I knew he was sort of our landlord, the question made sense. "Um, do you have a second to talk?" I gestured at the doorstep for us to sit.

Aston closed the door gently behind him. He had on another one of his tatty Aran sweaters, and his hair was in its usual untamed arrangement.

"Oh no. What is it, then?" he asked before we even sat.

I sat first, facing forward toward the street and garden beyond it so that I didn't have to look directly at his fluid blue eyes.

"Aston, look. I just wanted to say thanks again for what you did with Bae Yoon. That really meant something, you know?" I said swiftly before I could chicken out.

"Did it?" he asked slowly. He sat down beside me on the steps and also faced forward. We both looked at the garden.

It wouldn't be long now until it would burst into life, all green and blossoming and aromatic.

"To me it did." I was speaking too fast, but like sliding on ice, I couldn't stop myself now. I just had to ride it out or crash. "And I think we got off on the wrong foot. And I wanted to start again—if that was okay with you. And I hope—"

Aston interrupted me: "Who told you?" He stared at the pavement between his sneakers.

I didn't understand. "What?"

"You heard about my parents, I presume?"

I looked down, resisting the question. "I did. But that's not what this is about," I protested.

Aston stubbed the ground with the heel of his sneaker, looking like an unhappy little boy.

"I'm so sorry, by the way." My voice was slight, like I was trying to muffle my impotent sympathy. "It's terrible," I added. Words felt so inadequate.

Aston stared into an unspecific nothingness. "That's quite all right. You needn't have bothered. Thank you. Very much indeed. So what was it that this was regarding, then?"

I responded too rapidly, too defensively. "The guitar. Your guitar playing!" I sounded as if the idea just struck me.

He crooked his neck to watch me, his stare goose-pimpling my skin.

My words were twitchy, but I managed to chirp out my real feelings: "I like the way you play."

I closed my eyes, tilting my face sunward to sever all eye contact. But I still felt him staring at me, burning through my red-veined eyelids and my unbearably thinly veiled pity for all that he had been through.

"I wanted you to know that. It really bothered me for some reason. That's all," I added. "That's what I wanted to tell you. That's what this is about."

I turned to Aston, but now he looked away. He looked confused or maybe relieved. We sat side by side in silence. Somehow, this was okay.

When Aston spoke, he took his time. "So you enjoy folk music?"

"Love it. I really do. It sounds like home to me. I used to listen to it growing up; my mom played it nonstop on her sixties' turntable. She teaches her yoga to folk music. No sitar music in her classes."

He offered me a begrudging smile.

I continued: "And your playing—I don't know, it just really struck me. It reminded me how much I love it. And miss it in my life."

He took a moment and then dipped his head unhurriedly as if he understood. "If you like, I'm playing at the Arts Club on Gloucester Road next weekend."

I spanked my palms on my thighs. "You're inviting me to watch you play?"

"Very good, Yank," he said with his trademark cheek and bent semi-smile.

I gave him a wry smile back. "Can't." But before he spoke, I clarified. "I mean, I would love to, I just can't next weekend. I have someone coming to visit me. This weekend I'm free, though."

I didn't know I wanted to hear folk music so badly until I said that last part.

"Actually I meant this Saturday. You see, I play there every weekend. So Saturday at half nine, then? You may be home late."

"I can handle that," I said defensively.

"Surely you can," he said. "I'll come and fetch you. We can walk there if you'd like, of course."

I sprang up. "Sounds good. See you." I was down his stoop and halfway to my house before I recognized the bounce in my step.

— 30 —

This isn't a date. This isn't a date. This isn't a date.

I repeated it over and over like a mantra as I scraped my hair back into a careless ponytail. *This isn't a date, but why then have I been playing with my hair for the last ten minutes?* I gave up on my messy locks and let them tumble down my back as they pleased.

I was annoyed at myself for even *thinking* that this vaguely resembled a date—the whole pesky idea felt treacherous and unfair to Lochlon.

Then, my annoyance at myself congealed into sticky resentment: *This is all Aston's fault.* He was the one who white-knighted in and saved me from Bae Yoon, revealing himself to be a decent modern gentleman! Why did I have to take his niceness personally? And Elsbeth's stamp of approval only made it worse.

I stomped the ground like Gwendy when she didn't want to go to school in the mornings.

"Pull it together. This isn't a date," I said aloud into the mirror with resolve and a finger point.

"What isn't a date?"

I turned around and saw Mina in the doorway of my room. "Sorry, your door was open. I can come back if you're busy."

My cheeks colored. "No, Mina. Of course not, come in. Sorry about that. I was just giving myself a pep talk. What's up?"

Mina belly flopped on my bed and sent her glossed curls flying every which way. "Kika, do you think my parents will let me stay here for school break next week?"

We were all going to the south of Italy for the end-of-term holidays. The Darlings would be leaving one day earlier than me, since Lochlon's weekend visit coincided with the start of vacation. But as soon as Lochlon left on Sunday, I would meet them there. This was the first time since I arrived that I asked Elsbeth for anything, and she didn't seem to mind my arrival being a day later.

"You want to stay here? Why don't you want to go to Italy?" I asked.

"I'm just over it." Mina was over everything lately. Actually, that wasn't true; she was either "over it" or she "couldn't be bothered with it." They had become her two favorite and interchangeable expressions.

"Mina, you know I don't speak thirteen-year-old girl. You're going to have to translate for me."

"I just feel like staying home, you know? Plus, we go to the same place every year. Not like I'd be missing anything."

Actually, I didn't know, because I never felt like staying home. I, for one, was looking forward to the trip.

"Is it because it's an 'off-the-grid' trip?"

The other day, Elsbeth did this whole big song and dance where she banned the use of all technology during the trip: All phones, tablets, laptops, et cetera, would be left behind. Save for one emergency phone that Elsbeth insisted on carrying, but it would be left turned off. With all that family time, it was shaping up to be every teenager's dream vacation.

"Will you just ask my mom?" she begged in that drippy, world-weary voice.

"Oh, I know what it is." I hurdled onto the bed beside her.

"What?" she asked sharply, suddenly alert.

I took one of her curls and placed it under my nose to make a mustache. Her mouth twitched with the first hints of a smile.

"You want to stay home so you can have a party, you devious little teenager, you."

When she didn't respond, I was sure I'd cracked the code.

"Listen Miss Popular, I'm sure your rich kid friends throw grand fêtes all the time with their cool Euro au pairs from, like, Bratislava or wherever, but your mom is not going to let you stay home by yourself, which means I'll be here, which also means that there will be no parties."

Mina pulled at a strand of her hair and examined the ends with teenage aloofness.

"Sorry, that's just the way I roll." I shrugged, and Mina pouted, which reminded me that though she was technically an adolescent, she was still on the border of little girl territory.

"Ugh, fine. Whatever," she said. "So what are you doing tonight?"

"I'm going to watch some live music."

"Cool, can I come?"

I gave her an apologetic smile. "Sorry, I'm going to a bar, and I don't think Elsbeth would be all that happy about you around booze and boys."

"Kids are allowed to go into pubs here. I see it all the time."

I pulled a face. "You're right. You have no idea how creepy it is to be having a pint with a toddler running through your legs."

My mind went back to the first time I was in Ireland, and I witnessed a father give his baby—less than one year old—a sip of his Guinness. The baby did not enjoy it. I made a mental note to tell Lochlon the story, because he'd find it hilarious.

"Who are you going with?" asked Mina.

"You know Aston, the guy next door?"

Mina nodded. "All the older girls in my school think he's hot."

I narrowed my eyes. "He's a talented guitar player. I'm going to go to watch him play."

"Sure. Whatever," said Mina. She eyed my Dr. Martens and slipped her feet into them. "So is it, like, a date?"

I flamed red again.

"I'm just teasing you. I know you're with Lochlon."

"Right," I said gruffly. "I'm with Lochlon."

— *31* —

"Shall I order you a pint, unless of course you'd rather . . ."

"Sure, a pint sounds good," I said, twirling on my barstool. When I was with the Darlings, the girls and I always guzzled Shirley Temples. It felt different to be offered booze.

The bar was smoky and low lit with red bar lights that watercolored my hair pink. Aston caught the barman's attention. They chatted like old friends before he ordered for us both.

"So are you nervous?" I asked him.

"No. I play here all the time. Here and at the Zetland Arms by the South Kensington Tube on Thursdays—it's an absolute old man's bar, that. Not a bit like this place, mind you, but still good fun. I don't get nervous about playing. But public speaking is another matter."

I opened my mouth to respond, but then his body language sobered, becoming stiff and impatient.

"Kika, before the night goes any further, I must say something." He spoke over the music. "I meant to tell you earlier."

"Go for it," I encouraged, buying him time by taking a sip of the sudsy pint. I swallowed hard, the glacial buzz traveling straight to the center of my forehead.

"Right, well, I wanted to ask you to forgive me for being such a rude git the first time we met. I was such a fuckwit."

I rifled through my mind. "You mean that morning on the steps?" I wasn't expecting to hear about that morning again. Somehow, it felt so long ago that it was as if it involved different people entirely.

"Yes. You see, everything had gone tits up that night. I managed to get into a row with my mates. I had been up all night, so when I met you I acted like an utter wanker."

"It's okay."

"Rubbish. It really isn't. Not to make it some sort of excuse, but that night was . . . well, it was the anniversary of their deaths. I loathe that they call it 'anniversary.' Surely, there's a better word for it?" His face distorted inelegantly with bereavement.

From inside of me came the urge to hug him or shake him—anything to get him to change his facial expression. Instead, I said feebly, "There really should be."

Realizing that he had colored the mood, he put on a dignified smile. "Ah well. Can't be helped. But I do apologize. For it all." He spoke with a clear and rehearsed sort of sincerity. It let me know that this had been on his mind.

"And here I was thinking you were an alcoholic bum who just fell asleep on the stoop," I said grimly, trying to get him to cheer up. "Thanks for apologizing. It's cool. We're friends now."

He squinted at me. "Is that what we are, mates, then?"

I slowly nodded, testing out the friendship in my mind. "Mates it is." I offered my hand, and we shook on it.

Just then, a microphone squeak stole our attention away from each other. The crowd bent toward the blue-lit stage.

"Okay, well, it looks like I'm up, then. Get your hands ready to stuff your ears." He hopped off his barstool and ran his palms along his jeans.

I batted away his British self-deprecation. "Please. You're going to kill it."

He jogged up to the platform and swung his guitar onto his lean body, looking all self-assured and eager. And kill it he did.

~ 32 ~

"So what's this about some bloke coming to visit you next weekend, then?"

As it got later, the bar buzzed with boozy bravado. It was like everyone was sure that life would always be as beautiful and unplanned as it was on a Saturday night.

I took another pull on my beer before answering. "I never said a *boy* was coming," I said with a coquettish smile. Because I was talking about Lochlon, I thought I could get away with some innocent playfulness.

"Well, go on, then," he said.

"I'm kidding. It is a guy. His name is Lochlon. We met when I was traveling. He only returned home to Ireland recently, so we're going to catch up. Nothing crazy."

Aston blinked evenly, as steady as flashing traffic lights. We were then interrupted by another person complimenting his playing—this was the fourth or fifth person to do so since the end of his set.

"Well, I have to say that I am impressed. I knew you could play, but I didn't know you were a performer."

He leaned in. "You're too kind."

"I'm not being kind. I'm being honest."

He smiled. "You know, I do see that in you. You are an honest person. You don't hide much, do you?"

I shrugged. "I guess. I've been known to blurt out my thoughts—mostly because they just fall out of my mouth."

"I should try that more." Aston nodded to himself.

"Well, it's easy. Quick, tell me what you're thinking."

Aston shifted his vision away from me and scanned the crowd.

"No," I insisted, touching his arm. "Stop thinking about it. Just say it!" I snapped my fingers in front of his face to bring him back to me.

He squared his eyes to mine. "All right, if you're sure," he countered, mirroring my assertion. "I was just thinking about kissing you."

My heartbeat stuttered and skipped a beat. *Come again?*

Aston grinned and shrugged at my unconcealed shocked reaction. "What? If you truly want to know, I'm thinking about what it would be like to kiss you."

My mouth dried up, and I felt a lump building in my throat.

"Now you're thinking about it, too, aren't you?"

Shit, I am thinking about it. I didn't speak.

His fingertips strummed against the top of the bar. I couldn't help but watch how easily they moved. Aston moved his face closer to mine.

"That's cute," he said softly.

I ran my tongue over my teeth. "What?"

"You're picturing it right now."

"No, I'm not." I felt my skin get hotter, and Aston scoffed with amusement. But now, without being able to stop myself, I pictured Aston tilting up my chin with his nimble fingertips and moving his mouth nearer. The vision was so visceral that I could almost feel his lips delicately skimming mine, our mouths lightly brushing against each other before he parted my lips with his in a full-on, openmouthed kiss. I accidentally shivered.

I tried to swallow down the dry, chalky bulge in my throat. It wasn't dread or discomfort, I suddenly realized. It was *desire*.

Then, in real life, as if I forecasted it, Aston edged closer to me. As his lips got closer and closer to mine, I felt my gaze lowering. He was a few inches away from my mouth, and I licked my lips unintentionally, my body roasting hotter than ever.

But instead of kissing me, Aston stopped a mere inch from my lips. "You're beautiful when you blush," he whispered. I closed my eyes.

But then, a smacking sound jutted me awake. A hand slapped down on Aston's shoulder. "Great playing, mate!"

I jerked away from Aston's mouth and directed myself toward the interruption. *Go away!* I mentally yelled at the intruder, fizzling in disappointment.

Then a split second later, it hit me: *What am I doing? I almost just kissed Aston!* I straightened my neck. *I shouldn't be disappointed with the disruption—I should be relieved.*

Aston made eye contact with me and blew a small exhale out of his nose but otherwise hid his annoyance and turned to take the guy's hand. "Cheers, Thomas. Are you well?"

"Kika, this is Thomas, a mate from uni," Aston said, making a polite introduction. They began to catch up, and I used the moment to excuse myself to go to the bathroom. As I stood, I exhaled hard, only then fully understanding what I had almost just let happen.

WHEN I RETURNED from the bathroom, Thomas was gone. I wished he had stayed; I needed insurance that something like that wouldn't happen again. *I would be my own insurance*, I vowed. I was obviously just a little buzzed and caught off guard before. It wasn't longing I had tasted—it was just loneliness. And three beers.

Aston smiled at me. "Sorry about Thomas."

"No, no, it's fine. I understand that you have an obligation to your fans," I joked, trying my best to be natural and keep the conversation light.

"You really should do this. Make this your career," I said, pushing my stool away from Aston's. "You're good enough, you know. And everyone adores you."

"Everyone?" he asked.

I hummed along with the music and cursed myself for giving him that opening.

Aston rested his elbows on the bar. "Everyone's mad. But I would like to do this for the rest of my life. At least write music, if not perform it. Everyone expects me to take over the company one day. There's no rush—it's all run by a board of directors these days, thank goodness."

"You wouldn't want to be the boss?"

He shook his head. "No. Nor do I believe that my parents would have minded. They just wanted me to make my own choices. Even when I got into Oxford they didn't demand, 'You must go there because we went there' or insist I get top marks. They merely wanted to know if it was what I truly wanted."

"Was it?" I was grateful for the rerouting of the conversation. This was a safe, unromantic topic.

"It was. I went for musical theory, though, not business. But still, it is as if everyone's sort of waiting about for me to change my mind. But it's not likely to happen."

"I get it. I think people always hope for the best for you, but they have trouble seeing that the best isn't always the most obvious choice."

From under his pint, he ripped at the coaster, soggy and malleable with condensation. "You're speaking like someone with firsthand experience."

"The au pair gig is great, but it's not exactly my long-term dream," I admitted.

We were sitting side by side, so Aston swiveled his barstool to face me. He swung his legs open around mine so that my pressed-together knees were in between his splayed legs; the positioning felt both personal and protective.

"And so the plot thickens," he mused. "At the risk of sounding like an American, tell me, *poodle*, what is it that you want out of life?"

I released a sputtering sound while spinning my barstool away in the guise of crossing my legs. I couldn't just let my legs rest in the middle of his like that. It felt too familiar, too intimate.

"What do I want? Well, that's an easy one. I want to travel."

"Respectable," Aston said. "And I can well believe it, you being here and all."

"But before you say it: I know that traveling isn't a job. So I have this idea." I told him about Gypsies & Boxcars. I felt encouraged by his genuine interest, warm as an open fire, and I felt myself shedding layers.

Midsentence, my phone beeped, and I snuck a glimpse at it to see it was Lochlon texting me, but I left the message unread to be polite to Aston.

I concluded my pitch. "Anyway, I really think I could make it work." I was short of breath, and my cheeks flushed ardently.

"Too right," Aston said, breaking the trance. "You appear to have it all figured out. Not keen on traveling myself, though. Not my favorite thing."

I inadvertently jerked my neck back in response.

"I suppose I'm a bit of a homebody," he continued, undeterred by my reaction. "And I'm mad on London."

I resisted the urge to make a face. "Well, London *is* a great city," I said diplomatically. "But have you ever done any traveling?" I asked.

"A bit, with my mates at uni, and with my family growing up. But I never took a gap year or did any of that shite. Just didn't see the need."

The need. That was how I described my appetite for travel: an animalistic need, as primal and one-dimensional as hunger or lust. I couldn't keep the disappointment from spreading over my face like a stain.

"It's just such a hassle. And in this modern age, you can get plenty of experiences from the comfort of your own city," he said.

I held on to the barstool to stop myself from leaping down his throat in contradiction. I immediately thought of Lochlon, and I was reminded why I had been holding out for him this whole time: *This* was why.

Not everyone was like us. Lochlon and I were made of the same unrestricted spirit; we were the same train-hopping, impulsive travelers to the end.

As Aston blathered on about some amazing Chinese restaurant in Soho that was just like Shanghai, I chanted traveler-truths to myself. Lochlon and I had the same well-decorated passports, dust-choked mountain backpacks, and wandering, persistent, beauty-seeking souls.

We wanted to see the same second-string cities because we liked to spend our time seeing things others might skip over or miss. We were not scared of the road less traveled, but then again, we weren't too cool to take the path well-worn. Above all, we weren't afraid to get lost, to be without a plan, to be without the things that everyone else thought they needed. Our lives weren't something to be slogged across, but marveled through.

Aston paled against the distinct articulation of what Lochlon and I had.

But here I was, out with him on a Saturday night, drinking English lager and talking about my dreams. I lowered my eye-lashes thinking about the near-kiss.

"You're judging me, aren't you? You think it's dreadful. Look at you—you can barely stand it," Aston said with a curious lilt. He looked tickled by my reaction.

"No! I . . ." I wasn't expecting him to call me out. But then I shrugged. "I guess I am judging you a little." In the moment of honesty, I let it all out: "It's just that I don't really understand people like . . . you."

When I said that aloud, I heard how outlandish and condescending it sounded. He was his own person; he could do whatever he wanted. He wasn't my problem. I had Lochlon. And it was easy to love someone who loved the same thing as you.

In the meantime, I tried to be civil. "I guess it *is* silly for me to judge you. Lots of people don't travel. I mean, isn't there some statistic that says most Americans don't have passports?"

Aston shoved out a bark of laughter at my audacity. "Oh, is that supposed to be a consolation?"

My mind refused to come up with anything better, but I didn't care anymore.

"I do like skiing in Zermatt, but it's the skiing I like, not the traveling bit," Aston added.

The gap between us was obvious now, and I knew there'd be no coming back from it. But that was okay, because on my side, on my team, was Lochlon. The rosy validation of my feelings for him swelled inside me like a deep secret. No one could touch what we had.

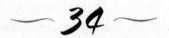

34

LEAVING THE CAB, the night air enveloped me, and I suddenly didn't feel tired even though it was 2 A.M. Aston dug out his wallet and waved me away when I tried to pay. I gave in easily.

"I really had a good time," I said, looking down at my purse.

"So did I. Really." Aston took one step closer. I felt as if he was trying to bait my gaze upward. I stayed firm and studied the ground.

He came in closer, moving tacitly and confidently.

I didn't move away, but I wanted to. Now that he was close, too close, he leaned toward me and bent down a bit, invading my space. But I still didn't take a step back. He was so close to me that his heated, exhaled breath mingled with mine. I held my breath so it wouldn't happen again.

Step away, I commanded myself.

He flicked his eyes over my lips.

I clenched my teeth. *Oh my God, he's going to kiss me. Move away, Kika.* But there it was; the same desire from earlier in the night cracked through me and surfaced again: *I want him to kiss me.*

"Aston," I whispered very softly in protest. Before he leaned in further, I took a step backward—finally. I drew the line and then placed myself determinedly behind it. "I can't, Aston."

"Why can't you?" He protruded his chin toward me without faltering. He wasn't at all uncomfortable or deterred, but he seemed very aware of the imaginary line I drew. I knew he'd never cross it without my permission.

The night wind breathed between us, inhabiting that physical space that I had just carved out. I fished my fingers into my pockets and took out the shiny keys.

"Is it because I don't like traveling?"

Despite myself, I produced a bold laugh that pinballed off the ancient houses. I was thankful that he broke the tension.

"No. It isn't. Although that is distressing," I admitted. "It's Lochlon. Sort of, anyway."

"That one who's visiting you? He's your boyfriend, then? I apologize, I didn't realize." Aston took another step backward now and put more chilly space between us that the night rushed to occupy.

"No, it's my fault. I should have said." I rattled the keys. "It's just that, truthfully, he's not my boyfriend. I don't know what he is, but I have to see. I owe it to him—I owe it to what we had—to see."

I heard the tinge of regret in my tone, and I tasted my own oily guilt. It wasn't that I *regretted* that Lochlon was coming—

God, no—I was *excited*, but I felt disloyal for not making this clear before.

Aston nodded. He kept looking at me unabashedly. He looked distractingly handsome in this lamplight. And it destroyed me to notice it.

"It was good of you to hear me play tonight." He took his hands out of his pockets.

"It was great. You were—" I started, but I stopped myself. My words were coming off as cheap.

"Good night, then, Kika." He turned around and climbed his steps.

At the door, he turned. "Go on inside. I couldn't leave you here on the footpath. It's quite late to be out here alone."

I parted my lips to speak, but I stopped when I saw Aston's face, which seemed to say, "Just don't." So I turned and walked to my door, deep matte navy like a passport. I felt him watching me.

He didn't leave the steps until he saw the light go on in my bedroom window above. I waved to him before pulling the curtains, but he didn't wave back. I left the curtains half open.

Before getting into bed, I remembered to check my phone. The text from Lochlon from hours ago sat there like a forgotten present: "Was just thinking about you. Wanted to let you know."

I didn't respond right away.

"Just one week! X" I eventually texted him back. He didn't respond, having long been asleep.

35

Normally, Elsbeth arranged for Clive to pick up Mina from school, but I had a surprise for her today.

Gwendy had a karate lesson after school, so I was going to take Mina to All Star Lanes, an American-style bowling alley and burger joint, where we'd have some good, old-fashioned, American fun. I felt a bit homesick myself, and there was nothing like greasy burgers and stinky bowling shoes to make you feel like you were in the good old US of A.

I heaved the front door closed behind me and galloped down the steps. I hastily glanced at Aston's house, but he wasn't around—thankfully.

With Lochlon coming this weekend, I hoped that I wouldn't run into him. I had tucked the memory of the night at the bar in a dusty corner of my mind not often visited. Aware that Aston could appear at any moment, I left the vicinity as fast as I could.

As I approached Harrington Gardens, I could hear the girls twittering like a flock of wild parakeets. They congregated in the garden just opposite the brick school. *Is there anything more uplifting than a gaggle of squawking schoolgirls at the end of a long day?* I asked myself.

I was early, so I whipped on a pair of sunglasses and leaned against the redbrick garden wall. I scanned the schoolyard garden, recalling the rapturous feeling of being done with school for the day and having the whole afternoon unrolled before me like a magic carpet.

I finally spied Mina in the midst of a crescent of girls. *Ah, the little queen bee.* But as I watched her a moment longer, I noticed she wasn't talking. All the other girls were laughing, *except* her; instead, her head was bowed as if in prayer. *Wait a minute. She isn't the queen bee; she is being teased!*

Just as I understood what was happening, Mina stood and walked away from her tormentors with her head held high. But the jeering girls—indistinguishable from one another in their uniforms—followed her, hissing at her back.

I was about to run to her when she looked up and noticed me watching. Even from where I was standing beyond the wall, I could see her face drop. She knew that I saw. And she looked absolutely devastated.

Before I could react, she abruptly about-faced and dashed inside the school. The gaggle of bullies hooted cruelly as she fled.

"Silly American cow," I heard one of the girls yell at her. My diaphragm tightened with despair, but just as quickly the sensation was swamped over by a surge of wrath.

Without thinking, I found myself swinging my legs over

the wall and charging over to the crew of mini mean girls, though Mina was now long gone and out of sight.

"Who did you just call an American cow?" I demanded in my loudest, most obnoxious American accent. I strained my neck out at each of the girls, challenging them to speak. "Do you not get that it's an offensive thing to yell at people?"

"Oi, we weren't talking to you, were we now?" ventured one of the girls with a smack of her gum.

The others laughed—but a lot lower and shakier this time.

"Well, that's the problem with having a big mouth. *Everyone* hears you."

The girls stared at me slack-jawed. I bet these rich brats never got disciplined in their whole lives.

"Listen to me, you bitches—actually, you're not even tall enough to be bitches; you're like, junior bitches." I laughed at my own gall. "You may think you're something cool, bullying other people, but I get what you're doing. You need to bully people so you're not the one getting bullied. You talk a big, mean game, but you're all *terrified* little girls . . ."

They didn't speak, but they appeared to be hanging on every word.

"Let me give you a life tip: Don't treat other people like shit. Because when you treat other people like shit, *you* get treated like shit in return. Get it?"

No one spoke. The ringleader clicked her gum, but with her mouth closed this time, muffling the cracking. Out of the corner of my eye, I noticed a teacher approaching us.

Get the hell out of here, I told myself. Still, I took the time to look each of them in the eyes with the most withering anger I could muster.

"Am I making myself clear?"

The teacher neared. "All right, junior bitches. I'm watching you," I said as I reversed, slung on my sunglasses, and sped out of the schoolyard.

Behind me, I heard the teacher reach the girls. She assaulted them with questions: "Who was that? What did that lady say to you?"

But all they did was mumble in response, "Nothing, miss. Nothing."

I made a quick left onto Gloucester Road, where I would be hidden from the school, and I settled in at one of the wicker café tables outside Café Forum. And I waited.

~ 36 ~

"SO I GUESS the secret is out." Mina sunk down into the café chair under the shade of the coffee-colored awning. I had texted her to come meet me whenever she was ready.

"That you go to school with a bunch of bitches?" I placed a hot cocoa in front of her. It was still cold in London, and it was looking like spring would take its sweet time to arrive.

She didn't touch the cocoa and instead rounded her scarf around her neck.

"No. That I have no friends." A small tear slid down her face when she finally took a sip of cocoa.

I wanted to hug her and tell her everything would be okay, but I also didn't want to spook her. She blinked back the tear with bravado and clumsily set the cocoa down, accidentally overturning it on the wobbly table.

"Oh no," she told the widening spill. Instead of trying to stop it, she started full-on crying.

I grabbed some napkins and alternated between giving one to her and one to the spill.

"It's okay, it's okay," I intoned as I mopped up the table.

"I know it's okay," she barked. But then she sniveled and fixed her school uniform skirt over her knees. "Sorry. Sorry. I can't believe I'm crying over spilled hot chocolate." She stared at the sugary confections piled high in the café window behind us.

"Hey, the waste of chocolate is a serious and terrible thing," I said only half joking, which got a good-mannered smile out of her.

"It's so stupid." She sniffed.

"I get it." I showed her my upturned palms. "Once I cried because I finished a chocolate bar."

Mina choked out a laugh. "But why?"

"Because I was sad it was done!" I protested, my steadfast assertion making her laugh out loud.

"When you were little?" she asked in disbelief.

I cocked my eyebrow. "It was, like, last week." Taking advantage of the moment, I switched subjects.

"Listen, Mina. I'm sorry you had to go through that bull-shit back there."

Mina puffed up her cheeks. "They are bitches, aren't they?"

"Well, junior bitches, but 'bullies' would be a better term for them."

"It's that Peaches Benson-Westwood! She's the ringleader. Everyone hates whoever she says to hate."

"So Peaches isn't your best friend, then?"

"She's horrible, but she's the most popular girl at school. She has *three* Louis Vuitton bags and a picture of her with Prince Harry in her logbook."

I rolled my eyes.

"Don't tell my mom. If she finds out that everyone hates me, she'll, like, faint or make me join a croquet team or whatever."

"Ha! She totally would. And she'd join with you."

"Because that's the way to make friends," she added.

I snorted a laugh.

"Promise me you won't tell her?" she asked with wet eyes. "No matter what?"

"Of course, I won't," I assured her.

"So, what did you say to them?" Mina asked in a different tone.

"I called them junior bitches."

Mina widened her eyeballs. "You didn't really!"

I shook my head, brushing it off. "They had no idea who I was. Don't worry."

"They've been teasing me since I started school. I don't know why—"

"Because they're insecure. Listen, it's all kill or be killed at your age. They're *Hunger-Gaming* you because if you don't tease others, *you* could be teased. They don't get that if they all stop playing the game, everyone would win."

I paused to drink my own hot cocoa before gliding it toward Mina like a puck on ice. "Aim for your mouth this time, okay?" I teased.

The frosty wind nipped up the busy street and urged me to raise my jacket collar. It was too cold to be sitting outside, but neither of us minded.

"So what should I do?" But then her face lit up. "If I can get my mom to get me a Louis Vuitton bag, then—"

I cut her off there. "Mina, that's not going to solve anything. You can't just get a new designer handbag to fit in."

She folded her arms. "Maybe I'll ask my mom."

"Yeah right, Elsbeth told me she thinks logo monogram bags are gauche as fuck. Obviously omitting the word 'fuck.'"

"Yeah, I'm pretty sure my mom has never said that word in her life," she added. "Can you just come to school with me and curse them out whenever they start?"

"I honestly would like nothing more. But no, I don't think I can pass for thirteen . . ." I gave Mina my most youthful smile. "We'll think of something," I told her, hopeful that it was the truth.

37

"WELL, WHAT WOULD happen if it were a movie?" I asked as I laced my ice skates in the waning dusk light. Mina and Gwen were ready to get on the ice (thanks to me). They eyed me impatiently, their legs in a wide straddle and hands on their hips in classic cheerleader stances.

"Hmm," Mina pondered aloud. "I guess if it were a movie, the most popular boy in school would become my boyfriend and then everyone would *want* to be my friend."

"That's a great plan, except you go to an all-girls school," I reminded her.

I swung Gwen over the partition, and she went flying onto the ice with little more than a "Whee!" The tiny nugget was fearless.

Notes of carnival music flurried around us. It was a bright, frosty evening, and we were at the ice skating rink in front of the Natural History Museum, which glowed violet and gold behind us. We were trying to come up with ideas to solve what we were calling "The Peaches Predicament."

I explained the situation to Gwen, because although I thought it was amazing that she adored her older sister, I wanted her to know that Mina's life wasn't perfect, either, and that even she could have trouble making friends.

"I'll punch Peaches in the baby-maker!" Gwen said, scissoring the air with sturdy karate chops.

"You most certainly will not!" I retorted while doing my best to hold in my laughter. While Gwendy went off to teach herself double axels, Mina and I tried to find a real solution. (Although punching bitches in the baby-maker was by far our best option at the moment.)

"Isn't Aston's grandmother the headmistress of the school? I could talk to her privately, or you could talk to a teacher. Is that out of the question?"

Mina skated away from me, which answered that question. "I don't want to give Peaches an *actual* reason to hate me, Kika," she said when I caught up to her.

I tugged on my gloves; my hands were slapped red by the cold wind. Children squealed, and hundreds of fairy lights glittered around us. I tried not to get distracted by all the mirth—we had problems to solve.

I thought back to instances in my own life when I was bullied or teased. Isn't being thirteen shitty for every girl? But then I thought of my mom—the best person I knew—and I asked myself what she would do.

Well, that was easy: She'd kill them with kindness. We had these nasty older neighbors who she won over by plying them with homemade juices and teaching them stretches made to relieve arthritis.

"Mina, I've got it."

She raised her eyebrow apprehensively.

"Invite her over for a sleepover!" I declared triumphantly.

"And then what? Get her to wash her hair with hair-remover? Draw a Hitler mustache on her face in permanent marker when she's sleeping?" she asked, enlivened.

"No, no, no," I protested. "Come on, Mina. Think bigger!"

"*Poison* her?" she asked with wide eyes.

I almost wiped out on the ice. "God, no! Mina, seriously?" I shook my head at her. "What kind of an au pair do you take me for?" I paused. "Don't answer that," I quickly added.

I pirouetted on my skates and clutched Mina's shoulders, forcing her to face me. "*You make friends with her.* In fact, it was what you did in your head to solve the problem: You *said* she was your best friend."

"Um, Kika, in case you didn't notice, Peaches Benson-Westwood hates me," Mina pointed out.

"But does she really, though? I mean, does she have a real reason to hate you, or is she just threatened?"

Mina shrugged and kept skating.

I hurried after her. "Look, picture this: You're the queen bee of the school and all of a sudden a new girl comes along. She's obviously cool and pretty, and worst of all, she has a kick-ass American accent and is from New York Freakin' City."

"I'm from Long Island."

"Same difference as far as these girls are concerned. Look, everyone was probably curious about you when you first got there, right?"

"Well, they did ask me about my American clothes. They're kind of obsessed with them over here."

"Right. This is what I'm thinking: Invite her over to the house to hang out. I'll help you. I'll be there the whole time to intervene if you need me. But I really think you guys can be true friends. I mean, why not?"

Unless she's a total monster, I said to myself.

Mina nodded but stayed quiet for a moment. "Okay, I'll do it. But we need to keep Gwen out of the way. I can't risk having her karate chop Peaches. I'd never hear the end of it," she said, sounding dangerously like Elsbeth.

～ 38 ～

WHEN THE DOORBELL rang, both Mina and I looked at each other with brave faces.

I had scheduled the playdate through Peaches' au pair. I knew I had to move fast, so we planned to have Peaches come over right after Mina's Mandarin lesson the following night. (I know, don't get me started.)

I reached for the doorknob.

"Hey, Peaches," Mina said like the good sport she promised me she'd be.

I waved hello to Peaches. Next to her stood a girl around my age. "Oh, hey, are you Peaches' au pair?"

The girl crumbled her features together. "Oh God no," she trilled. She quickly added, "No offense intended, of course. It's just that I'm Peaches' *sister*. Chantelle Benson-Westwood, lovely to meet you. I thought I'd pop over for a little chat."

Both Peaches and Chantelle pranced their way into the foyer without waiting for an invitation.

Peaches looped a strand of hair around her finger, looking bored—you could tell her parents made her come. Chantelle inventoried the room. She had the same English-rose complexion and that whole dark-hair-and-green-eyes combo as her sister, which made them look witchy and tubercular.

"I'm Kika," I announced with a charmed smile. I promised Mina (and myself) that I would play nicely.

"I'll let you get the girls sorted and then I'll take some tea." Chantelle dumped her coat on a decorative armchair in the foyer (located directly next to a coatrack) and swanned waifishly into the sitting room.

So if Peaches was the junior bitch, this must be the senior one, I thought to myself with an inner eye roll.

I trailed Mina and Peaches down the hall.

Peaches eyed me suspiciously. "You're the terrible lady who shouted at us."

"Guilty," I said with a psychotic smile frozen on my face. *Shit, she remembers me.*

"So you're the nanny, then?"

"I'm Mina's *sister's* nanny," I lied. "Mina and I are just good friends." Mina looked pleased at this.

"I see. I'd like a glass of orange juice now," said the demanding mini-monster. "Fresh squeezed." She had already mastered that face of professional champagne-coolness that expensive restaurant hostesses give you when you ask to use the bathroom in your grubby backpacker gear.

"I'll get it," said Mina sportingly.

"No. Make her. I'll want to see your room now, won't I? I'd like to see your American clothing."

"You guys go on. I'll set up some snacks," I said in an upbeat fashion. I knew what the junior bitch was playing at, and I would not let her get to me. There was still a real chance that she and Mina could become friends.

After setting up some snacks for the girls, I shelved my bitch face and grabbed two iced teas from the fridge knowing perfectly well it was not what Chantelle wanted. I joined her in the sitting room.

When I entered, Chantelle immediately started prattling on: "When Mummy said Peaches was coming over here for a playdate, I just said to myself, I must stop by and see Aston. Aston Hyde Bettencourt, just next door? We're quite good friends, you know. Since primary school, really, though I went to Harrington Gardens—same as Peaches and Willamina."

"Oh, cool." I picked a bit of lint off my sweater. I gave her a faraway smile and wondered how long she planned on staying. Celestynka would be over soon. Things were going well with her English lessons. (I recently taught her what "crunching numbers" meant.) And today we were going to do some mock interviews, and she had some questions for me about the budget she was making for my website.

I handed Chantelle the iced tea, but she held it away from her person with two fingers. I took an unladylike guzzle of mine and flopped my jean-clad legs inelegantly over the side of the stuffy armchair.

"He is an absolute delight. Isn't he?"

"Who?"

"Aston Hyde Bettencourt! You haven't been listening to a word I've said, have you?" she tsk-tsked in a cutesy voice.

"No, I was. Sorry." I actually hadn't been. "You were talking about Aston."

I was relieved not to have run into Aston since our night at the Arts Club. And I did my best to keep it that way. The hot water wasn't working in my room, and since Aston was in effect our landlord, Elsbeth told me to call him to have it sorted. But I wouldn't. Cold showers weren't so bad; they were sort of invigorating first thing in the morning.

I wanted to keep my mind on Lochlon and only Lochlon. Plus, I was going straight on our "no technology" vacation once Lochlon left. I hoped that enough distance and time would make everything normal again between Aston and me . . . whatever "normal" meant.

Chantelle made a stifled, contrived sound from the back of her throat.

"So you and Aston are friends, then? I'm certain I saw you speaking with him at the Wolseley party. That was you, wasn't it?"

"Oh yeah. You were there?" I asked, peering out the window in distraction. *Where is Celestynka?*

Chantelle looked affronted. "I'd be mad to miss it. It was marvelous fun."

"Yeah. Marvelous." *Who speaks like that?*

"Yes, yes, wasn't it? So are you all sorted in London? Do you have many friends here?"

Happy she changed the topic, I made an effort to be friendlier. After all, I had just heard a burst of singsong giggles coming from Mina's room. If she could play nice, so could I.

"London is really great. And no, I don't have many friends here, but it's cool. I make friends quickly."

She gave me a rapid-fire once-over in a single blink, which I didn't miss. "Have you been to Shoreditch yet? I'm a member of Shoreditch House, so I could take you one day, I suppose." She draped her arm over the back of the couch and reclined.

"One day," I said, knowing that it was an empty invite.

"But you're very naturally pretty," she said as a sort of pesky afterthought. "I'm sure you *do* make friends quickly."

"Um, thanks." I was unsure if etiquette required me to return the compliment. I wasn't sure it was a compliment.

Just then, we both looked toward the foyer at the sound of jingling keys. I felt a draft hurry into the room like a late guest.

"Celestynka," I called out, thrilled with the disruption.

Celestynka tip-tapped down the hallway and entered the sitting room. "Good evening, Kika," she said before noticing that I wasn't alone. "Oh, hello." She nodded to Chantelle.

Chantelle immediately looked Celestynka up and down in an undisguised evaluation.

Celestynka noticed and tugged her faux animal print coat tightly around herself. I made the introductions, but Celestynka quickly excused herself to go to work, the cheer gone from her face.

"She cleans the house dressed like *that*?" Chantelle asked loud enough for Celestynka to hear in the kitchen. She started cackling and covered her mouth.

"Don't be ridiculous." I shook my head. "She takes off her high heels first," I said in Celestynka's defense.

Chantelle bowled over. "Oh, come now, Kiki, she rather

does look like a stripper tragedy. She was wearing silver trousers!" She made no effort to lower her voice.

I didn't bother correcting her about my name. I stood. "You need to go now, Chantelle." *How dare she make fun of Celestynka?*

"I'm sure Aston will just be over the moon to see you," I said with overdone sweetness, beckoning her out of the house.

"Oh, come now, I was just having a bit of a laugh. She seems rather sweet. I'm sure she is an excellent scrubber," she said, dissolving into another eruption of self-satisfied giggles.

I desperately wanted to run my mouth at her, but thoughts of Mina stopped me. "Why don't you go over to Aston's and I'll call you when the girls are done playing?" I walked into the foyer and swung the front door inward on its hinges.

Chantelle composed herself and stroked down her hair, which was still magazine perfect. "Right. Well, Aston will try and keep me there *forever*, so do ring when you need me. Lovely meeting you," she said with well-bred, forged enthusiasm.

I slammed the door behind her and watched through the window as she went next door. When Aston opened his door, they clasped their arms around each other like best friends forever. My breath fogged up the cold glass, and I yanked the curtains closed.

39

"SO, HAVE YOU had a bit of time to read the pages I've sent you?"

I got up from my velvet chair and looked out the window. It was way past midnight, and it felt as if the rest of the world was in bed. Unpredicted early-spring flurries twirled in the glow of the streetlamps, cocooning the South Kensington streets in a silver-white silence. This cold spell would freeze the overeager crocuses and daffodils that were starting to peek out.

"Aren't you needy? I told you in the email that I loved those pages. Are you fishing for more compliments, Lochlon?" I rubbed my hands over my skin, soothing down the goose bumps.

"'Course. It gets me hot and bothered when you tell me you like my writing. Go on, then."

Lochlon sent me snippets of stories he wrote while we were traveling together. He was writing his own version of

The Sun Also Rises meets *The Rum Diary* (read: a book about traveling while drunk).

Unfortunately, he hadn't written since getting home to Ireland, but he promised me that he'd start again soon. "As soon as I get back on the road. I can't write here. No inspiration in Ireland," he'd like to tell me.

"I wrote that bit when we were in India. Got some brilliant work done there. Do you remember how lovely it was?"

"I think about it all the time," I said truthfully.

"And I." Lochlon made an irresistible smirking sound. "I still go mad thinking about you in that bikini. By the end of that trip, it was so worn that it was just falling off you." Lochlon was horny. That made two of us.

"So has everyone gone to bed over there?" I questioned.

"That's right, I'm just here all on me lonesome. Why so?"

"Just curious. It's snowing here. Well, flurries, really, but it's the first time I've seen snow here. It's very romantic." A passing car beamed fast-moving, buttery shadows over the blackened room.

"I wish I were there with you," he said quietly.

I sighed. "I have a fireplace in my room. We could make a fire and snuggle under the covers and watch the snow."

"You know if I were under the sheets with you, I'd not be watching the snow."

"So," I started overly innocently, "what would you be doing?" I was well aware of what I was starting. But I missed him. And I needed a way to keep my mind from wandering.

"Your clothes would be gone. That'd be the first thing."

"But wouldn't I be cold?" I teased the skin of my inner forearm with my fingertips.

"I'd keep you warm," he rumbled softly into the phone.

"Would you, now?"

"'Course I would. Now you got me thinking about you naked. Look what you've done."

"What have I done?" I naively asked.

But I just heard ragged breathing in my ear. "You're going to get it if you keep going on like this. God, is it Saturday yet?"

"I know. I can't stop thinking about seeing you again," I told him. I paced around the room. I was desperate to feel him again. The need ached inside me since India; it was like a broken bone that hadn't healed properly. I never told Lochlon that I hadn't been with anyone since him.

"Lochlon?"

I wanted to ask him if he had been with anyone, but then I stopped myself. We said in India that there was no point in discussing exclusivity. Still, I wondered . . . I *hoped* that he hadn't been with anyone else, even though I didn't really have the right to ask that of him.

"Yes, Kika?" he asked. I could tell by his slowed breathing that he was lying down flat on his back.

"I'm going to go to bed," I said.

"Are you sure? All right. Wish I could kiss you good night, at least."

"You can in a few days," I promised, confident that everything would fall into place soon.

40

"What is your funny face about?" Celestynka asked, drumming her glittery nails over the financial plan she was trying to explain to me.

Lochlon was finally arriving today, but I shook my head and tried to focus on the spreadsheet of monthly expenses that Celestynka had created for me. After hours of questioning, she was able to extract a budget for me and my website.

"This is so exciting," I said, spreading out my hands over the papers. There it was: 390 days until Gypsies & Boxcars would go live again—if I kept saving as I had been since I arrived in London.

Celestynka was more than just good with numbers; she had good business sense and she helped me get the steps in the right order.

With the money I'd save in a little over a year, I would be

able to hire a web administrator and relaunch the site starting with the British contacts I had been cultivating. After the relaunch, I would start taking mini trips for scouting purposes. I could afford two of these a month. My aim for these trips would be to find artisans with unique goods and photograph the items for the site. Though this was over a year away, I hoped I could work out a way to take these trips while still keeping my job as an au pair, since it was a guaranteed source of income.

But either way, with Celestynka's guidance, I had a concrete strategy to follow!

Celestynka clicked her tongue to the roof of her mouth. "I know you are excited about this, but maybe you are more thinking of Lochlon's arrival today."

I couldn't help stealing another quick glance at the clock. Throughout the whole discussion, I couldn't help but watch the clock every two seconds, thinking: *Lochlon's plane just landed. Lochlon is on the Tube right now. Lochlon is at his hotel now.*

I had felt a prickling heat spread over my skin when he had told me he booked a hotel. We were both hardcore backpackers and knew exactly what hotels meant: splurge, decadence, and, most of all—privacy. What is it about big white hotel beds that makes you want to have copious amounts of sex in them?

Everything was set. Immediately after Lochlon left, I would leave to meet the Darlings in the south of Italy. I had spent the morning packing so that once Lochlon departed, all I'd have to do was grab my bag and go to the airport.

"Okay, okay. I see. You cannot concentrate today." Celestynka smiled and collected the papers.

I couldn't even protest, so I just smiled dopily. "Thanks for everything," I told her. "This is exactly what I needed."

"You need something else, I think. Have a wonderful time. We will talk of this later." Celestynka left the house, and I filed away the papers and took a long, soothing breath.

This is it. After a whole year apart, it's really happening! I wiped my sweaty palms down my thighs and started making my way out the door. I was meeting Lochlon at Gordon's Wine Bar, and I wanted to be early. I locked the door behind me, wondering: *Will it be any different? God, I hope it won't be.*

— 41 —

I RODE THE humming Circle Line to the Embankment Tube stop, and I arrived at Gordon's Wine Bar with plenty of time to spare. The whole time my heart fluttered against my ribs like a jittery bird in a too-small cage.

I slipped into the slender alley called Watergate Walk, where little café tables were arranged in the shade just outside the cavelike candlelit bar. It was still early, and the sun hadn't set yet, so I chose a rickety table in a wedge of sunlight.

My nerve endings felt like a nest of activity. Whenever anyone entered the alley, I perked my head up like an impatient cocker spaniel.

Finally, I saw him approaching. From the distance, I recognized his posture, his height, his assured gait—the abstracts of him. He got closer and closer and started filling in with more detail.

We locked eyes and—*oh, he doesn't look the same!* I held my breath at the realization. *He's changed.*

From this distance, I wasn't sure how he was different, but I felt like a spell had been lifted from me. I swallowed down the feeling and quickly rearranged my face into a joyful expression before he got close enough to notice.

But it was too late. Something behind Lochlon's eyes shifted by the time he looked at me again.

Before anything else could happen, I jumped up from the table and dove into his arms.

"Lochlon," I called out, my mouth muffled into his shoulder as I rode out the emotions.

"Gorgeous." He lifted me off the ground and swung me in the air until I was giddy from the closeness of him: the smell of mineral soap and musk, the feel of his slept-in hair and lived-in denim—it cut right through the rotten, dissatisfied sensation I felt only moments ago.

Now I remember! He smells the same. Thank God he smells the same. I instantly felt better. *So what if he looks a little different? He is still my same Lochlon.*

"So good to see you," I said into his jacket, breathing him in, unable to pull away just yet.

"And how's yourself?" He peeled me off him and held me at arm's length, yo-yoing his eyes up and down. "You're looking very well."

I threaded a fidgety strand of hair behind my ear. "Was the flight okay?"

"Aw, you know," he said, batting the air. "I could do with a drink in me; that'll set me right," he said, striking his hands together. He hesitated before sitting. "Will I get the sauce so we can have a proper catch-up?"

I nodded, and Lochlon ducked inside.

Whirly and woozy, I felt like I had just come off a circling baggage carousel, and I took the opportunity to reset myself. *Come on, Kika. This is going to be great.*

A moment later, Lochlon returned with a bottle of red wine and a tight smile—lips pushed together in a line. I beamed back at him, pledging to make this weekend wonderful. *I know this man*, I reminded myself. *He's seen me naked.*

"Thought I'd go for the whole bottle and save us the trouble, so." He gestured with the wine bottle. "It's lovely out here. Grand weather."

The last of the day's sun spotlighted the alley as he poured the wine into the glasses up to the brims. He stopped to take a gulp before waterfalling more into his glass. While one hand rested possessively on the stem of his wineglass, he clasped his other hand atop mine in a quick smack.

Still uneasy, I dragged my hand from his and started rattling on to distract him from the gesture. "So I thought we'd go for a walk along the embankment after this, maybe see some sites or—"

I stopped talking when I noticed Lochlon steadily shaking his head. He downed the rest of his wine in one gulp. The action reminded me of a snake unhinging its jaw. I gagged.

"No chance, babes. I'm knackered. We're going back to the guesthouse, and that's all there is to it."

He spoke in that authoritative gruff that I normally found so sexy, but now it made me feel apprehensive.

"We'll have a bit of a lie-down," he said, and I searched for an underlying meaning in his tone. I don't know why, but it felt too sudden to be alone with him.

I ran my finger over the chip in my wineglass before lifting it. I cushioned the glass on my bottom lip and drank it all.

"Pour me another?" I managed with a light-headed, half-hearted smile.

— 42 —

WE TUMBLED INTO the stale guesthouse, both of us in hysterics at memories of Spain. I had just then recalled that the bartender in the hostel hated Lochlon with unbridled passion.

"Everyone adores me, got that whole Irish charm thing. What do you suppose his problem was?" Lochlon asked.

"Maybe it was because you used to throw lemon wedges at the back of his head whenever he went to mix a drink," I reminded him with another burst of laughter.

"I was only messing. But I did nick his phone. We had great craic that night, didn't we?"

I had forgotten about Lochlon's sticky fingers. I wondered why I never gave him a hard time about it.

Somehow, the alcohol sweet-talked us into a comfortable familiarity. Lochlon had drunk most of the bottle of wine at

Gordon's and then stopped off at a corner store to get a few pints to take into the guesthouse.

I had also forgotten how much Lochlon liked to drink, but he was doing his very best to remind me. I closed the door of the guest room behind us. He had already finished a beer on the walk over and held the next one in his hand.

"Slow down, tiger," I said playfully as he hurtled on the bed and popped open the Carlsberg. The beer hissed and erupted all over the bedsheets.

"Shite!" he stormed, launching himself off the bed, but his rapid activity only caused the beer to spill on his shirt in a foamy stream.

"Shite. Shite. Shite," he seethed in overreaction.

I felt a bump on my back and realized that I had reversed into the door.

"Feckin' spilled all over me shirt. Eejit!" He flicked the suds off his hand onto the dull, thin carpet.

"It's fine," I said softly, trying to distract him. I took a small step forward. *It's fine*, I cooed to myself, still not moving too far away from my spot near the door. But somehow I couldn't shake that initial feeling that it wasn't fine.

Now, below the harsh overhead light of the slightly seedy guesthouse, I could finally gauge just how much Lochlon had aged since I last saw him. He tugged the wet shirt over his head, not bothering with the buttons. It had only been a year, but his face was more wrinkled. His flesh was strangely puffy, and he had a small pooch on his stomach, which used to be flat. He abandoned the shirt on the floor and lay down on the bed. His pale skin and pink nipples looked strangely lewd. I looked down.

He looked hardened, I realized, like someone who had

been through a lot. But these observations still didn't satisfy me. He had changed in a way that I could not identify. Whatever it was, it made me sad.

Lochlon squeezed the empty beer can with his fist and then set it down on the bedside table. His mood had changed. He laid his head back on the old-lady bedspread looking wearied.

I crept over and perched pin-straight on the smallest corner of the bed, taking up as little space as possible. I tried to make myself reach out and touch him, to put my hand on his ankle as a comfort. But I couldn't do it.

It's just nerves, I concluded. My feelings hadn't shifted overnight. I dragged my sleeves down over my hands and looked him over.

As he lay there with his eyes closed, I looked at the white scar on his chin, a memento from a bar fight. It then dawned on me what it was that made him look so different to me: *He didn't smile anymore! He had barely even smiled when he saw me.*

When we were abroad, there was always a massive grin on his face, even when he tried to be a temperamental artiste. He had an endearing smile that could charm the meanest of taxi drivers and an impish half smirk that made just about anything sound like a great idea.

The realization snaked up my body until it reached my throat, where it squeezed tight. *Does this mean he is no longer happy?*

"Hey," I said softly. "Is everything okay, Lochlon?"

My mouth collapsed into a worried frown. I wasn't sure I had any more fake enthusiasm in me to adjust it.

Lochlon had only been in Ireland for about a month. *Did being home make him like this?*

"You seem a bit faraway," I continued, my tone petal soft and nonthreatening.

"Yeah, sure, grand. I just don't like you telling me to slow down with the drinking," he said, picking up another beer in protest. "Sounds just like Bernie, always giving out," he added before taking a long pull then brusquely wiping his lips with his knuckles.

Everything went silent for me then.

But Lochlon didn't seem aware of this. He fixed his gaze on my chest and then ran his eyes down me. I gripped my elbows.

"Jaysus, I missed you, you fit thing." He sat up and tried to slink an arm around my waist. The gesture had a predatory edge to it. "Take off them boots and get into bed with me."

I sprouted to my feet so that he couldn't reach me.

"Bernie?" The second syllable of her name came out in a whisper.

He flicked his eyes toward the window covered by dated frilly curtains. "A mate from home," he said casually, meeting my eyes for an instant before resuming staring at the window again, though there was obviously nothing to look at.

"You mean Bernadine, your ex-girlfriend, don't you?"

I turned away and moved toward the window that he couldn't stop staring at. I felt motion sick.

"You're back with her, aren't you?" I sprung open the ugly curtains. The view was just as bad as I expected, all concrete, wire fences, bare trees, and pigeon shit. I knew it then. He didn't have to answer; he had slept with her.

He rubbed the stubble on his face and blinked hard a few times, as if he had just woken up from a long nap. I expected some sort of violent protest, but he just traced the pattern

on the faded bedspread with his eyes. Overhead, the lightbulb produced a subtle, tinny din like a single, stationary mosquito.

Lochlon reached into his jeans pocket and retrieved a pack
of cigarettes and a lighter.

"You smoke now?" I asked incredulously.

Lochlon stood, hiked up his jeans, and began to circle like
a dog before sitting down.

"She's nothing to me. I don't even *like* her. She's just available. You know how it is when you go home after your travel . . ."
He trailed off and held the cigarette against the flame.

"No, Lochlon. Tell me how it is." I snatched his cigarette
out of his mouth and dropped it into his fresh beer, where it
sizzled like a mean snake.

Lochlon pursed his lips angrily, and for a moment I was
worried he was about to strike me. But instead he continued
babbling about Bernadine. "She's mad. It was only a few
times, after a session at the pub . . ."

Instead of concentrating, my brain insisted on reminding
me that I had expected this on some deep, inaccessible level.
There were slips and hints and red flags and dead-of-night
trepidation that I had stoically brushed aside in the light of
day. God, I hated myself in this moment for never asking him
about Bernadine before.

Lochlon kept talking. "Then she got herself up the duff.
She always was broody, that girl. I'd not be surprised if she
lied about being on the pill—pulled the goalie and all that."

"Lochlon, *what*?"

My lips moved, but no further sound came out.

Finally, I wetted my lips to speak. "You got her pregnant?"

I asked. My words sounded subdued and faraway, as if this was some scene playing from a TV left on in another room.

"Kika, listen to me, gorgeous—" He charged toward me, but I raised my forearms to block him. This wasn't some prime-time drama—this was my life.

"Do not call me that!" I exploded. I finally managed to raise my voice over the roaring din in my ears. The boom in my voice even startled me. *No, no, no. This isn't right at all. This isn't what's supposed to be happening!*

"How could you do this?" I cried. My shrill whine made Lochlon freeze in place. "Why didn't you tell me, Lochlon? This isn't like being in a shitty band—*this* is a deal-breaker. What the hell are you even doing here if you've been sleeping with her? Why did you even come to see me?"

He looked wretched. "Because I'm a total gobshite. She only just told me right before I left, right after Da passed. At first, I thought she was having a go," he said slowly. "But then Bernie says she'll name it after me da if it's a boy," he added quietly.

My joints buckled under the weight of this statement, and I dumped myself into an armchair, expelling a puff of ancient dust into the stuffy room. "Your dad died? Why didn't you . . ."

Defenseless, he flew over to me and knelt down in front of the chair, hands raised like a beggar. He didn't touch me, but this was still too close. I retracted my legs into the chair, my whole body recoiling from him like a turtle turning into its shell.

He recklessly shoved his hands into his greasy hair. "Kika, it just happened. I came right from the funeral to see you."

From my voice box came an unnatural sound. My mouth opened and closed like a fish trying to breathe out of water.

"Pay no mind, my da was a bastard piss artist—I told you

how he was—but me mam and me brothers and sisters are all torn up, like. I would've told you sooner. Kika, believe me, I wanted to confide in someone, in *you*. And then, right after it happened, I heard from Bernie, and—Jaysus, please, look at me. What am I to say?"

I lifted my eyes to see his face of violent, crimson shame. My attention was enough for him to keep talking.

Hurriedly, he added: "This isn't to change things between us, Kika. As soon as my da's estate is sussed, I'm going back on the road. I can't stay in Ireland. And I won't be staying with her!"

I realized I hadn't blinked in a long time. I tried to sort out the erratic and fidgety language overcrowding my brain. My eyes felt papery and dry; it was so stifling in this room—like there wasn't enough air for the both of us. I looked at the window, but somehow I knew that it was sealed shut.

"And Kika, I want you to come with me."

I wasn't sure I heard him correctly. I wasn't sure that any of this was really happening. My teeth filed against one another like in a nightmare. "I . . ." I started, but I couldn't yet speak.

"Come with me, Kika, please. In a few weeks, once I get everything sorted. Please, Kika. We'll go anywhere you want. Anywhere."

Is he really asking me to run away with him?

"You got a girl pregnant," I managed in a whisper.

"I promise you, Bernie and I aren't even a couple. I broke it off with her before I left Ireland to travel. I've told you that. She knows I won't stay with her, and this is just her way of trying to make me."

"But what about . . . the baby?"

I couldn't say "your baby."

He twitched his head to the side like a mule kicking. "I wish she wouldn't have the thing, but I've no say in the matter," he said. "She's after raising it on her own. I'm leaving again, Kika. And I've told her this. Won't you come with me? Please, Kika. We can finally be together again."

The insane thing was that before I heard this news, I was *just dying* for him to ask me something like this.

"Say you'll come?"

But now Mina's and Gwen's faces flashed in my mind. *I can't leave them.*

"I can't. I have to work—" I began with the most basic of problems. Then surprisingly, for reasons not readily known to me, my neurons flashed Aston's face across my mind's eye as well. I took to my feet, my pulse drumming in double time.

"Forget all that." He waved. "You don't have to work for those brats any longer. I know you hate being trapped in one place. I have an inheritance now, my shares of the farm. I'll mind after you. Please, just think—"

But I couldn't just forget it: I was so close to getting Gypsies & Boxcars off the ground again. I couldn't give it up now for this, whatever *this* was.

I don't want to leave: I like who I am here, I thought I heard myself say, but I couldn't properly hear myself think over Lochlon's incessant talking:

"You wouldn't catch me living in the back-arse of nowhere. I'm not to be a father and a farmer. I know zip about farming and the lot. They'll all expect me to marry her, but sure, I'm not up to doing that." His eyes were desperate and savage. "The unfairness of it!"

"When were you going to tell me all of this?" I asked.

"I was going to explain what happened as soon as I arrived, I swear it! But then I saw you and all the memories came back, and I didn't want to cock it up. I was just letting on, you know, pretending for a minute that everything was grand—"

"That's exactly what this is: *pretending.* Everything isn't the same. It can't be the same—you *obliterated* any hope of that!" I yelled. I snatched my coat, the idea of fleeing just occurring to me.

"Kika. I know I did, but can we not have a go? Just promise me you'll think about coming away with me?"

I shook my head. "I have to leave."

Lochlon got up from his knees. "Please, Kika. Will you consider it?" He tried to take hold of my arm, but I slickly slipped his grasp.

"No!" Suddenly his desperation and drunkenness sickened me. I felt my stomach turn in an acidy surge. "Just go to bed, okay? We'll talk in the morning," I said so that he would leave me alone. But at that moment, I was sure I'd never speak to him again.

Lochlon looked wild with rage and panic. It knocked me from my sour, nauseated haze.

Before he could try to stop me again, my adrenaline peaked and I pitched open the door. Seizing the greasy banister, I flew down the stairs. He called out my name like an eleventh-hour prayer, but I busted out onto the dark street and kept running.

VIEWING THE HOUSE in the darkness, with each bedroom light snuffed out, I thought of Mina and Gwen snuggled in their beds. I couldn't leave them now, could I? And what about Elsbeth? How could I desert her now when she saved me from tedious, jobless ruin?

I couldn't. I couldn't run away with Lochlon. How could I even have dreamed of it as a possibility? And it wasn't just obligation keeping me here—there was something else, too.

As a gesture of solidarity, I thumbed an email to Elsbeth on my phone, knowing she checked her email first thing every morning. I told her I didn't need tomorrow with Lochlon, and I would leave for Italy with them instead, if that wasn't a problem. I was sure Elsbeth would like to have an extra hand.

Travel as a fire-exit escape is but another of its many sparkly virtues. Sometimes when you're desperate for perspective, physical distance provides a space for that emotional distance to set into. Sometimes you just need to get gone. And I was good at getting gone quickly. I was good at getting far. It was always more fun packing than unpacking, wasn't it?

I hesitated at my door, realizing that I wasn't ready to go back upstairs yet. I couldn't face my room or my bed. It was too comfortable and dark and isolated there. It would be too easy to *think* there, to second-guess, to mull over.

I fingered the antique skeleton key on my key chain. The corpse-cold brass bit into the inner skin of my palm, and I walked toward the private garden instead. I was already out late. I could be out later. I was packed for tomorrow. And before I got into bed, I wanted to be thoroughly exhausted to ensure that when I closed my eyes only sleep would come—not a replay of the night.

The frosty metal gate groaned open in an eerie yawn. Overhead, the full moon blazed silver. I should have been spooked by the vacant garden, but I was too upset to fit in any other emotion.

The garden was thick with dead briars and ice-licked ivy. I sat on a clammy bench and held my head between my knees, thinking about everything I just lost.

"Kika?"

I perked up. There it was again, my name being called, and the voice grew closer this time.

"Kika?"

I lifted my chin from my knees. Ice dripped in measured plunks. For some reason, I was not afraid.

"Who is it?" I whispered back into the inky darkness.

A shadow split from obscurity, backlit by the weak blush

of the streetlamps on the road. My fingers seized the damp wood of the bench.

"It's me, Aston." He walked closer, very slowly. "I hope I didn't frighten you," he said in a bare-bones whisper. "You're all right?"

I nodded even though that was a barefaced lie. I was far from all right.

He dropped down next to me on the bench, as if someone had wrenched a rug out from under his feet. He rubbed the back of his neck.

I waited for him to ask me what I was doing, but when he didn't speak, I realized it was a suitable question to ask him as well.

"You know it's the middle of the night, right?" I asked faintly, trying my best to be jovial. The midnight garden was as soundless and otherworldly as a cemetery. It almost felt disrespectful to speak in these impossible shadows.

He shook his head. "Couldn't sleep. I'm a bit of an insomniac. Sometimes I come here when I can't sleep. I grew up playing in this garden."

I didn't respond, but Aston continued. "I suppose I couldn't sleep because I was thinking about you. I knew you'd be occupied this weekend with . . . him. So I didn't anticipate meeting you here."

"As my mom says, the best-laid plans are the ones that get screwed up first," I responded, ignoring most of what he said.

"So what happened, then, if I may ask? I trust it didn't go well if you're sitting in an empty garden in the dead of night."

Somewhere in the distance, a car canvassed the road with

a harpy shriek. I shivered, feeling the English coldness delve deep into my veins.

"I don't know what happened, to tell you the truth. I guess I'm still processing it all. He . . ." My tongue became uncooperative when I attempted to speak Lochlon's name; it felt too taxing, too heavy.

"Since he got back home to Ireland, he took up again with his ex-girlfriend, his childhood sweetheart. He said she was nothing to him, but he, um, got her . . . but she's pregnant," I finally managed. There was a literal pain in my chest. The admission sat there between us like a third party.

For some reason, I wanted to defend myself. I wanted Aston to know the whole story. So I continued:

"I know what you're thinking, but we met when we were traveling, so it wasn't like we were still a couple or anything. But you know, seeing him again wasn't how I dreamed it up to be. It's just a shock. I mean, even his eyes weren't as green as I remembered." Then quietly I added, "And he asked me to run away with him. To go traveling again—"

"You won't go, will you?" interrupted Aston.

"No," I said. "I mean, I don't think so . . . I don't know." I dropped my forehead.

Aston opened his mouth and then closed it. "Oh," he said. "This may sound bold, but . . ." Aston spoke gently. "I wanted to ask you. If you love him, what were you doing with me that night?"

That caught me off guard. "Aston," I started to grumble, but then I thought of the moment when Lochlon asked me to leave with him, and I had inadvertently pictured Aston's face.

"I never told you I loved him," I found myself saying.

"Well, do you?" He turned and looked as if he might touch me, so I withdrew my body to the end of the bench and made myself small.

"Aston." I didn't want to be having this conversation. He started to speak again, but I cut him off. "I can't think right now."

I got up, but Aston stood, too, and maneuvered himself in my path.

"Do you know what I think?" he asked impudently, knowing that I didn't want to know.

"I don't care what you think!" I said holding my hands up to my temples.

"It's just that—I think you *do* care. I *don't* think you love him. I think you loved the woman you were when you were with him, when you were traveling and free to do whatever you chose—"

"Stop!" My voice rocketed through the garden. I was rendered speechless by my own pained protest. It was so much shriller than I meant it to be. After a moment, I spoke in a forcedly quieter, calmer tone. "Please, stop. I can't . . . I can't hear this right now, okay?"

"Look now, Kika, I . . ." he said softly. "I just want you to know that you have options. It's okay if your feelings changed—"

"It's fine, Aston. Could you just leave me alone for a little bit?" My voice cracked.

Aston turned his back toward me, giving me a moment of privacy.

I fell back down onto the bench and bundled my limbs into myself. "I just need to be alone now," I repeated, when I was able to pinch the emotion out of my voice.

Aston inhaled thickly. "Okay. I'll go," he said. "But please understand, I'll be just inside my door. I can't leave you alone out here. And I won't go to bed until I see you go inside, understood?"

"Okay, thanks. I need five minutes. I'm sorry," I added.

"No. It's my mistake," he said delicately.

Suddenly, I didn't want him to leave. But I closed my eyes and listened to the icy dirt crunching under his shoes as he walked away.

Moments later, a ray of yellow light cut through the bone-like branches like a lighthouse's beam. Aston had put on the carriage lights in front of his house. I felt a little warmer knowing that he was waiting up for me.

I watched the ghostly vapors of muggy air from my mouth vanish into the bitter night. Then it was swiftly silent once again. The silence lasted forever. The silence lasted a split second. I wasn't sure how long it lasted, but I raised my head when I heard the rumblings of a car nearby.

I peered through the bare branches to see the taillights of a black cab skidding up my street. The cab bumped to a stop right outside my house.

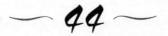

LOCHLON TOTTERED OUT of the black cab, hurling profanities at the driver at the top of his lungs.

My whole body earthquaked: *I have to stop him before he wakes up the entire neighborhood.*

"Lochlon. Here!" I darted across the frozen ground to the garden's gate and waved him inside so that the dead foliage would muffle his voice. Though he was the last person I wanted to see right now, I couldn't risk him banging on the door in the middle of the night and scaring the girls.

"Kika," he sniveled, wiping his face on his sleeve. "My lovely Kika." He moved toward me, into the garden. His fist choked the neck of a bottle of sloshing whiskey.

"You're drunk, Lochlon. Go back to the hotel. We'll talk in the morning," I begged him. "Please, go."

As I spoke, I walked backward, deeper into the garden to

draw him away from the houses so that our voices wouldn't carry.

Light caught the streams of wetness on Lochlon's face. My abdomen knotted with automatic empathy. Seeing his ruddy face streaked with tears and watching him stumble around reminded me of a wounded animal.

But then I thought: *Wild animals are most ferocious when they're hurt.*

"I can't go back. I know I have to, but I can't, Kika. I cocked it up, but I can't lose you as well. Please."

I brought my hands up to my mouth to blow on them for warmth. My fingers turned white from the cold. *I have to get him out of here as fast as I can.*

"Lochlon," I began, but he interrupted me.

"No, Kika." He dug his incisors into his lip and came closer.

I tried to back away, but I couldn't—my shoulder blades made contact with a stone wall covered in dense ivy and moss.

Lochlon just kept coming forward. "Kika, listen: I love you."

I sucked in a shard of air that only made it halfway down my throat. I had waited so long to hear him say those words to me. I had wondered for so long if he did actually love me. I had craved that declaration and obsessively pictured the moment he'd say it. But in my mind, the moment *never* looked like this. Or felt so offensive, so fraught with desperation.

He put his hands on my shoulders—one on each side of my neck. I tensed and willed the ivy to swallow me like in some fairy-tale forest.

I tilted my head away from him, but he didn't stop bearing down onto my shoulders with all his weight, as if he were trying to push me to my knees.

"I've always loved you, Kika. I'm not to know what took me so long to say it. I should have said it to you in India."

When Lochlon mentioned India, sentiment rushed toward me like a bullet.

But it's not love—it's nostalgia, I finally grasped. The sadness I felt when I first saw him was *mourning*; mourning for something long gone.

My stupid little heart finally peeped up: *I don't love Lochlon!* Over and over again, I repeated in staccato heartbeats: *I don't love Lochlon! I don't love Lochlon! I don't love Lochlon!*

A snatch of Aston's words soared to mind: *I* don't *think you love him. I think you loved the woman you were when you were with him, when you were traveling.*

Like eyes adjusting to the darkness and finally being able to make out shapes, the words began to make sense. I was in love with our story. Not with him. Not anymore.

"Kika, please." Lochlon's mouth was dangerously close to mine now. I inhaled the fiery booze on his breath. He lowered his hands from my shoulders to my upper arms, latching his meaty grip into the tender flesh of my biceps. I scrunched my eyes closed.

"You're hurting me," I whispered. *I'm in danger*, I sluggishly understood.

"Just come back with me, yeah?" he implored.

I tried to squirm out of his grasp, but he held me securely without letting up for even a moment. "To the guesthouse. Just spend the night with me, yeah? It will be just like India again. Promise."

He pressed me against the wall, pinned like a butterfly to

a page. He moved his mouth toward mine, trying to kiss me, looking deranged.

My eyes popped open in panic.

"Lochlon, no!" I twisted against his hold, but he thrust his whole body against me so that I was firmly trapped between his hips and the wall.

"Stop!" I yelled, finally gathering enough oxygen as his face was muffling my mouth. But he just smashed into me harder, grinding his hips into me.

"Get off, please," I sniveled now, but he was done speaking.

I was petrified by the look in his eyes, consuming and reckless, checked-out. *This was not the man I once knew.*

I cried out once more and pushed against him with everything I had this time. And suddenly, his body ripped away from mine. I hurled my palms backward against the wall to keep myself from falling forward to the ground.

Lochlon soared backward with stumbling speed and landed hard on the wet ground with a hostile thud. I let out a thankful whimper: *I am free!* My heartbeat spiked, unsure of what happened.

Just then, Aston whooshed toward me in a dark blur. He came to where I was slumped against the wall, and on impulse I flinched away. *Is it really Aston?*

I felt his hands on my face, and I registered the racing pulse in Aston's wrists. He put his face very close to mine and whispered, "Hey. It's me. It's me."

But my eyes couldn't focus.

"You're okay. You're shaking. Did he hurt you?" he asked. His eyes zipped down my body for any signs of trauma.

I swayed and let Aston hold me close until I could finally shake my head no.

Before I could speak, Lochlon whined behind us and attempted to stand. "Oi! Who're you?" he slurred.

Aston abruptly retracted his hands from my face and about-faced to watch Lochlon. He stretched his arm behind, signaling for me to stay back.

Lochlon's whiskey bottle had shattered around his legs, but he didn't notice the icelike shards crackling around him. He managed to stand upright.

On instinct, I groped for Aston's arm when Lochlon got to his feet. Aston reached backward and took hold of my hand.

But Lochlon remained in the same spot, swaying from side to side. He didn't come forward; he knew he had been defeated.

"Leave right now," demanded Aston with clenched teeth. "Go."

Lochlon brushed off the dirt from his trousers, and he looked suddenly sober and abashed. "Feck off," Lochlon said, the end of the words rising to an ugly high pitch. "Look, I didn't mean to—" He twisted his neck so that he could see me standing behind Aston. But I couldn't look at him.

"I would never hurt you, Kika. You know that, don't you?"

"Go!" Aston commanded in his unassailable, intimidating way.

Lochlon lurked away, toward the garden gate. When he reached the gate, he flung all of his weight into pulling it open. He turned back and eyeballed me once again.

"Kika?" he pleaded in a broken voice so despairing that I almost answered him.

But when I didn't answer, that violence returned to his face, and he snarled, "Jaysus, you're some woman. Fine. I'll be off."

Aston remained at attention, ready to pounce if Lochlon made a move in the wrong direction. His arm felt athletic and solid in my grip. I realized my fingers were burrowing into him. Aston gave my hand a short, reassuring squeeze.

"Feck the both of you, then." Lochlon banged the garden gate behind him. He stumbled out into the road toward the high street and managed to hail a lone black cab.

— 45 —

I SHUDDERED AND dropped Aston's hand. Standing there among the wreckage of my life, I felt foolish and confused. *How did this happen?*

Aston directed his body around to face mine.

I stepped back from him, awkward and unsure.

"You're not hurt?" he asked.

"No, no," I said. "I'm, I'm okay." I felt hesitant about my words, like each one was a tiptoed step on a wobbly bridge. I rubbed my arms as if to erase Lochlon's fingerprints. "I don't know what would have happened if you hadn't been waiting up for—"

"Right," Aston interrupted. "Don't think about that now. I told you I wouldn't go to bed without knowing you were safe, didn't I?"

I felt a warm tear melt down the hill of my cheekbone. My voice arched. "I should go."

"Surely you're not all right to be alone?" Aston said, coming closer to me. "Kika?"

"Don't," I said abruptly, my arm reaching out to block him in a reflexed sweep. Ashamed of this, I flicked my eyes up to meet his. He looked jolted.

I couldn't stomach it, so I ran.

"I'm sorry," I called as I passed him. I was close enough that had he wanted to grab my arm to stop me, he could have. But he didn't. I was so grateful that he knew not to grab me just then.

I rushed through the garden gate, up the three steps to my blue door, and I slid the key in the lock with only the sound of my own breath around me. Aston stayed in the garden and didn't follow.

GOD, WHY DID *I just run away from him like that?* I pressed my backbone against the inside of the locked door. I smeared the tears from my face and took my time to breathe.

I slinked upstairs to my room and clicked on my lamp by the window so that Aston knew I was there. None of this was his fault; I just couldn't be around anyone right now—I hoped he understood that.

I sat looking out the window and started picking through a box of pastel macarons until my mouth was numb to the flavors and all I tasted was sugar, sugar, sugar. Then I shut off my lamp, but I still kept watch.

An hour later, Aston emerged from the garden with his head down. I stood at my window, but he didn't look up. Instead, he walked straight to his door.

I collapsed into my bed fully clothed, fully exhausted.

A BUZZING PHONE ripped me from my feverish dreams. I buried my head under the covers, humid with sweat, and I let the throbbing ache of last night settle over me along with a repulsive sugar hangover. I reran the night's events; it was as masochistic as pressing on a fresh bruise.

I reached for my phone to put a stop to the insistent humming. It was still early, but I had a phone full of text messages from Lochlon, all liberally apologizing about last night. My head was foggy, but I was impossibly clear about one thing: Last night had nothing to do with me.

He didn't want to run away with me; he just wanted to *run away*. It killed me to realize it, but it was the truth. He cheapened what we had with a last-ditch go of asking me to run away with him just to escape his own problems.

Screw him, I thought violently and cruelly.

There was one happy text from Elsbeth in response to last night's email. "So glad you're coming with us today. We'll be leaving for the airport at precisely 8 A.M. No technology or no trip ☺."

I tossed my phone like a Frisbee to the foot of the bed and glanced at my stuffed backpack, pleased with myself for packing it in advance. In fact, I couldn't wait to get the hell out of here. Eight A.M. couldn't come fast enough.

My phone buzzed again, and I groaned aloud at its bleak persistence. I was actually welcoming this no-technology holiday.

"Come onto your terrace. Please," the text read. I spewed out a rainbow of curses.

"Please don't be there," I begged uselessly, swallowing down my surging fury. "Please don't be there. Please don't be there," I repeated.

I yanked the curtains out of the way and stepped out on the balcony barefoot. As if I had lowered myself into an icy lake, the cold from the tile jetted up my bare feet and surged upward until it reached my jaw, which plunged open in shock.

Like some screwed-up version of *Romeo and Juliet*, Lochlon was standing below my balcony on the street.

I shook my head at him furiously. "You have to get out of here," I whisper-shouted as quietly as I could. "You're going to get me fired. Is that what you want?"

Lochlon dug his hands in his coat pockets and looked up at me with big eyes.

"Please, Kika, come down. It won't take but a few minutes, then I swear you'll never hear from me again." He looked and sounded sober, but like me, he was still in the same clothes as last night.

My nerves jangled in the chilled morning air as he kept talking and gushing apologies.

I put my finger to my lips, gesturing for him to be quiet. Then I stuck my finger into the air as if to say, *Wait a minute*.

Before I could really think about it, I ducked inside, yanked on my boots, and raced downstairs to the street.

"Lochlon!" I spat when I got close enough. *Why won't he just go away?*

"I am leaving for a vacation with the Darlings soon. You have to leave right now." I was no longer afraid of him or even saddened by him. I was just straight-up livid. *How* dare *he try and mess up my life here?*

Lochlon took a step back and held up both hands in defense. "Please, Kika, just give me a quarter of an hour to say what I need to say. I promise if you listen to me I'll go and leave you be forever."

"Fine!" I started power walking away from the house with beastlike concentration. "I'll give you five minutes—that's it. Come on. You're going to wake up everyone. God, what the hell is wrong with you?"

I hated myself for giving him the chance to talk to me, but I felt like I had no other option. And in a few hours I would be unreachable—this thought was my life preserver just now. *I just have to get through five minutes of his bullshit and then I can get gone.*

Without speaking, he followed me into a little French café on one of the mews beside the house. The café was mercifully empty on this early Sunday morning. I dropped down into a table by the window.

He didn't sit and instead loitered above. "Shall I get us a coffee?"

I strummed my fingernails on the tabletop. "Fine, whatever. Just hurry, will you?" Dropping my head in my hands, I heard Lochlon walk toward the counter and order two coffees. Funny, he didn't remember that I take sugar and milk in mine.

He positioned a cup in front of my elbows.

I rubbed my hands over my face in exhaustion and then peeked out from behind my fingers. He sat across from me and blew at the rim of his own coffee. I remembered how he took his: black.

I pressed my forearms into the table and assessed him frankly for a moment. His front teeth slouched in on each other like two drunks holding each other up. I never noticed that before. He pushed my coffee toward me like a peace offering, but I didn't touch it.

"Lochlon. Do you have any idea how mad I am right now?" I asked.

He looked down but didn't interrupt me.

"Your behavior was unacceptable last night." The words sounded like something a parent might say, but I couldn't think of anything more appropriate. "You should have told me about your dad and about Bernadine before you came here. You omitted the truth and came here under false pretenses. Do you understand how unfair that is for me?"

His face looked like it had been punched.

"I cared about you, Lochlon. I wanted to be with you. I haven't been with anyone else *since* you!" I jeered maliciously, just to make him feel even guiltier. "And then, you get wasted and try to assault me—"

His head shot up. "No, Kika, I would never lay a hand on you. I—"

"Well, you did last night. You terrified me, Lochlon. I don't even know who you are." Once again, the words were a cliché, but there was simply no other way to put it.

He ground the heels of his palms into his eye sockets.

I kept my eye on the café counter, like the girl behind it was doing something incredibly interesting. I couldn't stand to look at him. It was too raw.

"So that's what I have to say. And I have no clue what else it is that you *need* to tell me so desperately"—I crossed my legs—"but you have five minutes to do so."

Lochlon inhaled at length. Facing the window, he looked outside like he was staring at some faraway distance in his mind. And maybe he was.

His Adam's apple dipped down his grizzled neck, and I was once again taken aback by my own lack of wanting for him. His scruffy neck used to drive me crazy. Now I felt only rage, which I suspected was masking the rotting scent of pity underneath.

"Kika, all right. Here's how it is: The reason I didn't tell you about Da or Bernie was that I was having trouble accepting my fate, see? In fairness, you'd want to refuse it, too. I'm sorry for not telling you sooner." He cleared his throat.

"I came here thinking that maybe this was a way out, that you'd come away with me. With you, things were always, like, grand, really perfect and that. You never even gave me a hard time about my past. But deep down, I knew I couldn't run away, but just for a moment there last night, I thought I could fight it. Do you understand what I'm saying?" His eyes were wet and searching.

"Lochlon." I sighed in exasperation. "That doesn't have to be your fate. It's not about abandoning your priorities; it's about reestablishing them. I'm glad that you're not running away from your responsibilities, but once you tend to them, you can still live the life you want, just with some changes. Don't just give up. You can definitely still write—"

He laughed darkly, nostrils flaring like a villain. "Oh, come off it, Kika! Traveling around the world and writing—it's a bloody *dream*, a bit of fun. I've a living to earn now."

He held his hand up as if he wanted to reach out to me, but I tipped my body backward. He closed his hand into a fist and dropped it on the table instead. He knew he wasn't allowed to touch me ever again.

"Where I'm from, people don't do those sorts of things. I have to marry her. I have to take over the farm and have a proper job, like," he said. "I've made my bed, and now I have to—"

"Fuck Bernadine in it?" I lashed, stripping the argument of any euphemisms that he could hide behind.

He ignored my outburst. It wasn't about me anymore.

"I have to live there, and I have to die there with the rest of that lot. That's all there is to it. You can't leave. Not where I'm from, you can't."

He spoke with a miserable, quivering vigor that showed me that he believed what he was saying—unlike last night when he was just desperate to bolt. But his resignation was uniquely devastating to me.

"If you think there's no other way to live your dream, then I feel bad for you," I told him, hoping to rile him up.

"But there *isn't* any other way. As much as I want to run away with you and start fresh somewhere new, I can never do it—and not because you're not mental enough to come with me; because it isn't possible."

For a passing moment, the morning sun outran the clouds and razored through the café glass, bathing Lochlon in a sepia shade of sorrowful light.

"I suppose I'm just destined to watch life on the telly. Like everyone else," he concluded with a short nod.

I fingered the lip of my coffee mug, steamy and wet. "Not like everyone else," I said.

He sighed in exasperation, deep and breathy like in sleep. "Will you stop going on about that traveling shite, Kika?" he said. "Life isn't like the way it is in films. One day you're going to have to get a real job as well, instead of minding well-off schoolchildren. You can't live like this forever. Your luck will run out just as mine has. I'm only telling you this so that you're not surprised—as I was."

I was so wrong about him. I thought we were both going after the life we wanted with everything we had. I thought we both loved traveling enough to rearrange our lives to make sure it was always a part of it. Turns out I thought wrong.

"You used to be on my team. You used to be one of my kind."

He wouldn't meet my eyes now.

"The old you could come up with a better solution than this—than just giving up." *Coward*, I thought. *Look how quickly you gave up on everything you ever wanted.* "And Lochlon, you know I don't plan on being an au pair forever. This job is a great way to make money for Gypsies & Boxcars, and sure, it's a means to an end, but it's a *wonderful* means. I have a real plan now. I've even been saving money." I flopped my arms into the air and let them fall limp.

When I mentioned Gypsies & Boxcars, he curled his

mouth. "It'll never work," he said under his breath. "You could never save a cent."

I shook my head in brazen disappointment. I wanted to say: *I expected more from you*, but instead I just stared him down, daring him to say anything more.

Lochlon gave me a mournful side-smile. "I suppose this is it, then, Kika."

"It is."

"Just promise me: When you're forced to stop traveling and settle down, you'll think of me then, won't you? Promise me that?"

"I'm done thinking of you, Lochlon."

Lochlon smiled again—unhappy but proud. "Well, then I am sorry for last night. It did me in thinking I could have hurt you—what a bleedin' disaster this whole trip has been, hasn't it? Pity, that."

I nodded glumly and left my gaze pointed downward.

When he didn't speak, I dragged my focus onto him: His eyes were fixed outside the window, and he wrinkled his brow.

I stared down at my hands in my lap and braided them together. There was nothing left to say. We both knew it.

And just then, I felt the back of his hand faintly stroke my cheek. It was so unexpected and unduly intimate that I froze against his touch, and it took me far too long to bristle away. But I did.

Disgusted, I searched his eyes and started to confront him, when I noticed that he wasn't even *looking* at me! He was looking *beyond* me—right out the café window at someone outside.

I whipped around just in time to see what was captivating him. When I saw, the gesture suddenly made complete sense.

I caught the briefest glimpse of a familiar coat sailing by just out of the frame.

Aston did not linger, peering into the café window; instead, he walked away robotically as if he had just seen everything he needed to see.

"WHY DID YOU do that, Lochlon?" I yanked myself up, thrusting the bistro table toward him. The table screeched like a hawk. His coffee spattered. "You saw Aston, didn't you?"

Lochlon didn't move from his seat and scrutinized the dark slick of coffee dripping between his legs.

With a clench-jaw reserve, he said, "I'm sorry I did that. It was too bold. I hope you're very happy together—have at it."

I choked, aghast. All I could do at the moment was stare at Lochlon and try to process the punitive damage he just caused, his hostile intent to injure. I knew now more than ever that I did not love this man. In fact, I suspect I *hated* him.

Lochlon's jawline tightened. He looked at me brazenly. "Actually, I'm not sorry for that, Kika. But maybe one day I will be."

What a bullshit apology. I grabbed my coat and pushed open the café door, the cold snapping on my skin like a rubber band. Before I left, I heard Lochlon say, more to himself than to me, "I'm well rid of you."

I shimmied into my coat as I whipped down the street. The damp air was cold enough to frost my lungs. I looked down at myself as I zipped up: still in last night's outfit. Lochlon was in the same clothes from last night, too. *Oh God, I hope Aston doesn't think we spent the night together.*

"Aston!" I called, though he was nowhere to be seen.

The streets were starting to thicken with bright-eyed families off to church. I had to get back to the house—the Darlings would leave without me—but I had to find Aston first.

Somehow, this is the most important thing to me, I realized as my rubber soles clung to the sidewalk. I loopholed around babies in strollers and old ladies with canes; past churches, sleepy chocolatiers, corner shops, launderettes.

My heart clobbered my chest urgently; my eyes teared up in the cold.

Just then, a stab of clarity pricked into me: Even before Lochlon came to visit me and mucked up my grandiose fantasy, Aston *meant* something to me. And I was pretty sure I *meant* something to Aston.

I like Aston! I self-confessed. And what I thought next surprised me further: *I like Aston despite the fact that he doesn't like traveling.*

My breath went in and out and in and out in speedy little huffs. He had gone back home; I was certain of it. I would find him and explain everything. But as I approached our row of houses, my leg muscles quivered and cramped to a stop. The Darlings' Audi was parked out front of the house, puffing out billows of warm exhaust—it was time to leave.

— 48 —

I NO LONGER had to check the time to know that we were due to leave this instant. Elsbeth sat in the front seat, and the girls sat in the back. (Mr. Darling was already in Italy.)

Before anyone could stop me, I made a break for Aston's front door. I banged the door, rattling the house while calling out his name. For a moment, I stepped out of myself and thought, *Damn, this girl is desperate.*

But I *was.*

Mina lowered the misty car window. "Kika, come on," she called. "We've been waiting for you."

I pushed my face to the peephole of Aston's door, but there were no signs of movement or light. He didn't go home after all—I was wrong.

"Get in the car, you big goon!" added Gwendy, pushing her head next to Mina's. My chest heaved, and I was unable to speak.

Now Elsbeth's window lowered. "Kika, there you are. We've taken your bag from your room. Get in the car right this moment or we'll miss the plane. We thought we were going to have to leave without you!"

I aimed one last desperate look up at Aston's windows, but it was clear that no one was home. I watched in slow motion as Elsbeth climbed out of the car toward me. She held out her gloved palm at me, the other hand cocked on her waist. I wasn't sure what she was after until she said with a formidable smile, "Phone, Kika. Now."

She was no pushover about this no-technology rule.

My backbone stiffened, planning my objection, but she nimbly tweezed the phone out of my coat pocket, right under the tip of my nose.

Before I could stop her, she trotted up the steps of our house and neatly slipped the phone through the mail slot. My heart plunged as I heard the bump of the phone hitting the rug. I opened my mouth, but Elsbeth interrupted:

"When you get back, everything will be waiting for you exactly as you left it. I promise," she said, shepherding me into the backseat with the girls. "Come this instant."

The girls' cheeks were rosy and doll-like from the car's blasting heat and the anticipation of the holiday.

"Yay, Kika!" Gwen said in her sweet, honest-to-God, genuine way that could make you forget, just for a moment, that your world as you knew it had just been dismantled. Gwen plunked down on my lap with a sigh of exaggerated pleasure, but Mina gave me a look that proved she experienced the same conflict over her phone.

"We'll get through this together," she said in earnest as she rested her hand on top of mine somberly.

"Very good then," clucked Clive after he heard the click of our seat belts fastening. Then, the luxury car swayed forward with whispering ease.

I squinted out the rear window as we left behind the row of white Victorian terraces fringed with skeleton trees.

I didn't see anyone. But I knew Aston was there somewhere. And I hoped he'd still be there when I came back.

ON THE M4 motorway, my fingers itched to call Aston. Luckily, I had his number written down in my notebook, since he was our landlord. The rough-edged thought that he may believe I had forgiven Lochlon and spent the night with him chafed against me.

"So you had a change of heart, then, lamb?" Elsbeth turned from the front seat and blocked the shushing stream of overbearing heat. "Do you want to talk about it later?"

For a moment, I thought: *How does she know about Aston?* But then I realized that she was talking about the change of plans with Lochlon.

I don't care about Lochlon; I'm too concerned about Aston, I wanted to object, but I couldn't tell her that.

"Talk about what?" piped Gwen. "Talk about me?"

I gave Gwen a friendly tickle. "It's all about you, isn't it, you little hobgoblin?"

She giggled and stretched out on the plush leather seats.

I balanced my forehead against the cool glass of the car window. The sky was bruised with black-and-blue clouds, and the glass was speckled with rain. I traced a raindrop with my fingertip until I couldn't feel anything but the sting of the cold.

"Any chance I can get that emergency phone, Elsbeth?"

"No way!" Gwendy exclaimed.

Elsbeth shook her head. "It's against the rules, Kika."

I coerced a deceptively sad smile onto my lips. It didn't matter. I would find a way to sneak off at the airport.

The wipers wetly swished across the windshield like a muffled metronome. I closed my eyes and fell asleep.

WHEN I WOKE up again, I saw that we had reached the airport but that the car was parked on the tarmac. It took me a moment to get it: Silly me; the Darlings didn't fly commercial, lamb. We were taking a private jet.

I got out of the car into the rain, making my way over to men holding glistening black umbrellas for us. We even had our own customs official.

One of the tricks of being a good traveler is to strike a balance between being prepared and still being able to be surprised. I didn't see this coming, but wasn't this just the most wonderful distraction?

This meant that there would be no chance of getting to

use a phone at the airport or on the plane, so I just would have to try once we landed.

Once aboard, I tipped my crystal flute to the stewardess, who had a chic little scarf tied around her neck, to accept a heavy-handed pour of champagne, or "champers," as Elsbeth called it.

"It comes with the plane," Elsbeth said, as if none of this was a big deal. But let me tell you, it *was* a big freaking deal. The bubbles tickled and fizzed at the bottom of my nose.

"Yum. It really classes up the joint." The environment was making it *very* hard for me to ruminate on my boy problems. I leaned back into the smart cream leather seat. "You know, Elsbeth, I've ridden in overnight trains in third class and hitchhiked in the back of pickup trucks with chicken crates, but flying private is a first."

Elsbeth clinked my glass. "It's not too shabby, huh?"

"It's hard to feel bad for myself when I'm flying private to Italy."

"So, is everything okay, then?" she asked with real concern.

"Well, it's over with Lochlon."

Elsbeth nodded, but then in a kind of ah-young-love brush-off, she added: "Well, things may change. Sometimes you don't appreciate what you have until it's gone."

"Like toilet paper?" I asked with a grin. "Sure. But not so much with Lochlon. I thought we were so alike, but it turns out I was so wrong."

"Are you sad?" she asked.

"I think part of me already knew it was done. It's been over a long time—it was over the minute my train pulled out of that station in South India, truth be told. But I didn't want to believe it, you know? So no, I'm not so sad."

When I heard my own feelings spoken aloud, I realized that was the truth. Now I understood that I wasn't waiting and desperate to see *Lochlon* again; I was waiting to see *myself* again—the self I was when I traveled.

I tugged at my seat belt. Lochlon couldn't bring back that girl (and to have gone away with him and tried would have meant ultimately to fail). I had to find her myself. And I *did* find her again, the moment I got to London.

"Well, it's better that you found this out sooner than later. You can't run on nostalgia, lamb," said Elsbeth.

"True." I nodded.

"And it's easy to fall in love in Paris."

"I met Lochlon in Barcelona," I corrected.

"Yes, I know, but you get what I'm saying. Everything's always chicer *en français*."

Thoughts of Aston popped into my head again and again. What bothered me most of all was that he didn't know how I felt about him. But until I got to a phone, I couldn't do anything about that, so I gave myself permission to forget it for now and enjoy the trip.

As if on cue, lace-thin clouds gave way to crystalline blue waters, and the windblasted limestone cliffs of southern Italy's fishing villages sharpened into focus. And here I was, still the luckiest girl in the world, despite it all.

"On to bigger, better adventures, right?" said Elsbeth, signaling for more champers. She rested her hand on the armrest and shimmied her fingers to make the high-altitude sunshine ballet across her manicure.

"Spoken like a girl who travels, Elsbeth," I said.

— 50 —

"So the villa we're staying at is outfitted with Vietri tiles and Murano glass lighting fixtures," gushed Elsbeth as we bounced along southern Italy's scrolling roads. She jabbered with the animated stamina of a teenager describing her prom dress. "And all the bedding is from Scandia Home, and the bathrooms are stocked with Carthusia products."

I nodded even though I had no idea what she was talking about as we nosed down the final curve. The car made a jagged stop at the outer gate of a villa clinging to a cliff. Elsbeth adjusted her oversized sunglasses, which made her look like a Waspy Sophia Loren.

"Elsbeth, you did not have to talk this place up," I told her as I climbed out of the car.

The whitewashed villa was traced in terra-cotta and sitting among lush tropical hanging gardens: handsome, ancient olive trees; thick palms and pines; lemon trees drooping with fruit; and flowers in punchy, flashy colors.

We entered through the foyer, which led to glass doors introducing a sun-bleached veranda. On the veranda, a tinkling fountain competed with a swimming pool that shone like a pillow-cut sapphire and overlooked the crescent of Positano and the cerulean Tyrrhenian Sea below.

("It's the Tyrrhenian, not the Mediterranean, lamb," Elsbeth corrected me. "A common mistake.")

I had been to postcard-perfect southern Italy once before but as a low-rent backpacker set on seeing the salt-preserved bodies in Pompeii and maybe making out with a hot Australian backpacker in one of Italy's trashy, fever-dream nightclubs.

This trip is going to be a teensy bit different, I concluded as the staff (yes, the *staff*) showed us to our rooms, though everyone but me had been here before.

The wonderful thing about Positano was that there was nothing to do. I couldn't wait to marinate in the Italian Limoncello sunshine—but of course I was here to work, I reminded myself. Though I was tempted to ask for a day or two for myself to do some scouting, I concluded that this was not the time to slack off on my au pair responsibilities. I had big plans for the girls this week, and I brought along boxes of watercolor paints, playing cards, and beach toys. I had planned day trips, seashell hunts, and beach games for us.

This was my moment to shine as an au pair extraordinaire by allowing Elsbeth and Mr. Darling to have their luxurious vacation while ensuring that the girls had a great time, too. Asking for time off now would seem flippant of me.

And so I would repurpose my acidic, hair-raising anger at

Lochlon as drilling motivation to ensure that I would go after everything I wanted in life—especially when it came to staying true to the promise I made to myself that I would try my hardest at this job.

Now, I just had to get access to *il telefono per un momento*. (I dug through the Italian dictionary for an hour to figure that one out.) I needed to tell Aston that I liked him, and then I could get on with it. You see, the longer I waited to do so, the more I doubted his feelings for me: *Did he* really *come off as strong as I remembered? And did he still feel that way about me after seeing me with Lochlon?*

51

"STOP BOUNCING UP and down." I wrangled Gwen to the ground, slathering her with sunscreen.

"Can't stop! Won't stop! Too excited!" she said, bobbing up and down like a Whack-A-Mole. "Can we go to the pool now? Can we? Can we?"

"Mina?" I angled my neck toward Mina's adjoining room, connected by a Turkish bath–inspired lavatory—all heated marble floors and glorious fluffy white towels. "Are you almost ready? Gwen is about to pee herself." My voice echoed off the imported tiles. My room, a Blue Grotto spectacle, was located right across the hall from the girls' rooms.

Mina walked into Gwen's room already in her bathing suit.

"As long as she doesn't pee in the pool," she said, looking peculiar without her cell phone; it was like she was missing an appendage.

Speaking of, the plan was to get the girls in the pool, then see if I could borrow a phone off a maid or a cook or someone.

Apparently the villa "came with" (sounds so wrong) a staff of ten, as well as a German shepherd named Mussolini, which also sounded a little wrong.

Yet so far, we saw no one besides the butler: a mushroom of a man with tiny legs that bloomed into a massive, operatic chest. He said a whole bunch of stuff to us including a whole slew of "*mamma mias*" (seriously didn't think Italians really said that), sprinkled with "*bellissimas*," then showed us to our rooms.

Elsbeth's first order of business was to get herself a seaweed wrap in the solarium. She said she'd meet us for dinner.

Mr. Darling was out driving a Ferrari or a cigarette boat, pretending to be in a Bond movie. (Not to sound unimpressed, but after a while all these ridiculous displays of wealth just blurred together.)

And me? All I wanted was to make a quick phone call and then take the girls down those winding stairs carved into the rock face and jump into the water, which was so frothy it looked carbonated.

Initially, I was a little surprised that everyone went off to do their own thing. Weren't they going tech-free to have family time? But then I realized that it was just a way to spend the whole day apart without having to stay in contact with one another.

"Are you guys sure you want to go into the pool instead of the ocean?" I asked the girls as they led the way to the patio.

"The ocean's too cold this time of year, Kika," said Mina, shaking an aerosol can of sunscreen. "But the pool's heated."

"Yeah, the pool's super fun," said Gwen. "Let's go." She

grabbed my hand. The girls had been coming here for years, so it was nothing special to them. But I couldn't ever imagine tiring of it.

On my count of three, both girls cannonballed into the pool, shattering the pristine stillness like glass. I clapped vigorously on the sidelines.

Another butler or waiter (I didn't want to call him a "servant" for God's sake!) came out onto the patio with freshly squeezed blood orange juice in too-fancy glasses.

"*Buon giorno,*" he greeted us politely and unloaded the tray of drinks onto a little frosted glass table beside my sun lounger.

I motioned for him to come closer to my lounge chair. "Excuse me, sir, but do you have a telephone I could borrow for a moment?"

He shook his head and babbled noisily, "*Mi scusi, mi scusi, non parlo inglese.*"

I motioned for him to lower the volume—I didn't want the girls to hear.

"Hmm, okay. Brrrrrrring! Brrrrrrrring!" I blared idiotically, forgetting all the Italian I learned a mere hour ago. I curved my hand into a phone shape and held it to my ear.

"Halo? Halo?" I said in an appalling generic foreign accent. I sounded way more Swedish than Italian, but it worked, and the young man began prattling in rattling-fast Italian.

"*Non abbiamo i telefoni. Sono state rimosse come richiesto.*"

"Kika Shores!" shouted Gwendy. She hoisted herself out of the pool and padded toward me.

The young waiter shrugged his shoulders up and down comically like a bird ruffling then smoothing its feathers. He backed away with a routine of little bows while repeating: *"Mi scusi! Mi scusi!"*

"You know you're not allowed to use phones," Gwen said with her fists planted on her waist. Drips of chlorine water spattered on the pavement.

"Sorry, Gwendolyn. I know," I said. "I just need the phone for one teensy second, though."

"No dice, lady." She picked up her blood orange juice and made a fish face around the straw.

"Mom called and made sure all the phones and computers were disconnected before we came," said Mina, getting out of the pool as well.

"No shit. Really? She can do that?" I asked.

"Um, yeah," Mina said, like it was obvious. "One year, when she decided that we were all eating gluten free, she had them remove all the pasta from the premises. She literally took the *pasta* out of *Italy*! Having a few phones shut off is child's play for her."

I looked at her, horror-struck.

Mina nodded. "We'll find some way to deal."

I wrapped the girls in downy towels, and we slurped our juice wordlessly.

"It's actually not so bad being without my phone," said Mina. "I guess it's just super annoying that it has to happen now when Peaches and I are *actually* friends. I mean, couldn't we have gone on vacation when I used to play Candy Crush on my phone and only pretend like I was texting?"

In a glorious turn of fate, Mina and Peaches had become genuine friends stemming from their mutual appreciation of preppy American fashion. As suspected, Peaches was just jealous of Mina—even though she'd never admit it. But once Peaches saw who Mina really was (i.e., someone who'd let you borrow her cool American clothes rather than just use them to one-up you), Peaches changed her attitude. Now I just had to hope that Mina would rub off on Peaches and not the other way around.

I positioned the girls' chairs under giant, ice cream–colored parasols straight out of a Fellini film.

"Speaking of which . . . where are the Snotty McSnots Benson-Westwoods going on their school holidays? Somewhere standard-issue faaaaaabulous I'm sure."

Mina shook her head. "Nope. They're staying in England—they're going to the countryside. Peaches says their estate is haunted so they're selling it. They have to clean out all their stuff."

"Selling a family estate? That doesn't sound like much fun."

"No," said Mina, crossing her blue-white legs. I chucked the sunscreen over to her.

"They've been selling lots of stuff. At first Peaches didn't like it, but now she knows she's getting all new stuff, so she's okay with it."

I raised my eyebrow. "What else have they been selling?"

"Peaches' nanny walks her home from school now because they sold the nanny's car. But it's okay because Peaches said they're getting something cooler. An awesome Italian sports car, a Linguine or whatever."

"Hmm." I nodded. "What else?"

"Peaches' mom made her sell her Louis Vuitton bags. She only has *one* Louis Vuitton bag left—the old one with the giant ink stain on the bottom. She said her mom took her others because she's getting a Paraty Chloé bag—the one that's made from real python skin. So she doesn't care about her Louis Vuitton bags anymore."

My mind drifted. I wondered if I would ever be the kind of girl to care about Chloé bags, seaweed wraps, or sports cars. I mean, just because Lochlon was going to be a farmer and father didn't mean I was going to just up and change one day, did it?

I would be lying if I said I wasn't blown back by how quickly he gave up the existence he wanted for himself. It's scary when someone similar to yourself morphs 180 degrees— it makes you think that one day it could happen to you.

But it won't happen to me, I assured myself, setting my orange juice onto the table and crossing my legs.

"So Peaches is happy," Mina concluded.

"Really, she doesn't mind? You'd think Peaches would be devastated having to sell all these things. Especially her precious bags," I said.

"Well, she's not allowed to talk about it. She only tells me because we're for real best friends now."

"I see," I said. "Are you girls hungry? I can go into the kitchen and rustle up some grub if you want."

"No, Kika." Gwendy leaped up and trotted over to a silver panel intercom affixed to a wall curtained in bougainvillea.

"You just press here when you want something." Gwendy sunk her chubby finger into a silver button.

"*Buon giorno, come posso aiutarla?*" asked a detached, static-tinged voice from the intercom.

"Hello, friend! This is Gwendolyn Prudence Darling III. Can we have more bloody orange juice and some delicious snacks?"

"Say please, Gwen," I added from the sidelines. (Just because we would have our every desire tended to didn't mean we could forget about our manners.)

"Please?"

"Of course, *piccola signora*. And where would you like it? At the pool?"

"Yes, please."

"Very good," confirmed the voice.

"Thanks!" said Gwen, looking very impressed with herself. I gave her a thumbs-up.

Mina turned to me to elaborate, and Gwen went back into the pool. "There's a button in every room that connects to reception. Just press it whenever you want anything. They speak English, but most of the staff don't."

"Thanks for the tip. Life here is not so bad, huh?"

"Nope, even without a connection to the real world, it's not too bad," Mina said, resting her hands behind her head.

A little while later, the same young waiter from earlier arrived with a tray of olives, tangy cheeses, and cured meats, along with another carafe of blood orange juice.

"*Qui ci sono gli* 'snack,' *belle ragazze*," he said merrily as if we had any idea what it meant. He set out the food with delicate care and beamed us a toothy smile.

"*Grazie*," said Mina shyly.

His thick eyebrows jumped. "*Si parli italiano splendidamente, signora!*"

Mina blushed violently. I surveyed him and guessed him to be around age fifteen or sixteen, and it occurred to me that Mina might be trying to flirt with him.

She shook her head at the young man, growing redder. "*Imparo a scuola*," she said meekly in a clumsy accent.

I lobbed a fat, oily olive into the air to catch in my mouth but then froze mid-throw when I heard Mina speak. "Mina, do you speak Italian?" The olive bounced off my nose with a greasy thud.

Gwen fell over in a fit of giggles—she always had a thing for slapstick.

"Not really, I just told him that I'm learning Italian in school. Don't tell my mom yet because she wants me to take French. But Italian is so beautiful, and next year I can take both languages." She looked shyly proud and leaned back on the swanky sun lounger.

"Bravo, Mina! How admirable. Ask him his name, would you? I feel bad bossing the poor kid around without knowing his name."

Mina bashfully turned to the young waiter to ask him, and he responded slowly, drawing out the syllables: "Beeee-niiiiii-to." He proudly stabbed his chest with his fingertip.

"Benito," we all repeated, and then we introduced ourselves.

"Tell him, '*Grazie, Benito*,'" Mina said to Gwendy, and she complied most cutely. Benito swooped out with a half bow and left us to bake in the sun, our tall glasses of juice growing sweaty with condensation.

"So, Mina," I began airily, "do you know how to say, um, I don't know"—I wafted my hand in the air as if wracking my brain for the first word that popped into my head—"like . . . um, 'cell phone'? Do you know how to say that in Italian?"

Mina lifted her sunglasses.

"No," she said flatly.

— 52 —

IT WASN'T UNTIL the night of the dinner party that I finally had my chance to get to a phone. The staff had prepared a gourmet feast in preparation for a few of Mr. Darling's colleagues who would be joining us at the villa that evening.

The terrace was laid with white candles and white wine, and the air was fragrant with a blend of fresh garlic from the kitchen and night-blooming jasmine.

"Italians eat late, so we do, too, when we're here," said Elsbeth, who was wrapped in a white pashmina, even though the terrace was dotted with heat lanterns.

"Well, when in Rome, or south of Rome," I added.

Over our heads, a grape leaf canopy was knotted and wiry with verdant twisting vines and fat dangling grapes. Over the grapevine trellis, constellations like darkroom photographs

were beginning to develop in an effort to outshine the wink-
ing lights of Positano.

I dressed the girls for dinner, and they looked like little
sun-kissed peasants in angel-white linen dresses.

Since we were around Mr. Darling's colleagues, I tried my
best to ensure that the Darling girls lived up to their sur-
name, but Gwen was already tired and cranky from another
long day in the sun.

"So, Gwen, I thought tomorrow we could leave the villa
and check out the Emerald Grotto. We can take a boat."

"Will I see mermaids?" she asked skeptically.

I pushed my mouth to one side. "Hmm, not sure."

"I want to see grotty mermaids, for pizza's sake!" She
balled her little hands into fists.

As Gwendolyn got worked up, one of Mr. Darling's friends
paraded by us. I glanced up just in time to see a shiny cell
phone sticking out the back pocket of his high-waist khaki
trousers. My eyes glued to the phone. *Finally, my chance has
come!* I stared at it with starry-eyed wonderment, as if the
phone was just *begging* me to pluck it right from his—

"Oh my God! Kika, did you just check out that old guy's
butt?" Mina interrupted with a blend of incomprehension
and revulsion.

I bolted out of the hypnotized trance, recoiling as I realized that it probably *did* look like I was captivated by that
guy's behind.

"No!" I refused. "Of course not."

"You totally did," she said in shock.

I was really looking at his cell phone! I wanted to shout, but if
the girls knew what I was after, they'd foil my plan.

"Ew! Old butts! Gross!" Gwendy added in a far-too-loud voice.

Mina folded over in laughter, and Gwen looked delighted with herself and copied Mina.

"Shh, you two," I whisper-hissed, but my overenthusiastic reaction just made them laugh louder. I poked Mina in the ribs. "Yeah, yeah, laugh it up, chuckles."

"Kika likes old man butts! Old man butts! Old man butts!" chanted Gwendy.

I held my head in my hands, traumatized, willing her to stop. I wanted to laugh, too, but I knew this would only embolden her.

Thankfully, the staff emerged with steaming trays of hors d'oeuvres, and Gwendy began jumping up and down, changing her chant from "Old man butts!" to "Feed me first! Feed me first!"

I was so grateful that Gwen stopped singing about old man butts that I didn't even rebuke her for her queenly mandates. As Gwen and Mina fearlessly devoured fresh oysters, I used the free moment to scout for the old man's butt—I mean his cell phone!

The guy with the phone was a jolly-looking, if not a bit puffy, man introduced as Amjad Nazari.

His sourpuss British wife, a willowy string bean of a woman named Primrose (Brits and their flower names!), hadn't acknowledged my presence once, unless you counted me in her blanket statement about the staff:

"The help seem rather slow tonight," she had told Elsbeth with a frown that was relegated to the bottom half of her face; her forehead had been Botoxed into paralysis.

My plan was simple enough. I'd wait for the tray of hors d'oeuvres to approach the semicircle of guests, and while they were distracted by the food, I'd simply pluck the phone from Amjad Nazari's pocket, send a brief text to Aston, delete it (this is of paramount importance), then, just as simply, return the phone. Easy.

The much harder part was figuring out what to say to Aston once I got the phone. I was thinking something along the lines of: "Hey, Aston, I just wanted to let you know that it wasn't what it looked like with Lochlon. Will explain everything when I get home."

Then maybe something like, "Oh yeah, and also: I have feelings for you. Maybe we could hang out sometime if you still like me?"

Anyway, the details obviously needed to be worked out, but I'd cross that bridge when I burned it—or whatever. Right now, I just needed to focus on getting that phone.

My chance came with a tray piled high with cured meats— Amjad Nazari couldn't keep his eyes off it. I tiptoed into position like a creeping vaudevillian.

Mr. Nazari leaned over the tray and dithered happily.

His wife, Primrose, said, "Think of your heart before eating that sausage, dear." Out of the corner of my eye, I watched as Amjad hesitated with his chubby hand suspended over the silver tray with ladylike deliberation.

This was my chance. I clasped my hands behind my back in a casual stance. Then, with my back facing his, I took a few baby steps backward to get as close as possible. I positioned my hand so it was in line with where his pocket would be, and I reached out my fingers and ever so stealthily pinched—

"Ooooooooooooo!"

Amjad jumped away from me, sucking in his behind. Propelling his chest forward, he knocked the tray out of the waiter's hold. Amjad grabbed his behind with both hands and sharply whipped around in my direction.

Holy shit. I just pinched that old guy's butt!

Everyone stared at me. Rounds of soppressata rained down on us from the heavens.

"I am so sorry, Mr. Nazari," I stammered in mortification.

"What are you doing, dear girl?!" he roared.

I opened my mouth. "Um, there was a bug, and I was just trying . . ." I looked over to see Mina's hand firmly placed over Gwendy's mouth. Thank God she wasn't free to sing the "old man butts" song or I would have jumped straight off the terrace then and there.

"Are you all right, my dear?" shrilled Primrose to Amjad as she sent a demonic glance in my direction.

I held my breath as Amjad craned his neck to look at his backside. Mr. Darling stared at me like I just ruined Christmas. I didn't dare make eye contact with anyone.

Amjad grumbled coarsely, "Now, now, honest mistake. You needn't fret about it, Prim." Amjad took his wife's hand in his and patted it kindly.

I giggled awkwardly, mumbled some excuse, and walked away as fast as I could without breaking into a full-on sprint.

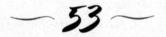

53

"Ok, I GET it. I'm not getting a phone this trip," I spoke aloud to the great cosmic comedian who had scripted this shit because *clearly* my life wasn't enough of a comedy of errors and shitty timing. I would just have to wait to tell Aston how I felt about him when I got home. I couldn't risk pinching someone else's ass. I slumped on one of the outdoor sofas and took Gwen protectively onto my lap.

"You don't *really* like old man butts, do you, Kika?" asked Gwen with a half yawn, as we both waited for dinner to just be over already. I willed my mind to erase what just happened. I didn't answer Gwendy.

For the rest of the evening, I collected Nordic-cold looks from Mr. Darling, but other than that, dinner passed without further incident, and finally, it was time for everyone to leave.

Unfortunately, this wouldn't be my last interaction with

the Nazaris. Tomorrow, they were coming with us on a little yachting trip for a few days down the Amalfi Coast.

On her way out, Primrose Nazari passed me with a cold stare. Behind her, Amjad trailed. He stalled in front of me and let his wife go ahead. I braced myself to be scolded.

When Primrose was farther away, Amjad looked me straight in the eye and gave me an unmistakable wink before rushing to catch up with his wife. My forehead smacked into my open palm.

AFTER PUTTING THE girls to sleep, I freed a lionlike yawn and padded across the cool terra-cotta floor toward my own room.

But the light from the veranda snagged my eye. I slipped outside soundlessly. The air was cooler now, brackish like fresh mussels.

The moonbeams crested off the dome of the church of Santa Maria Assunta, tiled like fish scales. I could hear the demanding roar of the sea below and the wet flapping of fishnets in wind. The silvery light skimmed off the chrome waves, and the tide nodded rusty fishing boats into one another, the distance shrinking them into pool toys. "Now you're just showing off," I said to the view.

I made my way into the kitchen instead of going straight to bed. I veered toward the fridge for a midnight snack and took out a cellophane-wrapped platter of meats and cheeses. I set it out on the butcher block. As I plopped salty cubes of pecorino and pepperoni into my mouth, I flicked through an Italian tabloid discarded on the table.

A black-and-white face in the spread of social photographs

caught my eye. I snatched the paper and brought it to eye level to make sure my eyes weren't playing tricks on me. *No. No. No.*

As I frantically searched the kitchen for the light switch, the paper crinkled in my sweaty grip. When I couldn't find the switch, I resorted to using the refrigerator and pried open the door to employ its humming blue light.

The photo was only a few inches wide and printed in grainy grays. The focus was blurry enough for me to need to double-check the fine print.

It can't be him. It just can't.

But then I remembered something Elsbeth once said: The press considered him an international playboy. *But he wouldn't be with* her, *would he?*

A rotten taste took over my mouth. I spat out the half-chewed meat. There, under the black-and-white photo, was a caption in Italian. There was no longer any denying who was in the picture:

> *Aston Hyde Bettencourt con ereditiera fidanzata,*
> *Chantelle Benson-Westwood, a Londra*

I boomeranged my vision around the kitchen as if there were someone around to decipher the Italian for me. I had to find out why they were together like this.

Even before reading the caption, I could tell it was Aston. His head was slanted down, away from the paparazzi's flashbulbs, and his hand was outstretched, tugging Chantelle through the crowd.

Chantelle was lively and waving to the cameras in true aristo-brat fashion. It looked like they were at a movie premiere or another major celeb event in Leicester Square. Why were they holding hands? And furthermore: How could this have happened so quickly? I had only been gone a little over a week!

I never missed technology more than I did at that very moment. I couldn't translate the words, and the villa staff was asleep in their quarters. I'd have to wait and get help tomorrow. In the meantime, this surely did not look good.

I glided the tray of meats and cheeses back into the fridge without eating another bite. Shockingly, I was no longer hungry. But I was never not hungry. Even after breaking up with Lochlon, I stress-ate a whole box of macarons. What was happening to me?

54

FOR A MOMENT, we all stood in a reverent silence.

The eye-squinting sun made the glistening mega-yacht look even shinier and whiter and yacht-ier.

"It's a one-hundred-seventy-eight-foot, luxury-crewed motor yacht," said Mr. Darling, breaking through our soundless awe. "It accommodates up to twelve guests in six luxury cabins and has five separate deck areas, a crew of fifteen—"

"Oh, stop it, lamb. You sound like a brochure." Elsbeth swatted her hand in Mr. Darling's face, righted her wide-brimmed sun hat, and charged right through the distinguished moment by sauntering up the sloping gangplank.

The yacht, simply put, was the coolest thing I'd ever seen, like, ever. I had to make a physical effort to stop saying "wow" as we toured the multileveled boat equipped with massive sun beds, a pool, a hot tub, and what could only be called an outdoor living room with teakwood sun beds and cubed white cabanas.

The inside looked like a South Beach hotel with crisp glass bars and Scandinavian furniture. There was even an Abachi wood sauna. (Like I knew what Abachi wood was; I was just quoting Mr. Darling.)

On the top deck, the girls and I laid out turquoise-striped towels on the sun beds around the pool and spent the day swimming and playing card games.

Elsbeth and Mr. Darling were tasked with entertaining Amjad and Primrose Nazari. Primrose was positively translucent in the daylight. Thankfully, I had been able to avoid them so far. They drank Campari in the shade while the girls and I giggled nearby.

"If only my boys were here to keep your girls company," trilled Primrose from under her shaded fortress.

She'd been babbling incessantly, but watching her speak was mesmerizing because of the Botox: The lower half of her face was a constant whirl of mouthy animation while the top was totally still. Watching her talk was like watching an Irish step dancer.

"The boys don't have their holidays now, Prim?" asked Elsbeth as I eavesdropped.

"Oh yes." Primrose hiccupped, already drunk. "But they're at boarding school—James is at Harrow and Jasper is at Le Rosey in Switzerland. And they stay at the school during their breaks. They just adore it there."

Or they want to be far away from you, I thought to myself.

Amjad interjected, "And they have made wonderful lifelong contacts with their networking. They are both to be neurosurgeons."

Elsbeth and Mr. Darling hummed appreciatively.

"And how old are the chaps now?" asked Mr. Darling. "Graduating this year, are they?"

"Nine and eleven," said Primrose.

I rolled my eyes behind my sunglasses.

Elsbeth gave Mr. Darling a coy side-eye, and he rapidly switched subjects. Something was up. But I had bigger problems to deal with.

The tabloid newspaper was tucked away inside my beach bag. I was waiting for the right moment and the right person to translate it for me.

"You lost, Kika," said Gwendy, sprawling out the winning cards with a grin on her face.

"You're telling me," I responded absentmindedly.

Gwendy suddenly yelped, "Benito!"

Benito, who had come along with the yacht staff much to Mina's delight, gave us a wink and went to refresh the Campari Sodas.

Mina checked her posture as Benito came over to us.

"Ciao, Benito," we chirped in unison, and Benito put on a big show of being very impressed with our toddler-level Italian.

I heard Elsbeth say to Primrose, "We've been coming here for years now, and I've never asked any of the staff their names . . ."

THE DAY OOZED on in a slow summer way, but soon enough the sun began to dip down behind the island of Capri.

The group oohed and aahed over the sunset, wisps and puffs of baby blues and cotton candy pinks that looked good enough to eat. Gwendy perched atop Mr. Darling's shoulders, and he gamely let her play bongo drums on his bald head. (Ah, parental guilt.)

But I was too distracted to properly enjoy it. I couldn't wait any longer. I poked Mina's arm and jerked my head so she would follow me. Mina was more interested in watching Benito on the other end of the boat than the sunset, anyway, so she didn't mind me pulling her away from the group.

"What's up, Kika?" she asked as we moved to the back deck where no one could hear us.

We took a seat on the polished wood benches where there was still a great view—I mean, we were floating off Capri: It was drop-dead beautiful any which way you looked.

Her hair shone with hints of fiery copper in the setting sun, and her cheeks were now tan and freckled from the long days in the Mediterranean. She looked fresh faced and healthy. I let the scene wash over me until I sharply remembered: *the tabloid.*

I reached for it and held the paper to my chest for a moment to prepare myself to look upon the upsetting picture again. "So, um, I found something and—"

"Lemme see!" Mina snatched the paper from me impatiently and pushed her sunglasses atop her head. "That's Aston," she said, unimpressed. "I've seen him in the paper before. He's like a gazillionaire."

"Yeah, but—" I began to explain, but she interrupted me.

"Hey wait, that's Peaches' sister. Look here," she said, pointing to the caption below. "Chantelle Benson-Westwood," she confirmed.

I nodded bleakly, and she kept examining the paper.

"Gosh, she looks awesome. Like Kate Middleton," she said, which was *wildly* unhelpful.

I seized back the paper with a snort and folded it so that only the caption was visible. I didn't need to see them holding hands for a moment longer than I absolutely had to.

"Can you read what this says?" I stuck my finger to the caption, and she read it aloud, slowly.

"It's something about Aston and Chantelle," she reported with a definitive head nod.

"Thanks Captain Obvious of the good ship *Duh*—"

"*A Londra*: That means 'in London.'"

I puffed with anticipation. "Okay, now we're getting somewhere. What else can you figure out?"

"Um, the only other word I know is *fidanzata*. It means 'girlfriend' . . . or is it 'fiancée'? Not sure . . ." she said, dropping the paper back into my lap. It slid off my thighs and onto the polished deck of the yacht. I didn't try to stop it.

— 55 —

"KIKA?" MINA ASKED. "Are you okay?"

A salty coastal gust whipped across the boat. I sat in stillness listening to the frothy water slurping against the ship's bow.

"I should get you and Gwendy some sweaters . . ." I said in distraction. I picked myself up and headed for the cabins, but Mina followed behind me.

"Mina, has Peaches said anything about her sister and Aston?" I asked. *This makes no sense—I haven't been gone that long.*

Our rooms were below deck, and we carefully navigated the steep steps.

"Nope," said Mina towing behind me. "Why? Are you upset? Do you like Aston or something?"

I stopped so abruptly that Mina rebounded off my back. "No! Do you like Benito or something?"

"No!" she said quickly.

We had the world's shortest staring contest until both of our faces went pink.

"I guess I kind of do like Benito," said Mina quietly. "How about you?" she asked hopefully.

I knew her confession meant I had to pony one up myself. I nodded meaningfully. "I guess I kind of do like Aston." I broke away and pulled out the sweaters from our bags.

"But what about Lochlon? He's not your boyfriend anymore?"

I shook my head in confirmation. "He wasn't for a long time. I just was holding on to this fantasy of how it used to be," I added, feeling like I owed her a bit of an explanation (and so she didn't think I was some boyfriend-dumping hussy—I was a role model, after all).

"But what are you going to do? Aston already has a fiancée."

"Oh, please. They couldn't have gotten engaged in, like, seven days," I snapped. "Sorry." I softened and petted down her windswept curls. I tossed her a sweater, and she threaded her arms into it. "I just don't think they could really be a couple. I know what it looks like, but I just have to talk to Aston first."

"Do you think he likes you back?"

"He did." I pulled on a sweater as well. "I don't know if he still does, though."

Before I really had a chance to process this, I linked arms with Mina. "Come on. Let's head back up. Gwendy must be cold."

As we reached the deck, we ran straight into Benito. "Benito," I said, grabbing hold of his arm to make sure he didn't get away.

"Mina," I called, and she timidly poked out from behind me. "Ask him which island is Capri."

"But I know which island—"

Benito's eye lit up at the word "Capri," and he motioned to follow him to the bow of the boat, on the opposite end of the deck.

"Go on," I whispered to Mina. "I'll keep watch. Don't do anything I wouldn't do."

She shook her head and followed Benito giddily. "You are so lucky that this guy doesn't speak English, Kika."

I gave her a sweet wave. From my safe distance away, I watched them talk in broken Italian while looking out onto the rocky seascape. Mina giggled ultra-girlishly, and I could tell that this would be the highlight of the trip for her.

I pulled my eyes away, giving them a moment of privacy. I went over to check on Gwen, who was with the adults on the other end of the deck.

"Gwendy!" I quarterbacked her a sweater, and she caught it with karate-honed reflexes.

"Thank goodness." She wriggled into the sweater. "I was freezing my—"

Before she could utter another word (most likely a bad one), I snagged her shoulders and trapped her in the fabric before she could weasel her head through. "Don't get lost in there, hobgoblin!"

She cried out in a muffled voiced and flailed her arms. Childlike silliness swished over me and lessened the dreadful feeling that I might have missed my chance with Aston. I banished the thought as Elsbeth strolled over to us with a full glass of sloshing wine.

I snatched a glance at Mina and Benito, but they were acting perfectly innocent and were out of Elsbeth's line of sight.

But her time was up for now. Mina caught my eye and knew

that my finger-swipe across the throat meant: *Wrap it up, and get your butt back over here.*

"Are you girls having fun?" Elsbeth asked just as Mina wandered over with a huge smile on her face.

I flung her a sly wink that she sent back with lightning speed.

Elsbeth bent down. She picked up the tabloid that I'd stupidly abandoned on the deck, flapping in the wind.

"Oh my, is that Aston Hyde Bettencourt?" she asked aloud, scrutinizing the photo.

"Yeah," answered Mina gravely. "And Peaches' sister, Chantelle Benson-Westwood. His fianc—girlfriend."

"You know, I *thought* those two were a couple. Lately, she's been over at his house constantly," Elsbeth said in a cheerful voice, her words walloping my gut.

"That is just what poor Aston needs, a society girl like Chantelle who will get him back out on the scene and make him *live* again. The Benson-Westwoods know everyone in London; they're in publishing, and they own all the lifestyle magazines and newspapers, so they know everything that's going on." She flipped over the tabloid to the front cover. "Why, they even own this paper."

She turned back to the photo. "They're just the type of people Aston *should be* cavorting with. Really quite wonderful, I think, don't you?"

She didn't specify who she was addressing, so both Mina and I grumbled inaudibly.

"She has the most lovely skin tone—like porcelain," she added.

I leaned into Mina. "You say porcelain; I say cadaver."

She stifled a laugh.

Elsbeth continued unaware. "He deserves to be happy after all that he's been through, poor lamb." Her eyes scanned the rest of the pictures as she took a healthy swig of her wine.

"And just look at Chantelle, dressed to the nines in Burberry Prorsum—mature but fashionable. She's the perfect fit for him, because he's always photographed, and he can't be with someone who'd be a liability to him—socially or otherwise, do you see what I mean?"

Mentally, I couldn't help but to inspect myself. With my wild hair and scuzzy bohemian clothes, Elsbeth basically meant that Aston should be with someone opposite of me. *I never wear stupid Blueberry Possum*, I thought.

Mina mangled her face at me. In response, I gagged my finger in my mouth and dropped my tongue in the universal gesture for *vomit*. Gwendy laughed at the both of us, though she didn't know what we were griping about.

"Well, lambs. I'm off to play with the adults. Kika will tuck you girls in tonight." She gave both girls kisses on the crowns of their heads before disappearing inside for more postdinner cocktails.

I took the liberty of crumpling the tabloid into a ball lest someone else come over and pronounce outright how amazing Chantelle Benson-Westwood was.

THE GIRLS AND I remained on deck awhile longer, now swaddled in sweaters and fleecy blankets. The wind relayed scraps of the adults' chatter and the pacifying tinkling sound of ice cubes in short glasses.

We watched the stars get brighter, each one happier and

266 · nicole trilivas

more twinkly than the last. When our eyelids went droopy, I ferried the girls inside to their cabin rooms. I folded them into their white beds before giving them good-night kisses of my own.

"Thanks for today," said Mina before closing her eyes. I stroked her hair off her forehead.

I automatically thought about Aston as the boat lulled the girls to sleep. It was a dangerous habit. If he really was with Chantelle, then I had no right to pine for him. But I would hold out until I saw it with my own eyes: I knew the tabloid could be wrong, and there was a chance Aston and Chantelle weren't a couple. But it was undeniable that they were out on the town together, which meant *something*.

If only I had been able to get to a phone sooner to explain why I was in the café with Lochlon, then maybe he would have never gone out with Chantelle.

With both girls asleep on the lower deck, I stole away for a moment to join the adults. I didn't want to be alone with my churning, repetitive thoughts anymore. They were clustered in the upstairs bar called the Sky Lounge, all steel and glass and fabulousness.

"But Switzerland seems so far," I heard Elsbeth say to Primrose, who now looked like a middle-school English teacher drunk on cooking sherry. "Is that really the best option? Mina *is* learning French, I suppose."

"Well, you can always go with English schools, but after doing my research, Switzerland is really the best option— especially for girls. They'll find it delightful. Don't worry for one moment longer."

I held back for a minute, hovering in the doorway.

"I know you're right, Prim," Elsbeth said. "Boarding school is the absolute right choice."

"Elsbeth!"

When everyone swiveled toward the door, I realized that it was me who had just blurted out Elsbeth's name in that reprimanding way.

"Kika, how long have you been standing there?" she asked, setting down her wineglass. She looked tipsy as well, and I hoped whatever she had just said was a product of the alcohol.

"Sorry. Hi, everyone," I said timidly. "I'm so sorry," I repeated, "it's just that for a minute there, I thought I heard you say that you were sending Mina to boarding school in Switzerland. It's been a long day. Obviously that's ridiculous." I started laughing feebly.

"Not just Willamina," said Mr. Darling. "Gwendolyn, too." He rose from his chair, posturing like an alpha gorilla.

"What?" I blinked rapidly.

He slowed his words. "Boarding school. In Switzerland. In September."

"What are you talking about? You can't send them away." I rushed the table. "You're kidding, right? It's a joke, isn't it?" I pleaded, looking only at Elsbeth.

Mr. Darling made a condescending chuckle for the benefit of his guests, and Elsbeth joined her hands together. Amjad and Primrose Nazari sat by awkwardly.

"Now, now, Kika, you're not to worry about your job," Mr. Darling fussed in a patronizing way. "We've already arranged—"

"*Screw* my job!"

Primrose wheezed as if we still lived in a world where saying the word "screw" aloud was unseemly. *Bitch, please.*

"You can't send the girls away," I said to Elsbeth, still not fully believing it.

"And why not, Kika?" Mr. Darling challenged.

I looked at Elsbeth, wordlessly beseeching her to say something. But she appeared to be captivated by the lipstick stain on the rim of her wineglass.

"This can't be your idea," I told her. "You'd never make them live alone in Switzerland, not when they're so young."

Primrose let out a scale of titters that got higher and higher. "American au pairs are certainly outspoken. Never you mind her, Elsbeth—"

"This is ludicrous," I interjected, still speaking only to Elsbeth.

Suddenly, she bolted upright like an exclamation point, and I let out a grateful sigh. *Finally*, I thought, *she'll set these maniacs straight*.

Elsbeth squared off: "You are quite right, Kika!"

But before I could let out a noise of relief, she barreled on.

"Your outburst *is* ludicrous. I'm very sorry you had to hear it this way, but you are not a part of this conversation or, to be quite frank, this family. Decisions regarding the education of the girls are mine to make with Mr. Darling. And your hostility is spoiling the night."

"Well put," said Prim.

I bombarded her with mute daggers. Elsbeth had never spoken to me like that before. I sucked my teeth. "Please, Elsbeth," I whispered. "You can't."

She glanced at Mr. Darling like she was looking for his approval. He nodded shortly at her, and she resumed talking.

"As Mr. Darling was just saying, we've made other arrangements for you work-wise, so please, not a word of this to the girls. I would hate for us to part on a sour note and have to give you a poor recommendation after all your wonderful work."

"There's a position open in Ronald Richmond's office. His PA needs an assistant. It's all sorted for you, Kika," Mr. Darling piped in like he just did me the world's greatest favor.

I grimaced openly.

"We will speak about it when we return to London, and that's final." Elsbeth sat back down looking shaky. She stared out at the sea with dead-fish eyes.

Primrose tapped her forearm in clumsy consolation. "Well done, darling. You must put these sort of girls in their places before—"

I turned around and barged out so I didn't have to hear another word out of Primrose, but I didn't move fast enough to escape hearing her call me a "right little bitch."

— *56* —

THE NEXT WEEK of vacation went by in a narcotic-like stupor, and before I knew it, we were on a private plane back to London. It was a lot less fun this time around.

Things were frigid and distant with Elsbeth, and she actively avoided me. I tried to talk to her about boarding school every chance I got, but it was no use.

The only information she gave me was that the girls were to finish out the school year in London, but by September— a mere few months away—the poor kids would be shipping out, me included, as there would be no need for an au pair once the girls were in Switzerland.

Once upon a time, I thought that the minute I got back to the Darlings' house in London, I'd run directly next door to Aston's. But now, more than ever, I worried that it may be too late.

I held my breath as I turned on my cell phone. *Maybe, just maybe, there will be something from*—nope. There was nothing from Aston.

Instead, a vile little message from Lochlon blinked onto the screen:

> Figured out a way to live your dreams yet? I didn't
> mean to be cruel. Only wanted to make you more
> realistic. Truly sorry for being so dreadful to you.
> Part of me wishes we never left India. Please think
> well of me. I will always think well of you.

It took everything in me not to text him back something nasty. Not being able to discuss things with Elsbeth had me gunning for confrontation. But I knew it was a bad idea, and so I said nothing and deleted his phone number. I felt an immediate, sweeping relief. *How wonderful for that to be so anticlimactic*, I thought, feeling myself brighten ever so slightly.

Instead of sitting in my room and feeling sorry for myself, I holed up in Mina's to unpack her bags while she was at school. But as I hung up her clothing, my feelings against her going to boarding school grew stronger and stronger.

They were still so young. Both girls hadn't adjusted well to a new country while living with their parents, so who knew what would happen to them in a dorm room in Switzerland with strangers! I thought it was great for girls to start traveling so young, but this felt all too Hansel-and-Gretel-left-in-the-woods for my taste.

Maybe Elsbeth was right, and this was the best thing for

them down the line when things like networking and contacts mattered, but I would never, ever want to choose it for them without *asking* if it was what they wanted.

And of course I'd be out of a job. I couldn't act like that wouldn't royally suck. Mr. Darling pulled me aside to tell me more about the job with Richie Rich. In an unconcerned, psychotic way, he couldn't grasp that being back in New York and having that bridge troll, Bae Yoon, as my *direct boss* was anything but a delightful solution. Why did a personal assistant need a personal assistant, anyway?

I could barely muster a smothered "thanks." I prayed that job wouldn't be my only option once I was "made redundant." (What a bullshit phrase.)

But regardless, without the au pair gig, I didn't have a work visa for the UK, so I would most definitely be leaving.

I had some money saved up—enough for me to get an apartment in New York City or for a few months of travel. Never had travel been so alluring, so irresistible. Like an old friend, travel was reaching out for me with glittery, shiny promises of great adventures. Never had I needed travel more than now. *Come away and forget about it all*, it cooed in my ear.

I could visualize the trip I would take: I could go to the bank right now, empty out my account, and book a plane ticket to wherever was cheapest. I could make my way down the spine of South America, where beer was inexpensive and hammocks abundant.

But instead of ending the fantasy there—down on some beach in Punta del Este, Uruguay, playing barefoot soccer—I forced myself to continue. After the beach, after the beers, after the boys, I would have to return home, come back. *Back.* There would always be a *back* to return to until Gypsies & Boxcars was profitable and self-sufficient. And the *back* after any trip I took now would be a deep, deep hole. I would have made no true progress and would have to start saving money all over again.

And so I turned away from the voice, telling it to shush. I would go back to Long Island and move in with my mom and take the job with Bae. I would leave my money in my savings account because it was my "more marshmallows money." I intended on keeping up with my goals for Gypsies & Boxcars—though losing this job meant it would take a lot longer to save for the relaunch.

So much for the schedule that Celestynka had made me. Regardless, I would do things differently this time in order to get to where I wanted to go—even if that meant staying still for a while.

I felt a mean little pinch in my chest when I thought that Lochlon would *love* this: He forecasted my return to office life with my tail between my legs. In fact, nothing would make him happier or more self-satisfied. I feared that he secretly thought that if *he* couldn't live our dream life, then neither of us should.

I closed the wardrobe door, the clothes hanging like listless ghosts. I felt tears pooling. Even now, I couldn't help but to think about Aston and feel that knee jerk of disappointment.

Just then, Mina's door swung open. Celestynka stood at the doorway in a lime green miniskirt and high ponytail, her arms filled with aerosol cans and dust rags.

"Kika," she said. "I did not know that you are back."

"Hey, Celestynka," I mumbled.

When she saw the look on my face, the cleaning products

dropped in a free fall from her arms. "What is happening?" She dashed over to me. "You break up with Lochlon?"

I shook my head, and the tears ruptured in hot, splotchy-faced misery.

"So Lochlon is okay?" she asked, confused.

"Oh no, we did break up," I added. But before she got a chance to say anything else, I spoke up quickly. "But it's not that."

Celestynka put her hands together to make a bowl shape and pleaded, "You no cry for Lochlon?"

Usually I corrected her English—she had gotten much better, but when she was emotional she regressed.

"No, I'm crying because ... because ... everything is messed up."

"Tell me all," Celestynka commanded, patting the bed-spread beside her.

"The girls are being sent to boarding school in Switzer-land!" I choked out. "But you cannot tell anyone," I added, taking ahold of her wrists.

Celestynka pulled away and clutched her chest. "Why does Ms. Elsbeth want to send her babies away?"

"I don't get it, either, but come September both girls will be shipped away, and I'll be out of a job."

Celestynka shook her head. "But this is no right. They have you leave America to work here."

I sniffed back my tears. "Well, they'll get me another job back home, in an office." (This realization led to a fresh burst of feelings.) "But I'm just sad for the girls."

Celestynka made a disappointed ticking sound.

"Oh, and also, Celestynka," I added with a miserable sniff. "You should probably know that I've fallen for Aston."

Celestynka jumped off the bed. "Aston! But this is wonderful! How—"

"No." I wiped my nose on my sleeve, finally getting control of my emotions. "It's not wonderful. Aston already has a girlfriend: that Chantelle Benson-Westwood with her fancy wardrobe and shiny Kate Middleton hair and shit-ton of money enough to buy—"

"Chantelle Benson-Westwood?" Celestynka repeated in perfect pronunciation.

I surveyed her. She was suddenly very clear-eyed. "Yes . . . how do you know—"

She shook her head into a motion blur. "I have Polish friend who is the child-minder for Mrs. Benson-Westwood."

"Ah, so you, too, must know all about how perfect she is with her great media fortune and—"

"Chantelle is no right!" she said with real heat in her voice. "She has no great fortune, Kika. My friend, she tells me everything. Chantelle is bad, bad girl."

"What are you talking about?"

Celestynka's eyes bugged out like a cartoon. "They lose whole fortune! Is great secret, but my friend knows because they talk in front of her because they think she's stupid and knows no English. They have no more money now."

Celestynka let her knees release, and she thudded back down on the bed next to me, but I leapt up with a flourish.

"Oh my God," I proclaimed. "You must be right, because Mina is in the same class as Chantelle's sister, Peaches, and she told me that Peaches had to return her Louis Vuitton bags and her other fancy-pants crap. And she said they were selling her country estate." Mina's words came back to me gradually. But then I sat back down. "But still, even without money, as Elsbeth pointed out, Chantelle knows the right people—"

"Fuck that!" Celestynka interjected by stamping her fist onto her thigh.

For a moment, I radiated with nothing but pride as her English teacher: She had used the word "fuck" perfectly! I gasped in admiration and almost broke out into applause.

"Do you not see, Kika?" Celestynka then rattled off sentences in fast-moving, impending Polish, and then stared at me like she just straight-up forgot she was speaking in a language I didn't understand.

"This girl, this *Chantelle*"—she said her name with scorn—"I am thinking she is only wanting to be with Aston for his fortunes."

My mouth dropped open.

"You must tell him. You must," she beseeched.

But before I could answer her, the door slung open again. This time it was Elsbeth.

57

"WHAT'S ALL THE racket in here?" Elsbeth challenged, filling Mina's room with her noxious black mood.

When Celestynka saw it was Elsbeth, she made apologetic mumblings and lowered her head. Shimmying her hips to put her skirt back in place, she hurried over to collect her cleaning supplies, muttering, "Sorry, sorry, Ms. Elsbeth."

"You ladies are being awfully loud when I'm trying to read," Elsbeth said as Celestynka scurried out of the room. Elsbeth obviously had the problem with me, not Celestynka.

"Sorry, Elsbeth," I said without meeting her eyes. I hurriedly stowed the rest of Mina's clothing in her drawers. I wanted to get away from Elsbeth as soon as possible. Just as Celestynka had done, I scampered past. But Elsbeth shadowed me into the hall.

"Kika, a word, please."

"Sure," I said, entering Gwen's room. "I'll just unpack Gwendy's clothing, and—"

"Sit. Please!" she ordered, exasperated at my flurry of movement. It sounded just like she was reprimanding a misbehaving dog.

I obediently folded down on Gwen's bed.

Elsbeth pulled out a desk chair and sat, crossing her legs at the ankles. She expelled a saintly, long-suffering sigh before speaking. "Kika, I understand you're not happy about the girls going away to school, but we have made our decision. This is the best option for later in life when they will use the connections—"

"They're seven and thirteen," I implored. "They have their whole life to network. Elsbeth, can't you at least *ask* them? It would be different if they wanted to go, but they—"

She held up her hand. "Enough. That is quite enough." She screwed her eyes shut and opened them a moment later as if resetting herself. "This is not up for discussion. All I want to know is if you can do your job until September or if this will continue to have a negative effect on it."

Instinctually, I knew that whatever I said next was crucial. But I had to speak up for the girls. Elsbeth had to know this was wrong. Everyone else could coddle her, but I would not. I wouldn't make this easy for her. I wouldn't make this neat or tidy. So I spoke the truth, though every word was another shovelful of dirt that would deepen the hole to my own grave.

"No, Elsbeth." I got the feeling she wasn't told that very often. "It's not okay. Of course this is going to affect my job. I can't just pretend—"

"That's all I needed to hear, Kika." Elsbeth studied her

lap. "I think it's best if we went our separate ways." She paused. "Of course we'll give you a good reference, and Mr. Darling will make that phone call for you to make sure you have a job in New York . . ." She let her voice trail off.

"Oh, lamb. I know this isn't ideal for you," she said, for the first time sounding like herself. "But I cannot have you in my ear for the next few months trying to talk me out of this. It's settled. Their tuition has already been paid, and all the arrangements have been made. Do you understand that, Kika?"

I stood, and my arms dropped to my sides in a rag doll flop. "No, Elsbeth. I'm sorry, but I don't understand. And I never will."

She toyed with her wedding band. "I thought as much. You're welcome to stay for the rest of the week to get your plans sorted, but we've booked your plane ticket for Friday at seven P.M. Mr. Darling and I have agreed that this is more than sufficient and fair. We will tell the girls on Friday when they return from school—right before you leave, so as not to distress them sooner."

I couldn't say anything. She had cobbled together the whole plan even before talking to me about it. There was no detail left to grapple over. It was decided.

Elsbeth got up and walked out, but not before looking back at me with a look that proved she was sorry, though she'd never say it.

I WENT TO my room and lay on my bed and memorized the ceiling. It was officially done—and so much sooner than I anticipated. I remembered the promise I made to myself after

I was fired from VoyageCorp to give this job my all. I guess my all wasn't enough.

I thought of Bae Yoon at this moment. Wouldn't she do everything in her power—including lying to Elsbeth about her feelings—to keep her job? To make herself relevant? To keep moving forward, progressing with that blistering speed that came so naturally to her?

But I was no Bae Yoon. I would always have to speak up with my true feelings. And that would be my downfall.

"Is everything okay?" texted Celestynka when she left the house, not daring to come by my room to say good-bye.

"Yeah, it's fine. You didn't get in trouble, did you?" I texted back. I couldn't bear to tell her that I was leaving on Friday.

My phone buzzed practically right after I punched the "send" key: "All is okay. Ms. Elsbeth just tells me to chat less, clean more. I don't mind. But you are all right? You will talk to Aston now?"

I thought to myself: *He does deserve to know that the nasty Chantelle may be using him for his money.*

"You must tell him the truth. Even if he is angry with you for it or does not believe you," she instructed me as if she read my thoughts. "You also must tell him your feelings," she added.

My insides cramped and quivered at the thought of seeing him again. *Yeah, okay, I get it,* I told my belly. *I do like him. But what good is it now that I'm leaving?*

"I don't know. I'm getting cold feet," I finally texted Celestynka back.

A few minutes later my phone vibrated with a response: "Put on socks, then! But after, you must talk to Aston."

— 58 —

I WAS ALREADY half seduced by spring in London, I realized as I closed my door with a clack and walked toward Aston's house. Spring had come while we were away, and baby green and butter-yellow buds had begun to fatten up the trees. *It's too bad I'll never see the season in its full glory.*

The night before, I had decided I would tell Aston what I knew about Chantelle. I still wasn't sure if I would admit to my feelings for him, though. I dragged my feet along the pavement.

The girls had just left for their early-morning choir practice before school, and the neighborhood was still wrapped in a thick quiet. *God, I'll miss it here.*

Because I was looking up at the trees, I wasn't watching where I was going, and I almost bumped into someone.

"Oh!" I stopped short.

When I saw who I virtually collided with, I was charged with an ache so potent that I staggered backward. I blinked a few times hoping she'd go away. But there she was, Chantelle Benson-Westwood. And she had just emerged from Aston's front door at this early-morning hour.

Why? Because life's like that, that's why.

When Chantelle saw me, she smiled deeply. I pressed my nails into my palm, leaving a constellation of crescent moons in my flesh.

She flattened her hair and flashed me a long, proud look but put on a show of being embarrassed.

"Kika! My, my, I hadn't the slightest idea that I'd encounter anyone at this hour of the morning." She folded her coat over her body as if gift wrapping herself and then blotted the smeared mascara from under her eyes.

"I'm afraid you caught me on a bit of a walk of shame," she confided with a nasty twinge.

The crescents grew deeper. "So the gossip rags were true," I said with no inflection. I told myself that I wouldn't believe that Chantelle and Aston were a couple until I saw it with my own eyes, but now I wished I had just believed it to have spared myself the agony of seeing Chantelle leaving Aston's with a postcoital glow.

Chantelle nodded demurely. "Oh, so you've heard, then? Aston and I are a couple now." She wiped the sides of her mouth in a sexual but restrained gesture that was not lost on me.

"Were you going in?" She motioned at his door. "You may want to give him a moment. He just went into the bath. We had *quite* the night," she said with a hateful smile.

I flinched.

"Well, I think he'll want to hear what I have to say," I said, stalking past her, the gift of movement finally restored to me.

"And what's that, Kiki?"

I knew she said my name wrong on purpose. I whipped back and fired: "I know you're using him. I know there's no money left!"

Chantelle didn't speak for a moment, and we stared at each other in a showdown. But then she threw her head back and laughed like it was the funniest thing in the world. The alarm clock–like cackles grated on my very soul.

"Deny it all you want. I know on good authority—"

She reeled in her laughter. "Oh no, dear, you're quite right, the money is gone. I can't believe you thought it was some big secret. Aston is well aware."

I shook my head in confusion. "Well, he's certainly not dating you for your sparkling personality, so what the hell is going on?"

Chantelle squished her eyes into vicious little slits. "What you don't understand is that the Benson-Westwood family has been a member of the English aristocracy since before your silly little country even had a flag. Our name, our heritage, our lineage is something no one can buy, no matter what size the fortune," she boasted. "What I have with Aston is a partnership: He has the means and I have the name. I don't expect an *American* to appreciate the significance of this."

She said "American" in the same way that stuffy intellectuals said "Kardashian."

"I don't believe you," I said, but my words lacked the punch and gave me away.

She coolly shouldered past me and clacked down the street.

"It's over, Kika," she said, sliding on a pair of designer sunglasses in a melodramatic way. "As you Americans would say, 'Get over it.' Good effort, though. Let's try and be friends, shall we? I'm practically your neighbor now," she said cheerily as she stretched her fingers into cropped leather gloves.

I turned and watched her flounce down the tree-lined street, looking like she'd just won. (And hadn't she?)

Was Aston really that shallow? Were she and Elsbeth right about his need to be with someone of proper breeding? I smacked Aston's red door with the flat of my open palm, but Chantelle was right: He didn't answer.

59

TRYING TO GET my shit together was a mini-tragedy. There was a lot of throwing of clothing and slamming of drawers. I spent the rest of the day in the special hell that is being made to leave before ready to. I felt like a thuggish bouncer was jostling me out of the VIP room.

I kept going back to Aston's house, but he wasn't there. Or maybe he was there, and he just didn't want to see me. I distracted myself by taking a long, heated walk to Celestynka's flat to say good-bye to her. But her weeping was more than I was prepared for.

"But Kika," she said with black mascara tears, thankfully keeping her voice down because the babies were asleep. "This is not fair!"

I shrugged. *No, it isn't fair. But the world likes to screw with my best-laid plans.* I didn't bother to say this aloud, because I didn't know how to explain it to Celestynka.

"I am so sad that my good news is no longer good enough," Celestynka said, nursing a kiddie cup of iceless vodka.

I stared at the drink she poured for me in a cup decorated with clowns and considered guzzling it in one go. "I need some good news now more than ever," I told her. "What've you got?"

"Well, because of your teaching, I received a job."

I snapped awake. "You got a job?" I had recently helped her with her CV, but I didn't realize she already interviewed and got the job.

"Celestynka!"

She gnawed at her fingernail, testing out a smile, though her eyes were still gloomy.

"I didn't want to stress you out," she said, sounding like a native English-speaker, now. "It is at a bank. I start next week. Full-time."

I threw my arms around her. "I'm so proud of you," I beamed, squeezing her tighter. This tiny lift of joy reminded me that things would be okay.

Things would get better, wouldn't they? Even if I had to leave, I would look back on this experience and think it beautiful after I had the distance that came with time, wouldn't I?

Damn it, I was starting to sound like my mom.

UNFORTUNATELY, I LEFT all the mirth at Celestynka's. I got home to find that the last few days I had intended on dragging on unmercifully. Elsbeth instructed Clive to pick up the girls from school this week, so I had little to do but mope.

"The girls are going to have to get used to you not being here," she told me.

I boiled over with rage at her for not giving me the chance to say good-bye properly. Elsbeth said that they'd be distracted at school all week if we told them now, but I knew she was just doing it to spare herself the fuss. I was dreading Friday when I'd have to tell them good-bye and then leave right after. What a cruel surprise.

There was only one last chance to get Elsbeth to change her mind: The card up my sleeve was to tell her about Mina being bullied. Surely that would convince her to take the girls' desires into consideration?

But I gave Mina my word that I would not tell. So I shoved the opportunity away with hard determination. *I won't betray her. Not even now.*

As for Aston, with heartsick resignation I concluded that there was no longer a reason to tell him how I felt. But I wouldn't leave without telling him what I knew about Chantelle—I didn't believe her when she said Aston knew about her lack of funds. And because of all the times he helped me, I felt like I owed him this at the very least.

My plan was to catch him at the Zetland Arms. He played there on Thursdays, so with any luck, I would find him there tomorrow. He couldn't avoid me then, and I couldn't leave without telling him.

I waited for the girls to come home from school, and I thought, *Damn it. I'll miss them most of all.*

~ 60 ~

THURSDAY TOOK ITS sweet-ass time to arrive. I approached the Zetland Arms as the setting sun bronzed the city, skipping gold against the pub windows and cobbled streets.

When I saw Aston sitting at a high-top table toward the back of the pub, my heart squeezed with greedy want. It was like looking into the lit-up window of a pretty house and wishing you lived there.

Look at him sitting there by himself, brooding and miserable, I told myself to egg myself on. *That's what dating Chantelle Benson-Westwood will make you look like.*

I whipped through the door, all business, before I lost my nerve.

"You're avoiding me," I said as I plopped down at his table, rattling his pint glass.

A ray of dying sun sliced through the smeared window,

setting him aglow. He looked up at me sparkle eyed, and for a moment, I was sure he was going to smile at me. *Oh God, please do it!* I pleaded.

But he didn't smile. His stoic features stayed unmoving. He stared at me like an impenetrable statue, and suddenly I felt less poised. I gulped hard and gave myself a terse nod of encouragement. *You have to tell him*, I implored. *Tell him now.*

"Kika," he said without emotion. I expected him to contradict me, but instead he said, "Yes, I have been avoiding you."

I leaned back in my chair. "Well, too bad. I have something to ask you." I whacked my palms on the sticky tabletop. Before I squandered my spurt of courage, I asked, "Why are you with Chantelle? She's just after your money!"

Aston moistened his lips and looked at me, but he quickly traded it for looking out the window.

I used the chance to examine him. His lips were full and glistening. I couldn't help but stare at him, at his lips, and think about how they'd feel on my—*God, Kika, pull it together.*

"Say something," I insisted.

In his resigned manner, Aston took his time speaking. "We'll get to that, but there's something I have to ask you first. Is that quite all right?"

"Okay . . ." I said, already feeling my pluck ebbing, disarmed by how much I suddenly craved to touch him, to press against him.

"What does it even matter to you who I'm with? Haven't you a boyfriend?" he asked, scrutinizing my reaction.

My tongue stumbled, caught off guard. *Why does this always happen to me when I'm around him?*

I watched myself from above: A brave hand reached for his

pint glass. I found myself taking a massive gulp of his beer. I was horrified to find myself still gulping away like a frat boy. Oh my God, by the time I set down the pint, it was nearly finished. I snatched back my hand appalled at myself. What did I just do?

"Aston, I am so sorry, should I get you another—" I started to apologize, but he shifted his feet on the ground and leaned forward onto the edge of his high stool.

"Just answer my question," he stated firmly, ignoring the beer that I had just emptied down my throat.

"Well, that's part of what I came here to tell you," I said with flayed hands and a bit of a beer buzz now. "After that night in the garden when you . . . came to my rescue"—I shyly flicked my eyes up, and I swore Aston's expression softened for a split second—"Lochlon came to the house first thing that morning. I was so worried he was going to wake up everyone that I agreed to talk to him at the coffee shop, just to get him to go away, you know?"

"Kika," he cautioned, tilting forward. "He could have *hurt* you—"

"I know," I interrupted, but for the first time I saw his point. With shaken confidence, I continued. "I shouldn't have gone with him. But he was sober and wouldn't leave, so I agreed to listen to his bullshit. It was stupid; you're right."

I didn't look at Aston as I said this next part: "But his apology made no difference to me—I was done with him. I've been done with him for a long time. I guess I just didn't want to believe it."

I flicked my gaze up. "But that morning he saw you pass by the café, and he deliberately made it look like we were back together just to mess with you—with us—but Lochlon and I resolved *nothing* that morning. I promise." I said this with real energy, piercing my own pupils into Aston's. "It's over."

I added quickly but quietly: "Not like you still care or anything, but I wanted you to know. I tried to tell you sooner. As soon as I understood what Lochlon did, I went to your house trying to find you, but the Darlings were waiting for me to go to the airport for their holiday. They took my phone—it was this whole no-technology trip. And I tried to contact you while I was in Italy. But then I saw the papers."

"What papers?" he asked.

"Some society column that showed pictures of you and Chantelle together."

Aston's face darkened.

"I hoped it wasn't true, and so I tried again to tell you when I got back to London."

Aston didn't speak, so I continued.

"But as soon as I reached your house that morning, I ran into Chantelle leaving. And I just figured you obviously didn't care anymore, because . . . you know, because you and Chantelle were having . . . s . . . sleepovers." (I apparently was not old enough to use the word "sex.") I stopped talking abruptly.

Aston surveyed his near-empty pint before opting to kill the last dredges. He shook his head then.

"What is it?" I asked.

He placed the empty pint glass down like he was positioning a chess piece, and then he looked up at me.

"Kika," he said with a tinge of annoyance shading his tone. "It appears that we both fell for the same rather stupid trick." He fingered the clammy paper coaster.

"What?"

"Chantelle pulled a Lochlon, I'm afraid," he explained.

"What do you mean? I saw her leaving your house the morning after."

Aston gave a chesty scoff. "That's precisely what she wanted you to think she was doing: leaving after staying the night. But she had most likely just arrived moments before you did."

"But she made it seem like—"

Aston interrupted me. "But she didn't, don't you see? She came over first thing that morning because she had gotten my message that I wanted nothing to do with her, and she was making a final effort to change my mind.

"But of course I rebuked her again. And as far as those pictures of us together, well, they must have been taken ages ago. The Benson-Westwoods are in media, so she must have had them planted so that people would assume we were together."

"So it's true that she was after your fortune? I heard it from Celestynka that her family lost all their money."

Aston swiveled his head, affronted. "Well, I'd hope she was after me for more than just that. It isn't like I'm Quasimodo after all."

I laughed too loudly at this, but I was just so relieved.

"When I confronted Chantelle about being after your money, she said that she had the pedigree, and you had the fortune, and it was the perfect arrangement."

Aston grunted. "She tried that with me as well. After she realized she couldn't, shall we say, 'seduce me,' to put it politely"—he rolled his eyes—"she then pitched the power-couple idea to me."

"So you turned her down?"

"Of course I turned her down! Can't stand the woman. And my granny thinks her ghastly as well."

"Your granny?" Immediately, I pictured a pearl-clutching, tea-sipping matriarch with a Norman-Bates's-mother-like grip on Aston.

Like Aston could hear my thoughts, he added, "But not to worry. Granny likes you."

"She does?" I asked, astonished. "You told her about me?"

"Yes, of course. Granny knows everything about this town. She's at the Harrington Gardens School for Girls, and she said since you've arrived, the Darling girls have never been better."

I grinned.

"Besides, you're rather likable, you know, for a Yank, that is. And Granny doesn't 'give a toss about Chantelle's aristocratic bloodline.' This is a direct quote, mind you."

I couldn't help but let the corners of my mouth raise at the mention of him telling his granny about me. I immediately redrafted the image of her in my head. This was a lady with spunk!

"I cannot imagine that you believed Chantelle. What era do you think we're living in, Kika? This isn't *Downton Abbey*."

"Well, I didn't know," I protested. "And you *did* tell me straight-out that you went to Oxford. So I thought that crap meant something to you."

Aston blinked his eyes briskly. "Fair enough."

I let out a little burst of air, unaware that I was holding my breath this whole time.

"So then, Kika, you have yet to answer my question fully:

Why does it matter to you who I'm with?" He rested his chin atop his knuckles.

I used the moment to gather my feelings. Now that I knew Chantelle was out of the picture, things were suddenly different.

"Well, you know, I didn't want to see you with someone who was after you for all the wrong reasons," I said, running my nail along the wood's grain. I picked up the coaster, cool and wet like a basement.

I felt his eyes blazing on me. "Was that it, then?"

"Yup," I peeped, too quickly. "Well, there's also the fact that there's me," I added.

"And what about you?"

"Aston," I whined, trigger shy. "You're really making me work for it, huh?" I said under my breath. My heartbeat accelerated, the confession building like a drumroll.

"I haven't the slightest idea of what you're talking about, Kika," he said with unconvincing naiveté.

I fluttered my lips. "I guess there is the fact that *I* like you, Aston."

He glided the beer coaster away from me. "Do you, now?"

With nothing to distract me, I nodded without lifting my eyelashes.

"Kika?" he asked with the stern menace of a headmaster.

"Of course I do!" I stumbled out.

Aston reached across the table and lightly used his thumb to tilt my chin up so that I was forced to lock eyes with him. "I've always fancied you, Kika," he told me.

I could feel my pupils widening. "Always?"

"But you must know! Why do you think I was avoiding

you? I feared you were too silly to realize that you felt the same way about me."

Before I could say anything, he leaned over the small expanse of table. The conversation was far from over, but in that moment it didn't matter. His lips touched down on mine in a kiss that, moments before, I thought to be impossible.

— *61* —

"But it was supposed to be happily ever after," said Aston.

I had ruined the moment by breaking the news of my impending departure tomorrow. "Not this time," I said.

We stood outside the Zetland Arms under hanging flower baskets and puddles of lamplight. The night was colder now, but notes of dank springtime still puckered the air. Aston paced. I slouched against the wall.

"You can't leave tomorrow. I've only just kissed you the once. What are we to do?"

I gave him a lopsided smile. "Make up for lost time?" I closed my eyes and glided forward on my tiptoes.

But no kiss came. I snapped open my eyes in irritation. "Aston!"

"Oh. Right. Sorry." He stopped circling and came in close, using his hands this time. He took his time and moved slowly, like a moan. This kiss wasn't like our first one, tender with sugary fairy-tale swoon. Instead, things were suddenly steamier. I involuntarily flexed my spine and slinked my body against his like a cat.

He gently pressed the heel of his open palm against my back, slowly insisting that I feel him against me, adamant that I know how much he desired me. He took me in an open-mouthed kiss that lasted, that rolled up and down like a tide, that teased something out of me. The taste of him melted like salt against my tongue. I felt my inner thighs clasping together in reply to his lips on mine, his hands brushing against me over my clothing. *I want him*, I found my skin saying. *Want. Want. Want.*

"Mmm," he hummed as he peeled his mouth away from mine. "What was it that I was saying?"

"How it's an outrage that I'm leaving tomorrow," I said miserably. I broke from his embrace and headed south to walk off the sultry, lusty zinging in the cool night.

I didn't know where I was headed, but I just knew that I had to move before I threw my body on top of his right then and there.

"Right. So what can we do?" To catch up, he trotted behind me. "There must be something."

"Aston, trust me. I thought long and hard about this. There's nothing we can do. Without my visa from the Darlings, I can't work here. And I need an income."

Aston nodded and dug his hands into his pockets.

I halted. *Will I really lose him now?*

"Kiss me like that again, Aston," I asked.

He licked his bottom lip in a devilish way. "Like this?"

With brisk confidence he pulled me up against him. "Is this what you want?"

"Oh," I gasped, startled by his force. I hugged his arms to stabilize myself. I wanted to feel him again. I wanted to make sure this was really happening.

He put his forehead to mine with a dark smile. "Tell me, is this what you're after?"

I nodded, slack-mouthed.

"No. Say it." He grinned.

My mouth felt ashy. "I want this. I want you."

Then his open mouth was on mine. Lips, tongue, an arousing nip of teeth to the bottom lip. His hands journeyed up my rib cage as I pushed my chest against his. But then, he abruptly withdrew. I panted for air and didn't let go of the nape of his neck.

"Kika," he piped unexpectedly, breath hot and moist in my ear. "Spend tonight with me . . ."

The streets were deserted now, and my mind filled in the next steps and blotted out his voice. From the flavor and potency of that last kiss, I could draft the flowery sex scene perfectly: I visualized us rushing home, the longest five-minute walk of our lives, leading up to full-eye-contact sex where all that urgent, pent-up infatuation would be released.

Eyes half closed, I pictured my hands burrowing under his sweater, impatient to pass my fingertips through those faint blond hairs of his lower stomach, teasing the line where his skin meets his jeans—but I stopped right there, mid-fantasy, while our clothing was still on.

As flushed as it was making me, I couldn't do it.

With my hands flat against his chest, I shook my head faster than I meant to. As much as I wanted him, I was too fearful of it moving too fast—especially since it was all ending tomorrow. I couldn't stand the raw loneliness, which—like a physical presence—would sit next to me at the airport tomorrow, along with the dull ache between my thighs as a last reminder of him.

Sure, it would be darkly intense and rosy romantic tonight, but in the unsexy and plain fluorescent light of day, it would make it that much more devastating to leave.

My head felt weighty and weary at the thought of being a million miles away from him. We could have been so much more.

"Hey," he said, trying to hook my waist, but I wrenched away and looked at the gravelly street. If I had any chance of sticking to this, I couldn't let him touch me there. I only could control myself at a good, safe distance away from him.

"I want to, Aston. I really do. But if I'm leaving—I just couldn't bear it—"

He bent his face down toward mine. Things were so different in close range.

"No, Kika, I hadn't meant that. Rather, I meant stay with me tonight—we'll go to a pub or just walk around the city all night. It needn't matter. I only meant I wanted to be with you." He ran his fingers over his scalp, through his windswept hair.

"Not that I wouldn't want to do the other thing. Christ, I'm gagging to be alone with you," he added, "but tonight, just being around you is enough. You're not leaving. Not yet, anyway," he said firmly. "And I'm sure we'll think of something to sort it. But we mustn't give up and go home just yet."

I nodded to appease him, but I wouldn't get my hopes up about finding a way to stay here.

"So you're game for a bit of a walk, then?" he asked me, snaking both hands around my hips and pulling me toward him like we were about to dance. A current of lust sped through me again, but this time I didn't back away from it.

— 62 —

I WAS ALL deep sighs and wistful eyes that night. The clock moved faster than it should have as we walked south, down toward the River Thames. Midnight came and went with the chiming from Gothic bell towers.

I thought: *It's officially Friday, officially my last day in London.*

We followed the river east, past the sparkly bridges all lit up in the night like lacy spiderwebs catching moonlight. We walked through silent, aristocratic neighborhoods fitted with quaint churchyards where long-dead souls rested. Aston told me about what it was like to grow up around here, and I told him long tales of my travels. We covered miles.

We talked as we ambled along the river on the embankment promenade, the asphalt pathway glistening before us.

Strings of bistro lights, like pearls on a chain, illuminated our way through the misty night, the fog diffusing the glow.

A busker played a violin somewhere nearby. I wondered whom he played for, and I thought: *It's just for me, one last love letter from the city of London to me.* Why were cities always at their prettiest right when you were about to leave them?

"I wouldn't want to spend my last night in London doing anything but this," I told Aston, feeling sentimental.

He slipped his hand in mine. The pads of his fingers were callused from tugging at nylon guitar strings. He rubbed them along the outside of my hand, and I found the act unusually sensual. I couldn't help but wonder how those fingertips would feel stroking the sensitive skin behind my kneecap or the curve of my hip. But would we ever get to that?

We stopped to watch the River Thames, dark as ink and throwing back the city's reflection in shimmering whorls. We didn't know what time it was besides very late or very early—depending on how you wanted to see it. London was a foreign film set that night, photogenic and filled with dark magic. Just as I suspected when I first arrived, the city was now mine, filled with my ghosts and my memories. And tonight I would be making my final one, leaving my last impression.

"Hey, don't be so hopeless." Aston flexed his hand against mine. We stopped under one of the fussily decorated lamp-posts, and the light made him look heartbreakingly attractive. "This doesn't have to be your last night, remember?"

I plumped my lips together in admission. "But it is, Aston." There was no use pretending that we'd come up with a way to keep me here.

"But why?" he asked, pained. "You won't even try and strategize with me."

It was true. Each time he brought up an idea to keep me here, I poked a hole in it.

"I'm a traveler." I shrugged. "It's part of what I do. I leave. I'm hardwired this way," I said in resignation.

Travelers come and go, and if I learned anything from what happened with Lochlon, it was that I should leave *without* looking back. Make clean breaks. Just go.

"You don't have to always leave, you know. You don't have to leave to prove anything," he told me, facing away from the river now.

As he stepped away from the beam of lamplight, the darkness swallowed him up. "Who are you trying to prove or defend your life to, anyway?"

"To everyone!" I said, surprised by the way my voice slashed through the night.

"Who's everyone? Everyone believes in you, Kika. Why don't you see that?" Aston flexed his fingers into a fist and then released them.

The violinist stopped playing, and now I could hear the water of the Thames gulping at the wall below.

"Not society. Not the world. Not . . . not Lochlon," I stuttered, without risking turning away from the view.

Aston kicked his lean frame off the chest-high wall. "Oh, so that's what this is about?"

"No. It's not. It's not that at all," I said absolutely. "It's that he used to be *just* like me. His priority was to travel, and now he's the opposite of me. He just gave up. I cannot and will not just give up the desire to build a meaningful life around travel."

Aston was quiet, and I thought the worst. *I should have never brought up Lochlon.* Silence passed between us.

But a fight is good right now, I reasoned with cheap abandon. *A fight would make it easier, less emotionally costly to leave him tomorrow.* I knew these kinds of thoughts made me a coward, but I let myself think them, anyway.

But instead of obliging me with hostility, Aston spoke with kind consideration: "I think I understand."

I didn't say anything.

"You're scared it could happen to you if you stay too long in one place. You're trying to prove it to yourself, too, aren't you?"

I rubbed my hands together. The fact was, I didn't know how to answer that.

"Kika, I know you're worried about being hurt again because of what happened between you and Lochlon. But don't let your identity as a globe-trotter act as an excuse to give up on this and leave. Don't lean on your wanderlust as a cover-up for being scared."

"I'm not *scared*!" I turned around now, away from the showy river. I tucked my hands into my armpits. "I just don't see what we can do." I felt like I was butting up against the same wall again and again like a mouse in a maze. "But I'm not scared. Why would I be scared?" I tittered tensely, the words fizzing and manic in my mouth.

Aston spoke delicately, and with a small shrug, he answered, "About us. About what we could be."

I meant to tell him: "That's ridiculous."

I meant to tell him: "This has nothing to do with what happened between Lochlon and me—I'm over it."

But instead my mouth asked: "But what if it doesn't work out?"

It slid out in a rickety, high pitch. I didn't recognize the voice as my own. *Do I really feel this way? Am I really scared?*

I was. I secretly knew that the most spineless part of me believed that if I traveled far enough from here and moved fast enough, then the regret of leaving might never catch up to me.

But Aston had to go and call me out on it. And now I was forced to admit it to myself, because I was supposed to be traveling *toward* the life I wanted, not away from the life I was too scared to want.

Aston shrugged with one shoulder. "If it doesn't work out, then it doesn't work out. And we can say we tried, didn't we? But being a traveler means being open to things as well. I mean, well, doesn't it? Isn't that why you came here? You tell me."

I thought about what he said. And damn it, he was right.

"Okay." I nodded with my whole body. "You are absolutely right. What should we do?" I asked it hopefully; this time I'd contribute. This time I'd try.

"Well, first we can get coffee," he said mirroring my determination. "Come on. We can't think without a good dose of caffeine, can we, now? I know a coffee shop that's open all hours."

He took a few steps forward, away from the path, away from the river, and away from where I stood alone. *Could I really do this?*

When he saw that I wasn't following him, he turned around.

"Hey," he said. "I'm scared, too, but this could be really good, I think."

I looked down at my boots. If I really was the girl I claimed to be, I would at least *try*. And because I didn't want to let that girl down, that girl who I was at my finest hours, I extended my hand and clasped his palm to mine. My mouth curved in an unself-conscious smile. "You may need caffeine to think, but I need sugar. Let's go."

— 63 —

"I WANT TO show you something," Aston said with his hand on my lower back as we zigzagged the leafy streets, past the Seven Dials sundial pillar. The roads were empty and wet. A spring shower had begun pitter-pattering through the canopy of new leaves above our heads lit up by orange streetlamps. "You're not in a hurry for that coffee, are you?"

"I've got all night for you." I tilted my face toward the English rain. *And please let me have tomorrow, too*, I thought.

"Good." Aston turned down a small cobblestone side street. When he noticed that I was a few paces behind him, he stopped and took my hand. His face was flushed. "Come along," he said. "I think you'll like this."

It occurred to me then: Aston and I weren't from different worlds at all. He may not identify as a traveler, but he sure could act like one.

We trotted down a lane so narrow that if I spread my arms I would have been able to touch the bricks on both sides. He stopped at an arched wooden door and took out a set of rattling keys.

"Where are you taking me?" I asked.

He pressed his finger to his lips. Just then, it started to pour. I stopped talking and let his mysterious energy overtake me as the icy rain pelted my cheeks.

The old door swung open. Taking my hand again, Aston tugged me inside. He closed the door behind us, shushing out the pouring rain and pitching us into blackness. A gasp slipped out.

"Don't move," he told me, holding my shoulders as if to show me he knew exactly where I was. "I'll get the lights and turn on some heat for you."

"Where are we?" I whispered.

But he didn't answer and instead left me standing there alone. My eyes adjusted to the dark, and I began to get a sense of the room's geography. Opposite from where I stood it was lighter: There must be windows over there. It felt like a low-ceilinged, narrow space—but cozy. It smelled of wood and paper and age, not unlike a library.

Just then, an antique desk lamp flicked on with a metallic bounce. From overhead came a slight buzzing as a cluster of candle-faint Edison bulbs turned on. Even though it was very dim, I squinted my eyes in response to the new light.

I mapped my surroundings: Rows of vinyl records lined the shelves. Polished wood guitars and posters advertising gigs long passed decorated the walls. I looked up and saw a tin ceiling, the bare bulbs dropping down like fishing lines. I was right—opposite me stood a wall of loft windows: little glass rectangles that were covered by curtains, but beyond them was the street and the pattering of rain. We were in a record store.

I swiveled myself toward Aston. He took out a lacquered black vinyl record from its paper slip and blew on it.

"How do you have keys to this place?"

He ignored me for a moment and cradled the record into a record player. The needle scratched and squeaked before the warm analog notes took form.

I ran my hand over the dusty sleeves of black LPs, time-worn or dressed in flimsy cellophane. The moaning of wild, wild horses pushed through the snug, warm atmosphere. And I thought, *You're right. Even wild horses couldn't drag me away from all this tonight.*

Aston took a guitar off the wall and sat on a wooden stool, tuning it up in twanging plucks. His tendons rippled and swelled under the thin skin of his hand as he caught the strings and made them quiver.

"That's beautiful," I mumbled as he joined in with the drowsy, moody melody.

He looked up at me and smiled like he just remembered I was there.

I sank down on the Oriental rug and sat cross-legged in front of him. "Are we supposed to be here?" I asked.

Aston shook his finger over a fret. The note answered me.

"'Course we can be here. I own the place." His fingers moved with ease and traditional grace. "Used to come here skiving off studies, so when I found it was for sale a few years ago, I couldn't let it be turned into a Body Shop."

I lay back on the carpet, spread out like a snow angel, and

let the music cover me like fresh snowfall. The smoky lights, secondhand records, woozy heat, and vibrating strings—they made me feel like things were happening, real, important things. I actually felt myself *living* life at that moment.

The song concluded and looped white noise, but Aston kept strumming, transitioning into another song, equally melancholic, equally beautiful. The music he created felt intimate, like a lover whispering in your ear.

Aston hummed a bluesy melody above me, his pitch as smooth as lived-in bedsheets. But then, he stopped playing his guitar.

With my eyes closed, I lifted an eyebrow, not wanting to break the enchantment. Something inside me went quiet in peaceful contentment.

Sitting up, I found him watching me. I looked down, playing with the carpet between my fingers. My mind whooshed when I realized what I was about to do.

Nearing the turntable, I found a cherished album close by. And soon, a sad, dusty cello in a minor key meshed with a heartrending acoustic guitar and a ghostly female vocalist.

"That's an original." Aston watched me over the curve of his guitar. There was a smile in his cadence when he spoke to me. The cello hushed, and the lamplight cast otherworldly velvety shadows over the towers of old records, arranged like a cityscape around us.

I walked over to him and took the guitar out of his hands, leaning it against the wall. He let me take it.

Feeling sure of myself, of my body, of my movements, of my intentions, I positioned myself in front of Aston. The needle skipped a groove on the record but continued undeterred a moment later.

"Kika," he said in a low, smoky voice that came from the depths of his throat. "We don't have to."

I held still for a moment, and I knew that if I wanted to stop now, he would let me. But I straddled myself down onto his lap and kissed him.

"I want to," I told him, breaking off the kiss.

Instead of speaking again, I guided his hands to where I wanted them. I made a faraway noise when his warm palms first skimmed over my bare skin, lost in the sheer, simple stupor of being touched. The music made me braver, but I couldn't recall a time I wanted anything more.

64

IN THE FIRST small hours of morning, the rain stopped and we left the record shop and went to Soho, our fingers coiled together the whole time. We sat in an Italian-style coffeehouse filled with people too preoccupied to go home or with no homes to go to. Shoulder-to-shoulder they rested—all-hours cab drivers with nicotine eyes and electric-blue-haired teenagers returning from neon nightclubs.

On the other side of the filmy window, the early morning threatened to arrive, while oblivious parades of drunken partygoers passed by with far less on their minds than us.

A television played a soccer match in machine-gun-fast Italian. Aston flipped through a morning paper left in our booth. I thought of what had just happened back at the shop, about that pulling feeling in my heart when he tucked me against his chest afterward, when we were just bare skin on bare skin. I could have slept there all night, with my ear against his thrumming heartbeat.

"What has you smiling, Kika?" he asked, eyeing me over his paper.

I didn't realize I was smiling.

"Go on. Tell me." He folded the newspaper in half, hiding a sleepy yawn behind it.

"You," I admitted. "And me. We'll think of something," I said finally.

"Of course we will," he said. "I thought, say nothing manifests, perhaps we could, I don't know, go on one of your trips together. Scout some handicrafts and whatnot—if you have to leave the UK, I mean."

"But I thought you said that you don't like to travel?"

"Well, I think I may like to travel with you." Thankfully, he curled his gaze downward before I was forced to jump over the table and drag him back to the record store.

"Just an idea, anyway. I'm quite sure we'll find a solution." He shrugged and gathered up the newspaper again. As he started reading, I stole a bite of his pastry even though I already finished two of my own. (I regret nothing.)

He would never be more handsome to me than he was right then—at 4:30 A.M. on a Friday morning; the smell of strong espresso thickening the air; the neon lights splashing through the windows, coating his cornfield-blond hair and making him look like someone poets wrote sonnets about.

We talked adamantly then, each of us moving from option to option: I could maybe come back and get a job under the table; Aston would get visa information from his company's lawyers; or we would look into au pair agencies.

We talked and talked and talked, both of us certain we'd figure something out as the night trudged toward unavoidable daybreak.

But time had its way with us that day, and we wouldn't come up with a fleshed-out solution. We needed more time, and as much as it hurt to admit it, we had been outwitted.

So hand in hand we watched the sun break like an egg over the Thames that morning, staining the dawn with orange and melancholy.

Bloodshot veins made Aston's eyes even bluer, and his ridged jawline had cultivated a plain of powdery golden stubble as fine as May pollen.

This is some strange version of what it'd be like waking up beside him, I imagined privately, my stomach leaping at the thought. If only there were more of these drowsy early mornings to come. But for now, this dawn was all we had.

— 65 —

WE PAUSED IN front of our respective houses. Before going inside, I promised Aston that I'd stop by his house when I was done packing so that I could say good-bye to him—officially, but temporarily, until we could find a better solution than this. Good-bye for now, which was always my line, wasn't it?

"Well, that's it," I announced to myself. I tugged my backpack straps taut and marveled at how my whole existence could still be condensed into one bag. I ceremoniously held my final paycheck in both hands.

You could never save a cent, I heard Lochlon say. But I already told Clive that we would be stopping at the bank on the way to the airport. Another deposit. *Take that,* I thought. *Just watch me rewrite my narrative even in the face of lost momentum.*

All that was left for me to do now was to articulate those

overwhelming good-byes: first to Aston, and then to the girls when they got home from school this afternoon.

I wrote each girl a long letter despite Elsbeth's wishes and hid it between their bedsheets so that they'd find it before going to bed tonight. No matter what Elsbeth said, I would have my good-bye with them.

As for Aston, well, there was no letter for him because he already knew how I felt about things: We were put on pause. Walking away from it now felt like a sudden loss of electricity. We were plunged into a blackout, jumbled and unprepared.

But I was proud of our flailing: I was glad we blundered around blind and let our fluttering fingers feel for walls, grasping at anything we could. Our floundering proved that we were making the effort.

Though I was going back to New York, I was under orders to call Aston as soon as I landed. All I could do was believe that we would figure out a way for this to work. What else could I do? If I didn't believe in it, there was no point. Always, even after a hundred heartbreaks, we still want to believe, don't we? And so I'd be a believer. I'd risk it all, and I'd bet it all. Again, and again, and again.

"You never know," Aston told me as we parted ways this morning, facing our front doors. "We still have a few hours left. In football, things change during stoppage time all the time."

"I'm not sure I get your sporty metaphors," I told him with a bent grin. But I couldn't help but to cross my fingers and hope he was right.

I thought of Aston's words when I heard a pounding at my door and perked up.

"Come in," I called, begging for something—anything—

to push down the chalky lump that had been stuck in my esophagus since returning to the house.

"Elsbeth!" My breathing caught hopefully when I saw the state she was in: *Is this the last-minute miracle I'm hoping for?*

Unfortunately, this didn't look like it could turn into a happy ending.

Elsbeth's hair had broken loose from her ballerina-tight bun, and her face was ghostly pale. As she entered my room, she brought with her a buzz of anxiety so insistent you could hear it.

"Are you okay?" I asked, alarmed. Elsbeth never looked so untidy. (Of course, what she calls unruly, I call Tuesday, but never mind that. For Elsbeth, *this* was highly undignified.)

But she was too winded to answer. She hurried at me, fastened her hands on my shoulders, and led me to a set of chairs.

Once she sat me down, she dumped herself down into the other chair, holding her hand to her head like some swooning Jane Austen heroine. I had the impulse to offer her some smelling salts or a thimbleful of sherry, just to complete the picture.

"Good God. I just ran here from Harrington Gardens. Sprinted, really. And here I thought I was in amazing shape. I am going to fire that personal trainer—"

"Are they all right?" I interrupted.

"What?" Elsbeth fanned herself.

"The girls—you said you went to the school."

"Yes, they're fine. Oh, let me just start at the beginning." Elsbeth patted her cheeks and did what my mom would call "a round of Ujjayi breathing."

"I received a message this morning instructing me to go to my daughter's school to meet with her teacher. The message said that it was 'high time I found out what was going on,'" Elsbeth said, making air quotes with her fingers.

"Obviously distressed, I jetted over to Harrington Gardens just as fast as I could. I tried to find you to see if perhaps you knew what this was in regards to, but I couldn't find you anywhere this morning," she said in one breath.

I scrunched my brow in anticipation.

"So because Gwendolyn had been having problems, I assumed the message was about her and went to see her teacher first. Of course, she made me wait for approximately an hour before she was able to sit down with me. I didn't want to alarm Gwen, so I hid like a refugee in the school hallway— the whole thing was very theatrical really." Elsbeth looked slightly impressed with herself.

I whisked my hand in the air for her to get on with the story.

"Gwen's teacher told me how *amazing* she's doing, and really, Kika, this is all your influence. She has been getting along smashingly with the other kids and behaving herself. As you can imagine, I was just so pleased—with her and you, Kika."

"Well, that's great to hear—" My shoulders collapsed in anticlimax. *This is what she got me all wound up about?*

Elsbeth pointed her finger at my chest insistently. "But that's not all. You're not off the hook yet."

I pepped up, despite the warning.

"Still concerned about the message, I dashed across the street to the upper-classes building—Mina's school. And that's when the *real* surprises came out." Her mouth pursed.

I swore to myself. It must have been Mrs. Benson-Westwood who had called her. She must have gotten the school involved after she heard about how I lectured Peaches and the rest of the junior bitches.

My back straightened, and I strategized my objection, ready for a fight. But then I remembered: *I am already fired. I'm already leaving on a jet plane; don't know when I'll be back again, and all that jazz.* And so I kept silent, feeling wildly liberated by the "fuck it" mood that was settling in.

"Mina's teacher was available to have a sit-down. Kika, only *you* would have any idea about what I learned. I cannot believe that she had been bullied for so long and no one alerted me. And you *knew*, Kika. And what you did—"

"I did do it, and I'd do it again!" I hurled myself out of my chair in a demonstration of guiltlessness. "And you know what, Elsbeth, if you were there, you'd have done the same thing. So I don't want to hear it."

Elsbeth clasped her pearls (or where her pearls would have been had she been wearing some). "Kika!" she wheezed.

My knees told me that I made my point, and so I plummeted back into my seat, the wind having been knocked from me.

"Why, Kika, that was *just* what I was going to say!"

My mouth opened. "Um, seriously?"

Elsbeth clapped her hands together in exhilaration. "You *fixed* it as if you were her mother. And actually, Mina's teacher thought you *were* her mother. You see, she saw you at the school that day when you gallantly stuck up for Mina. She said whatever you said to those girls had a great effect on them, and since that day the teasing lessened and then ultimately tapered off completely.

"Oh, Kika, you *saved* my girls. I had no clue what was going on. I got so caught up with the social scene here and the parents and parties and . . . and . . ." She stopped talking and looked at me questioningly.

I sat stunned. "I just did what anyone would have done."

"No, Kika. No one can do what you do. And that is the truth. I don't want you to leave."

I nodded sluggishly. "That's nice, but if the girls are leaving in September—"

"Kika, they're *not* leaving. The boarding school idea is a huge mistake. I was peer pressured," she claimed with enlarged pupils.

We both smiled at the statement, the conflict evaporating into the space between us.

"But I was, Kika. All of Mr. Darling's colleagues' children go to boarding school, and the parents all harp on about how they make 'connections that will last into their futures,'" she said in an intonation that evoked Primrose.

We both rolled our eyes at the phrase.

"But now I see that they just say that . . . that . . . *poppycock*" (of course even now Elsbeth wouldn't swear) "to make themselves feel better."

She reeled in her tone for a moment. "Well, maybe it *is* right for them, but it's not for *me* or *my* girls."

I leaped up and launched a full-contact hug on Elsbeth's delicate form. "Oh, thank God. I didn't want to say anything about Mina being bullied because I promised her that I wouldn't betray her trust. But I was so worried about her going to boarding school and having to deal with being the new girl again."

Elsbeth nodded knowingly. "You know, Kika, when you protested boarding school, I couldn't handle it and fired you because deep down, I felt it was wrong, too."

"I know you did. I could tell," I said enthusiastically.

"I am truly sorry. Please say you'll stay?" Elsbeth prompted like she didn't already know the answer.

"Yes, I'll stay—of course I will!"

"That's my girl. Now get these bags unpacked before the girls get home—I don't want to startle them," she said in her bossy but somehow comforting way. "And don't forget those letters you snuck in their beds."

66

I KNOW HE'LL be here, I thought as I pushed open the garden gate without shutting it behind me. I didn't even bother knocking on his door first. *He'll be here.*

Spring had come to the garden overnight. Aston stood with his back toward me. The sunshine glinted off flowers jeweled with condensation, and the pollen in the air gave the whole place a dreamlike haze.

I hurried toward him. My boots, sprinkled with cherry blossom petals, slapped the wet grass, the suctioning making a sort of kissy noise with every step.

"I knew you'd be here," I said lightly, stopping just behind him, my boots yielding to the dewy earth. He didn't turn around, and I used the concealed moment to tell him exactly how I felt.

"It means so much to me that you're where I thought you'd

be," I gushed with hearty emphasis, so needlessly sincere that it was cheesy as all hell, but I didn't even care. "It makes it feel so *right*." When he still didn't turn around, I took a few more steps forward and reached out to touch his shoulder.

He wheeled around, and suddenly, I was face-to-face with those hypnotic bright blue eyes and—

"*Fuck me!*" I yapped in alarm. I was *not* face-to-face with those hypnotic bright blue eyes. I vaulted backward as I realized I was actually face-to-face with a teenage boy.

Oops. Wrong guy. I physically recoiled in embarrassment.

The teenager gawped at me. "Fuck you?" he repeated. His tongue was suspended mid-lick over the paper of a hand-rolled cigarette, which—it now became apparent—he was rolling facing the tree to avoid the wind.

"Was it me you were talking to?" he asked again. Strangest of all was that he sounded vaguely hopeful.

"Um, no, sorry," I protested with a red face. I took rapid steps backward. "Best be going now," I said, hiding my face behind a curtain of hair. *What is wrong with me?*

I heard cackling behind my back and peeked up apprehensively. I turned to see Aston unsuccessfully trying to hold in his laughter. The teenager used the opportunity to hightail it out of the garden.

Scrunching up my eyebrows, I stomped over to Aston. (This time I was positive it was him.)

"Well done. You always talk to underage schoolboys like that?" He broke apart in hard laughter now. "You saucy thing! I think you just sent him into early puberty."

I whacked him on the arm. "You sat here watching me pour my heart out to the wrong guy, and you didn't even stop me?"

"Couldn't. It was too funny," he said, rubbing his arm. "I had to let you crack on, surely." He chuckled and stretched out his arm where I smacked him and examined his bicep. "Wasn't expecting to get hurt."

I overlapped my arms defiantly, but it was hard to fake a bad mood right now in this sweet stupor.

"Come on now, I thought I'd at least get a 'thank you' or maybe a little snog?"

I nodded, facing my eyes downward in an effort to conceal my grin. "So, Aston Hyde Bettencourt, who'd you get to leave Elsbeth that message?"

"My granny, would you believe? She works at the school, so she knew what was going on. She'll be delighted it worked," he told me, enthralled.

I laughed at his enthusiasm. "You brought your poor granny into this?"

"Brought her into this? She's *been* in it. That woman knows everything. It was her idea. She can hardly wait to meet you. So you are staying now, aren't you?"

"But how did you know that Elsbeth would change her mind?" I backtracked.

"As Granny said: 'Does that Elsbeth Darling understand what Kika did for those girls?' She saw how they changed since you moved here, as did I. There was never any laughter on this street until you arrived. She said that lately it has been like old times around here, when my parents were still alive. That's what Granny said." He sunk his eyes in a moment of introversion.

"Plus, Miss Chantelle Benson-Westwood has very loose lips and was rather quick to note that Mina used to be a social outcast until her sister—a Benson-Westwood—got ahold of her and 'changed her life.' She thought she was making the winning point to convince me to take up with her. The nerve of that woman."

I shook my head in disgust, and Aston continued.

"I must say, I was quite excited to use her own stories against her, and so I was able to find out that you were truly the one who rescued Mina, as it were."

"You sneaky bugger!"

Aston sniggered. "Love, you haven't been in London long enough to pull off saying 'bugger.'"

I made my face blank.

"So, what's it to be? Will you stay?" he asked, sounding boyishly hopeful.

I started casually, my hands hugged at my back. "Well, I *was* thinking it might be fun to see you play next weekend."

"Really? Was that all you were thinking?"

"And maybe again the weekend after that."

He deftly angled his pointer finger into the loop of my jeans like a fishhook and tugged me toward him. Then he ran his knuckles along the curve of my face. "More like it," he said.

I threw my arms around his neck, my heart feeling that same undeniable and important pulling. I kissed him with everything I had, holding nothing back. Even while it was happening—the weight of lips on lips, color slapped high onto cheeks, and pink petals pinwheeling through the air—I saw the kiss for what it was: a beginning.

This was not the end.

There was too much left to do, too much still to see to call

326 · *nicole trilivas*

this the end. My career was not yet crafted; there were marsh-mallows that still needed to be collected. And all my wild, wild loose ends still needed to be tied into Pinterest-perfect bows. But there was that pulling, and so I knew my direction. And all girls who travel know that it's not about arriving; it's the getting there that's the good part.